"You'd better eat more than that, MacKinloch," Nairna ordered him. "You need to get your strength back."

"And what will I be needing the strength for, *a ghaoil?*" Bram asked, taking her fingertips.

Her face colored, and she held out a bite of fish, offering it to him. When she pushed the food into his mouth, her thumb brushed against his lip.

The soft touch brought him into a deeper awareness of her. He ignored the clan members gathering, and the sounds of their conversation grew muted. He looked into Nairna's worried green eyes, and kept her fingers locked in his.

"Bram, are you all right?"

No. He was tired, irritated at having to be around so many people, and his mind couldn't stop thinking about the night he would spend with Nairna. The bawdy conversation was doing nothing to alleviate the sexual hunger he felt for her. He remembered the silken skin and the sweetness of her kiss. Even more, the way she'd clung to him when he'd kissed her only deepened his own arousal. He wanted to be alone with his wife right now. He wanted to explore her body, to learn the mysteries of a woman's flesh. Unless she kept her hands off him, his control was going to break apart.

When her hand came up to stroke his cheek, all semblance of reason snapped.

* * *

Claimed by the Highland Warrior
Harlequin® Historical #1042—May 2011

Author Note

Ever since I saw the movie *Braveheart,* I longed to write a Highlander story of my own set during the era of William Wallace…only, with a happy ending! Bram MacKinloch is a prisoner of war during this troubled time, and he must save his brother from the English who captured him.

After seven long years, Nairna believed she'd lost her childhood sweetheart. But Fate gives her a second chance at love and a family. She tries to help Bram overcome his sleepless nights and horrifying memories, despite his belief that he doesn't deserve happiness. It's the story of healing and hope, and how two people can rekindle a lost love.

A friend of my father's was a prisoner of war in the Vietnam conflict. His wife never knew what happened to him and he was believed dead, until his shocking return years later. I can only imagine the feelings in her heart, and *Claimed by the Highland Warrior* was inspired by their true-life love story.

There are a few additional things I wanted to note. During the early fourteenth century, the Scots did not wear kilts, plaids or tartans; these came centuries later. Also, though they likely understood English, amongst each other the Highlanders would have spoken Gaelic. This is why I've left out the Scottish burr that's common to many romances, since it wouldn't have been part of a Highlander's speech.

This past summer, I visited the Scottish Highlands and took many pictures that inspired my new miniseries You're welcome to view the photos at my Facebook page, www.facebook.com/michellewillinghamfans. You can also visit my website at www.michellewillingham.com for excerpts and behind-the-scenes details. I love to hear from readers and you may email me at michelle@michellewillingham.com or via mail at P.O. Box 2242 Poquoson, VA 23662 USA.

MICHELLE WILLINGHAM

Claimed by the Highland Warrior

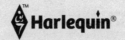

TORONTO NEW YORK LONDON
AMSTERDAM PARIS SYDNEY HAMBURG
STOCKHOLM ATHENS TOKYO MILAN MADRID
PRAGUE WARSAW BUDAPEST AUCKLAND

Recycling programs
for this product may
not exist in your area.

ISBN-13: 978-0-373-29642-2

CLAIMED BY THE HIGHLAND WARRIOR

Copyright © 2011 Michelle Willingham

www.Harlequin.com

Printed in U.S.A.

With many thanks to Sharron Gunn
for her help with researching the medieval Highlands
and for being willing to answer so many of
my questions. Thanks to my editor, Joanne Grant,
and to my agent, Helen Breitwieser, for their
continued support and for challenging me with each
and every book. Both of you have helped me
to grow as an author, and it's deeply appreciated.

Available from Harlequin® Historical and
MICHELLE WILLINGHAM

And in ebook Harlequin Historical Undone!

*The MacEgan Brothers
**The MacKinloch Clan
†linked by character

Chapter One

Ballaloch, Scotland—1305

Bram MacKinloch couldn't remember the last time he'd eaten or slept. The numbness consumed him, and all he could do now was keep going. He'd been imprisoned in the darkness for so many years, he'd forgotten what the sun felt like upon his skin. It blinded him, forcing him to keep his gaze fixed upon the ground.

God's bones, he couldn't even remember how long he'd been running. Exhaustion had blotted away the visions until he didn't know how many English soldiers were pursuing him or where they were now. He'd stayed clear of the valley, keeping to the hills and the fir trees that would hide him from view.

His clothing and hair were soaked, after he'd swum through a river to mask his scent from the dogs.

Had there been dogs? He couldn't remember anymore. Shadows blurred his mind, until he didn't know reality from the nightmares.

Keep going, he ordered himself. *Don't stop. Not now.*

His footing slipped as he crossed the top of the hill and he stumbled to the ground. Before he rose, he listened hard for the sound of his pursuers.

Nothing. Silence stretched across the Highlands, with only the sound of birds and insects breaking the stillness. He grabbed at the grass, using it to regain his balance. After he stood, he turned in a slow circle in all directions. From the top of the hill, he could see no one. Only the vast expanse of craggy green mountains and the clouded sky above him.

Freedom.

He drank in the sight, savouring the open air and the land that he'd missed these past seven years. Though he was far from home, these mountains were known to him, like old friends.

Bram steadied his breathing, taking a moment to rest. He should have been grateful that he'd broken free of his prison, but guilt held him captive now. His brother Callum was still locked away in that godforsaken place.

Let him be alive, Bram prayed. *Let it not be too late.* If he had to sell his own soul, he'd get Callum out. Especially after the price he'd paid for his own freedom.

He started moving west, towards Ballaloch. If he kept up his pace, it was possible to reach the fortress within the hour. He hadn't been there in years, not since he was sixteen. The MacPhersons would grant him shelter, but would they remember or even recognise him?

Cold emptiness filled him, and he rubbed at his scarred wrists. The days without any rest had taken their toll, causing his hands to shake. What he wouldn't give for a dreamless night, one where his mind no longer tormented him.

But one dream held steady, of the woman he'd thought about each night over the past seven years.

Nairna.

Despite the nightmares of his imprisonment, he'd kept her image fixed in his mind. Her green eyes, the brown hair that fell to her waist. The way she'd smiled at him, as if he were the only man she'd ever wanted.

A restless sense of regret pulled at him, as he wondered what had happened to her over the years. Had she grown to hate him? Or had she forgotten him? She would be different now. Changed, like he was.

After so many years lost, he didn't expect her to feel anything towards him. And though he'd never wanted to leave her behind, Fate had dragged him down another path.

He reached to finger the edge of his tunic, touching the familiar stone that he'd kept hidden within a seam. Over the years, he'd nearly worn the small stone flat. Nairna had given him the token on the night he'd left to fight against the English. So many times, he'd clenched the stone during his imprisonment, as if he could reach out to her.

Her image had kept him from falling into madness, like an angel holding him back from hellfire. She'd given him a reason to live. A reason to fight.

Regret lowered his spirits, for it was unrealistic to imagine that she'd waited for him. After seven years, likely she would have put their memories in the past.

Unless she still loved him.

The thought was a thread of hope, one that kept him moving forwards. He was close to the MacPherson stronghold now and could take shelter with them for the night.

He imagined holding Nairna in his arms, breathing

in the soft scent of her skin. Tasting her lips and forcing back the painful memories. He could lose himself in her and none of the past would matter.

As he crossed down into the valley, he saw Ballaloch, nestled between the hills like a gleaming pearl. Bram sat down on the grass, staring at the stronghold.

And then, behind him, he heard the sound of horses.

He struggled to his feet, his heart pounding. When he glanced behind him, he saw the glint of chainmail armour and soldiers.

No. The thought was a vicious command to himself. He couldn't let himself be taken captive. Not again. Not after so many years of being a slave.

He tore down the hillside, his legs shaking. But his weak body betrayed him, his knees surrendering as he fell to the ground.

The stronghold was right there. Right within his reach.

Anguish ripped through him as he fought to rise, to make his legs move.

But even when he managed to run, they overtook him with their horses, dragging him up. Gloved hands took him by the shoulders, and as he fought, they dropped a hood over his head, blinding him.

Then they struck him down, and all fell into darkness.

'Something's wrong, Jenny,' Nairna MacPherson muttered to her maid, staring out her window into the inner bailey. Four horsemen had arrived through the barbican gate, their leader dressed in chainmail armour and a conical helm. 'English soldiers are here, but I don't know why.'

'Probably Harkirk's men, come to demand more silver from your father,' Jenny answered, closing the trunk. 'But don't be fretting. It's his worry, not yours.'

Nairna turned away from the window, her mind stewing. 'He shouldn't have to bribe them. It's not right.'

Robert Fitzroy, the English Baron of Harkirk, had set up his garrison west of her father's fortress, a year after the Scottish defeat at Falkirk. There were hundreds of English outposts all across the Highlands and more emerging every year.

Her father had given them both his allegiance and his coins, simply to safeguard his people from attack.

Bloodsucking leeches. It had to stop.

'I'm going to see why they're here.' She started to move towards the door, but Jenny stepped in her way.

The old woman's brown eyes softened with sympathy. 'We're going back home this day, Nairna. I don't think you're wanting to start a disagreement with Hamish before ye return.'

The arrow of disapproval struck its intended target. Her shoulders lowered, and she wished there were something she could do to help her father. They were bleeding him dry, and she loathed the thought of what he'd done for his clan's safety.

But Ballaloch was no longer her home. Neither was Callendon, though she'd lived there for the past four years while she'd been married to the chief of the Mac-Donnell clan.

Iver was dead now. And though she'd had a comfortable life with him, it had been an empty marriage. Nothing at all like the love she'd known before.

A tendril of grief slipped within her heart for the man she'd lost, so many years ago. Bram MacKinloch's death had broken her apart, and no man could ever replace him.

Now, she was mistress of nothing and mother of no one. Iver's son and his wife had already assumed the leadership of the clan and its holdings. Nairna was an afterthought, the widow left behind. No one of importance.

The unsettled feeling of helplessness rooted deep inside. Loneliness spread across her heart with the fervent wish that she could be useful to someone. She wanted a home and a family, a place where she wouldn't be a shadow. But it felt like there was no place that she truly belonged. Not in her father's home. Not in her late husband's home.

'I won't interfere,' she promised Jenny. 'I just want to see why they're here now. He's already paid the bribes due for this quarter.'

'Nairna,' her maid warned. 'Leave it be.'

'I'll listen to what they're saying,' she said slowly, feigning a nonchalance she didn't feel. 'And I might try to speak with Da.'

Her maid grumbled, but followed her below stairs. 'Take Angus with ye,' she advised.

Nairna didn't care about a guard, but as soon as she crossed the Hall, Angus MacPherson, a thick-chested man with arms the size of broad tree limbs, shadowed her path.

Outside, she blinked at the afternoon sunlight and saw the English soldiers standing within the inner bailey. Across one of the horses lay the covered body of a man.

Her heart seized at the sight and she hurried closer. Was it a MacPherson they'd found?

Their leader was addressing Hamish, saying, 'We

caught this man wandering not far from Ballaloch. One of yours, I suppose.' The soldier's mouth curled in a thin smile.

Nairna's hand gripped the dagger at her waist. Her father's face was expressionless as he stared at the soldiers. 'Is he alive?'

The man gave a nod, motioning for the other soldier to bring the body closer. They had covered their captive's face with a hood.

'How much is a man's life worth to you?' the Englishman asked. 'Fifteen pennies, perhaps?'

'Show me his face,' Hamish said quietly, sending a silent signal to his steward. Whatever price they named, Nairna knew her father would pay it. But she couldn't even tell if the prisoner was alive.

'Twenty pennies,' their leader continued. He ordered his men to lift the captive from the horse and hold him. The hooded prisoner couldn't stand upright, and from his torn clothing, Nairna didn't recognise the man. The long dark hair falling about his shoulders was their only clue to his identity.

Nairna drew closer to her father, lowering her voice. 'He's not one of ours.'

The soldiers gripped their captive by his shoulders, and another jerked the man's head backwards, baring his throat.

'Twenty-five pennies,' the Englishman demanded, unsheathing a dagger. 'His life belongs to you, MacPherson, if you want it.' He rested the blade at the prisoner's throat. At the touch of the metal against skin, the prisoner's hands suddenly closed into fists. He struggled to escape the soldiers' grip, twisting and fighting.

He was alive.

Nairna's pulse raced as she stared at the unknown

man. Her hands began shaking, for she understood that they would show no mercy to the stranger. They were truly going to execute him, right in the middle of the bailey. And there was no way to know if their captive was a MacPherson or one of their enemies.

'Thirty pennies,' came her father's voice, reaching for a small purse that his steward had brought.

Their leader smiled, catching the purse as it was tossed at him. The soldiers shoved the prisoner to the ground, but after he struck the earth he didn't rise.

'Go back to Lord Harkirk,' Hamish commanded.

The English soldier mounted his horse, rejoining the others as he fingered the purse. 'I wondered if you were going to let him die. I would have killed him, you know. One less Scot.' He tossed the bag of coins, his thin smile stretching.

Angus moved forwards from behind Nairna, his hand grasping a spear in a silent threat. Other MacPherson fighters circled the English soldiers, but they had already begun their departure.

Nairna couldn't quite catch her breath at her father's blatant bribery. Thirty pennies. She felt as if the wind had been knocked from her lungs. He'd handed it over, without a second thought.

Though she didn't speak, her father eyed her. 'A man's life is more important than coins.'

'I know it.' Nairna gripped her hands together, trying to contain her agitation. 'But what will you do when they come back, demanding more? Will you continue to pay Lord Harkirk until they've seized Ballaloch and made prisoners of our people?'

Her father strode over to the fallen body of the prisoner. 'We're alive, Nairna. Our clan is one of the few left untouched. And by God, if I have to spend every last coin to ensure their safety, I will do so. Is that clear?'

She swallowed hard as Hamish rolled the man over, easing him up. 'You shouldn't have to bribe them. It's not right.'

There was no difference between the English soldiers and cheating merchants, as far as Nairna was concerned. Men took advantage, whenever it was allowed. She knelt down beside her father, trying to calm her roiling emotions.

'Well, lad, let's see who you are,' Hamish said, pulling off the hood.

Nairna's heart stopped when she saw the prisoner's face.

For it was Bram MacKinloch. The husband she hadn't seen since the day she'd married him, seven years ago.

Pale moonlight illuminated the room and Bram opened his eyes. Every muscle in his body ached, and he swallowed hard. Thirsty. So thirsty.

'Bram,' came a soft voice. 'Are you awake?'

He turned towards the sound and wondered if he was dead. He had to be, for he knew that voice. It was Nairna, the woman he'd dreamed of for so long.

A cup was raised to his lips and he drank the cool ale, grateful that she'd anticipated the need. She moved closer and lit an oil lamp to illuminate the darkness. The amber glow revealed her features, and he stared at her, afraid the vision would fade away if he blinked.

Her mouth was soft, her cheekbones well formed and her long brown hair fell freely across her shoulders. She'd become a beautiful woman.

He wanted to touch her. Just to know that she was real. Longing swelled through him, mingled with bittersweet regret. His hand was shaking when he reached out to her. As if asking forgiveness, he stroked her palm, wishing things could have been different.

She didn't pull away. Instead, her hand curled around his, her face filled with confusion. 'I can't believe you're alive.'

He sat up and she moved beside him. With one hand clasped in hers, he touched her nape. The light scent of flowers and grass seemed to emanate from her, and he leaned closer, drinking in the sight.

God help him, he needed her right now. He threaded his hands in her hair, lifting her face to his. He took her mouth in a kiss, for she was the hope and life he'd craved for so long.

Nairna's heart was beating so fast, she hardly knew what to do. She tasted the heady danger within his kiss, of a man who didn't care about all the lost years. Bram had never been much for talking, and without words, he told her how much he'd missed her.

He kissed her as though he couldn't get enough, as though she were an answered prayer. And in spite of everything, she found herself kissing him back.

God above, she'd never expected this. Not in a thousand years. It was as if she were seeing a spirit, and when he bent to take her lips again, he convinced her that he was indeed made of flesh and blood.

A tangled knot of emotions warred inside her. She gripped his lean shoulders, unable to stop the tears. She'd grieved for him, raged against the injustice of losing him. And when she'd finally accepted the dull ache of loss, Fate made a mockery of her grief by returning him.

She was torn between happiness that he was here and her guilt of betrayal. She'd married someone else. And though Iver was dead and there was no shame in kissing Bram, it felt strange.

His mouth moved against her cheek, along the line of her jaw. A spiral of desire tightened within her breasts, spearing down between her thighs. And when he pulled her down on top of him, she felt his heated arousal pressing against her.

'Nairna,' he whispered. His voice was husky, a deep bass note that rumbled against her throat. Her skin flushed, while warmth pooled within her body.

She didn't know where these feelings were coming from, but they terrified her. Bram's hands moved down her back, bringing her hips against him. The sensation of his arousal cradled against her womanhood made her moist with wanting, her nipples tightening beneath her gown.

His mouth captured hers in demanding possession. Every part of her body was attuned to his touch and the longer he kissed her, the more she wanted him. She envisioned lifting her skirts, feeling his hard naked body against her own.

Confusion warred inside her, for she wasn't supposed to respond this way to a man who was virtually a stranger. Caught between past and present, she didn't know whether to trust her heart or her mind.

Bram's palm moved down her cheek, stroking her in a caress that evoked the feelings she'd tried to bury. His face was harrowed, as though he'd seen things he shouldn't have. And he'd grown so terribly thin.

'Bram, where have you been all this time?'

He didn't answer at first. Then he sat up, keeping her on his lap. His hands framed her face, as if he were trying to learn her features. She covered his hands with hers, staring into his eyes. Willing him to tell her the truth.

'I was a prisoner at Cairnross.'

She'd heard of the English Earl and his cruelty. Her heart bled at the thought of Bram enduring captivity for so long, in such a place.

'I thought you were dead,' she managed.

He touched her as if he were afraid she might disappear. His roughened palms abraded her skin, his fingers trembling. 'I thought you would have married another by now. That you'd found someone else.'

I did, she nearly said, but stopped herself, not wanting to hurt him. She'd married Iver, desperately wanting a home and a family of her own. But now, it shamed her to think of what she'd done. It made her feel like she'd committed adultery, though she knew that wasn't true.

Her cheeks grew hot and she didn't know how to tell him about the marriage. A tear spilled down her cheek, but whether it was from grief or joy, she couldn't tell.

Bram's thumb brushed it away, and his hands moved down her shoulders, resting upon her waist. He drew her into his arms, caressing her back. 'You've grown into a woman since I saw you last.'

Nairna's skin prickled. A latent fire seemed to rise up from within her, burning her flesh with need. His mouth bent to her throat, and she bit back a shuddering breath at the kindled sensations. His thumbs stroked lazy circles over her spine.

But when he moved to the upper curve of her breasts, she panicked.

'Bram, wait.' She stood up, pushing him away. 'I need to know what's happened since you—'

'Tomorrow,' he whispered, rising from the bed.

He looked wild, his eyes blazing with fierce need.

He reminded her of a savage tribesman who had come to claim his woman at last.

For a long moment, he stared at her, as if he didn't know what to do next. Before she could voice another question, he walked towards the door. He turned back again, his hand resting against the door frame. For a breathless moment, he studied her, as if making a decision.

Then he left, without a word of explanation.

Chapter Two

Seven years earlier

'For God's sakes, Bram, keep your eyes upon your opponent!' his father roared.

Bram blinked, staring at Malcolm MacPherson who was attempting to stab him in the training match. He balanced his footing, trying to determine where the dirk would slash next. Though both of them were sixteen, Malcolm had a stronger instinct for fighting.

Bram lunged left, only to be slashed from the right. The blade didn't cut his skin, but skidded off the chainmail armour his father had made him wear.

He adjusted his position, trying again to find Malcolm's weakness. For a time, he successfully defended himself, predicting where the next strike would come. He'd sparred often enough in the past, but not in front of so many people. He could feel the MacPherson chief watching him, as if determining his worth. His cheeks warmed, for he'd much rather fight a single opponent with no one staring.

As the fight wore on, his attention began drifting again. He moved out of habit, and from his peripheral vision, he spied a maiden walking towards them. It was Malcolm's sister Nairna, who was only a year younger than himself. He'd seen her before, but he'd never really *noticed* her.

She wore a gown the colour of new spring grass, with an embroidered cap covering her long brown hair. The strands fell to her waist, and as she moved, he found himself entranced. He could sense her watching the fight.

He barely missed the blade that came slashing towards his throat. Bram threw himself to the ground, grunting when Malcolm rolled him over and pinned him.

'You let yourself be distracted by a girl?' his opponent taunted. 'Or were you wanting to wear her skirts?'

The insult sent a haze of red surging through him. Bram released his rage, using the momentum to force Malcolm off him. In a ruthless motion, he twisted the young man's wrist until he disarmed him, then lifted his dirk to Malcolm's throat.

'She's your sister,' he gritted out. 'Show some respect.' He held his position long enough to demonstrate that he'd held his own in this match, before rising and sheathing the blade.

He strode away, not bothering to speak with his father or the chief of Ballaloch. His father had brought him here to visit over a fortnight ago, and Bram didn't know why. He wasn't included in the conversations between the two chiefs, but he knew they were watching him.

He kept walking, not even looking where he was going, until a hand pressed a dripping cup of water into his palm. Bram stopped short and saw Nairna standing before him. For a brief moment, her eyes met his, before she released the cup and walked away.

The water was cold, quenching his thirst. He hadn't even known how thirsty he was. Casting a glance backwards, he saw that Nairna had not brought a drink to her brother, or anyone else. Why?

He drained the cup, feeling his face warm. Shy and thickheaded when it came to girls, he preferred to remain unnoticed, fading into the background. He didn't know how to talk to them, and, more often than not, he avoided them.

But it wasn't only girls who made him uncomfortable. He rarely spoke and hated being around larger groups. Though his father had chastised him for his reticence, ordering him to talk with guests and behave as a future chief, Bram never knew quite what to say.

Fighting was easier. As long as he could wield a claymore or a dirk, no one cared about his inability to converse. And in the middle of a cattle raid, it was rare for anyone to be watching him. They were too busy saving their own necks.

He made his way back to his discarded tunic, where he'd left it by the wall. He set down the cup and saw something round inside the folds. Wrapped in cloth, it was still warm. Bram glanced around him, but saw no one nearby. Inside lay a small loaf of bread.

His stomach rumbled as he tore off a piece, devouring the food. Nothing had ever tasted so good, after he'd been training all morning.

Nairna had left it for him; he was sure of it. As he finished eating the bread, he wondered if she'd had another purpose. If, perhaps, she cared for him in that mysterious way that women did.

He couldn't stop the incredulous lift of a smile, though he felt like a complete fool.

Over the next sennight, their secret courtship continued. One day, he would find that a torn tunic had been mended, while another time, he would reach into the fold of his cloak and find a small handful of fresh blackberries.

Since it wasn't right to receive gifts without giving any in return, he began leaving Nairna pretty stones or dried flowers, outside her chamber door. Once, he'd traded for a crimson ribbon and she'd smiled the entire day she'd worn it twined in her brown hair.

He couldn't understand why she'd chosen him as the subject of her affections. But the longer he stayed with her clan, the more she fascinated him. She never bothered him, never tried to speak with him directly. But the quiet kindnesses she showed had somehow made it impossible to stop thinking about her.

One afternoon, he found her huddled beneath a tree during a rainstorm. No one else was about, and from the basket she carried, it was clear she'd been collecting wild mushrooms.

Bram dismounted from his horse and untied his cloak, holding it out to her. 'Here. You look cold.'

She shook her head. 'No, it's all right. The rain will stop soon.'

He ignored her and walked closer, holding it out. Nairna took one end over her shoulder and held out the other. 'Share it with me.'

He didn't want to. The idea of sitting beside a beautiful young woman made him uneasy. He'd likely embarrass himself by saying something foolish.

But then Nairna raised her green eyes to his. 'Please.'

The softness in her voice reminded him of everything she'd done for him. Against his common sense, he sat beside her, leaning his back against the tree.

Nairna held out the cloak, drawing the end over his shoulders. 'Do you mind?' she whispered, huddling close to his side for warmth. He put his arm around her, keeping her wrapped in the woollen cloak. The rain was cool upon his face, and the cloak kept the worst of the weather away from them.

Had it been pouring down rain, he'd not have noticed. Every fibre of his attention was centred upon Nairna. Her head rested against his shoulder and she didn't try to fill up the space with meaningless words. His heart hammered with nerves, but he reached for her hand.

'My father came to speak to me this morning,' Nairna murmured, her palm cool against his. Her voice sounded nervous, as though she were afraid to speak.

Bram waited for her to continue, as he traced the contours of her palm.

Nairna coloured, squeezing his hand as if to gather strength. 'He said that…I am to be married.'

Whatever he'd been expecting, it wasn't that.

A hollow darkness invaded his mood and he couldn't stop the feelings of anger and unfairness. Though he'd only known her a few weeks, he felt protective of Nairna. *You're mine,* he wanted to growl. He'd skewer any man who tried to touch her.

'You're not getting married,' he said tightly. 'You're too young.'

'I'm fifteen,' she admitted. 'But you don't understand. They want an alliance between—'

'No.' He cut her off, not wanting to hear it. A possessive jealousy ate him up inside, firing up his temper. He removed the cloak, letting her hold on to it while he paced. He needed to think, to make decisions.

But Nairna rose, walking close to him. She took his hands in hers, and her face reddened. 'Bram, no. They want me to marry *you*.'

Shock struck him speechless and, slowly, the blood drained away from his anger. He took a breath, then another, trying to wrap his mind around her words.

'It's why they brought you here. So that we could... get to know one another.'

Married. To this girl, who would belong to him. The very thought made him dizzy, afraid that he wouldn't please her. She didn't truly know him. He wasn't the sort of natural leader his younger brother Alex was, nor did he fight as well as his father wanted him to. He had too much to learn and, though he was sixteen, he'd felt the sting of mediocrity. If they married, he had no doubt at all that he'd disappoint her.

Nairna looked down at their linked hands. 'Say something. If you don't want to wed me, then I'll talk to my father.'

He couldn't find the right words. If he tried to speak right now, not a word would make sense. He reached out to her nape, sliding his hands into her hair.

Refusing to wed her would be the right thing to do, but he couldn't relinquish the rigid need to be with her.

When dismay filled up her eyes, he leaned down and kissed her for the first time. He tasted the rain and her innocence, and when her mouth moved against his, a reckless desire raged through him.

He wanted her to be his, though she deserved better.

And when her arms folded around his waist, her face pressed against his chest, he vowed he would do everything he could to be the husband she wanted.

Chapter Three

Present day

Bram spent the remainder of the night within the stable. He didn't sleep, though he'd tried. His eyes burned with the aching need for rest, but slumber eluded him still. His conscience taunted him that he could never rest, not with Callum still a captive. And despite the fierce need, he couldn't command himself to sleep.

He still heard the screams in his memory, the unthinkable images branded into his mind. Darkness held nothing but horror for him, and he supposed it was little wonder that he couldn't trust himself to close his eyes.

Instead, he'd spent the hours thinking about his wife. The years had transformed her from a bright-eyed girl into a woman who took his breath away. Her kiss had melted away any ability to think clearly and it was a wonder he'd managed to leave her at all.

Even now, his hands were shaking at the thought of

touching her. He'd wanted nothing more than to lay her down upon the bed and claim her body with his.

And though he had that right as her husband, she wasn't ready to lie with him. Not when they were strangers to one another.

His father's advice on their wedding night drifted into his mind. *You'll know what to do,* Tavin had said. *Trust your instincts.*

If he'd surrendered to his instincts last night, he'd have pulled back the coverlet and used his mouth to taste every last inch of Nairna's body. And wouldn't that have shocked his innocent wife?

He wished to God that he'd had even a single night with her, but there'd been no time after he'd left the wedding. His eagerness to fight alongside his father had meant abandoning his new wife in their wedding bed. They'd never consummated the marriage, though their families hadn't known it.

So many foolish mistakes.

Now, he understood why his father hadn't wanted him to join in the battle. A hotheaded, untrained lad of sixteen wasn't ready to face English soldiers. Tavin MacKinloch had shielded him, taking the sword that would have ended Bram's life.

He'd fallen to his knees before his father's body, not even caring when he'd been captured. The blood of his father had stained his hands and there was naught that would bring Tavin back again.

The only atonement was to keep the promise he'd made, to look after Callum. The back of his neck began to itch, as if the heavy iron band still encircled it. Bram swallowed hard, forcing away the dark memories.

His gaze settled upon his scarred wrists. No doubt Nairna would be horrified when she saw the rest of him.

The more he thought of it, the more he wondered if he had any right to be here.

Did she still want him as her husband? She'd pushed him back last night and he didn't know if it was shyness or an aversion to him. What if she'd gone on with her life, remembering him as nothing more than a mistake she'd made, years ago?

Bram closed his eyes, lowering his gaze to the ground. The desire for a life with Nairna went bone-deep, as if she could somehow bring him redemption.

Though he hadn't slept at all, an anxious energy filled his veins with the need to be with her again, to convince himself that he hadn't been dreaming.

Footsteps entered the stable, and Bram jerked to his feet, his hand reaching for a dagger that wasn't there.

Hamish MacPherson, the chief of Ballaloch, stood at the doorway, his eldest son Malcolm behind him. Nairna was nowhere to be seen.

'You didn't have to sleep in the stables, lad,' the chief chided. With a shrewd gaze, he inspected Bram from head to toe before gripping him in an embrace of welcome. 'It's good to see you again. By God, we all thought you were dead. Where were you all of these years?'

'Cairnross,' he answered. Raising his wrists, he revealed the scars of his years of captivity.

From the grim look on Hamish's face, the man understood. 'I won't ask how you escaped. But you're fortunate Harkirk's men didn't strike you down.'

Bram said nothing, for he remembered little of what had happened after he'd been hooded. One moment, he'd felt the cold metal of a blade against his throat, and the next, he'd opened his eyes to find Nairna standing over him.

The chief kept talking, and the words blended together. Something about them being glad he had returned and more words about Nairna. Bram tried to piece the conversation together, but hunger and lack of sleep made it difficult to concentrate.

A sober expression came over the chief's face and he made the sign of the cross. 'It's a good thing that Iver MacDonnell is gone, God rest him. That would have made a mess of everything.'

Bram had no idea what Hamish was talking about, and at his blank look the chief cursed. 'She didn't tell you, did she?'

'Tell me what?'

'Nairna married the MacDonnell chief four years ago. He died last summer.' Hamish shook his head, adding, 'Though I suppose their marriage was never legal, since you were still alive.' He rubbed the beard on his face, thinking to himself. 'I'll speak to Father Garrick about it and ask what's to be done.'

Bram didn't hear anything else Hamish said. A low buzzing filled his ears and he felt as if someone had knocked him to the ground.

She'd married someone else. And worse, she'd said nothing about it.

It grated upon Bram's temper, the knowledge shredding apart his control. He'd wanted to believe Nairna had waited for him. That there had never been anyone else.

He'd been wrong.

Rage tore down any rational feelings. It made him wish the MacDonnell chief were still alive, just so Bram could kill him for touching what belonged to him. The bastard had claimed her virginity, and the longer he thought about it, the more Bram's anger grew.

It took everything he had to keep his face impassive, burying the fury deep inside. When he saw Nairna, he fully intended to confront her about it.

'I'm taking Nairna back with me,' he told the chief.

'You'll want her dowry as well,' Hamish commented, his mouth twisted into a dark smile. 'Seeing as you left before you could collect it.'

God's bones, he hadn't even thought that far ahead. Right now, he was itching to talk to her, to learn what had happened during the past seven years. And why she'd married another man.

The coins weren't important, but until he knew what the circumstances were at Glen Arrin, it was best to be prepared. 'I'll take the dowry with me when we go back.'

Hamish raised an eyebrow. 'She won't have as much as before. And she'll lose her widow's portion when her stepson learns that the marriage wasn't a true one.'

Another disconcerting thought occurred to Bram. 'Did she…have any bairns?'

'There were no children from the union.'

Hamish looked uncomfortable and Bram let out the breath he'd been holding. He half-hoped it was because her husband was impotent. 'Where is Nairna now?'

'Inside her chamber. She sent us to find you.' The chief reached out and touched his shoulder. 'But you needn't worry about the MacDonnells. I'll talk to their chief and work out the details of Nairna's property.'

'She's not returning to them,' Bram swore. 'They can keep whatever they want, but Nairna stays with me.'

The corners of Hamish's mouth twitched. 'I'm glad you've come back, Bram. For I'm thinking you're just what Nairna needs right now.'

Nairna's hands were buried in her trunk, while she sorted her stockings by colour. First, all the dark colours, then the lighter ones, and last, the heavy woollen stockings she wore only in the winter. She rolled them up into tight, neat balls, arranging them into rows. Though she'd already packed her belongings yesterday, this was the only thing she could do to keep her nerves under control.

Last night after Bram had left, she'd lain awake, thinking about him. It almost seemed as if she'd imagined him kissing her. For so long, she'd held on to memories of the past, but those visions were nothing like the man who had taken possession of her lips, seizing his right to touch her.

He'd kissed her until her body had responded, her skin growing heated at his rough mouth and tongue. Something unexpected had awakened inside her. It was as if he were coaxing her to surrender her tight control and bend to his will.

Iver had never kissed her like that.

Her cheeks burned with shame when she thought of the man she'd believed was her second husband. Had she sinned, by giving her body to him, believing they were lawfully wed? Was she meant to forget those married years, as if they'd never happened?

Her mind turned in circles until she didn't know what to think anymore. She'd given her heart to Bram once, long ago. And though she was confused about what she felt for him, she couldn't deny the fierce hope rising inside. He'd come for her, as soon as he'd been released. He wanted her, despite all the years that had passed.

It might be possible to resurrect the buried feelings. And perhaps…there was hope that Bram could fill her empty womb. Her heart softened, for she wasn't ready to abandon the dream of having a child. Not yet.

Would he take her home with him now? As his wife, she would be expected to join him and live with the

MacKinloch clan. Bram's family lived further north and she'd only visited once. The men were hot-tempered fighters, fierce men whom the English feared. Her stomach tightened with uneasiness.

It will be all right, she reminded herself. There was no need to be anxious about it. Better to think of it as her second chance for a home and family of her own. And Bram would be there, at her side.

Nairna rose and went to the chest where she kept her belongings. Inside, she withdrew a faded crimson ribbon. The edges were frayed and worn.

She held it in her palm, as if she could grasp the lost years. The ground beneath her feet seemed to have split apart. No longer was she a widow, but, instead, a wife. And where Bram went, she had to follow.

She threaded the ribbon into her braids, tucking the strands around it.

The door opened and her maid Jenny interrupted. 'They've found yer husband.'

Nairna let out a breath, her shoulders relaxing. 'Good. He'll need food, fresh clothing and a bath.'

Widowed and elderly, Jenny was like the mother Nairna had lost so many years ago. And though her gnarled hands made it hard for the woman to serve, Nairna didn't have the heart to dismiss her.

'I'll see to it, then.' The old woman paused at the entrance, her voice turning concerned. 'Are ye glad to have him back, m'lady?'

'I am, yes.' Nairna ventured a smile, but truthfully she was worried.

'Well, that's good to hear. And at least ye won't fret about the marriage bed, since ye already know what to expect.' Her maid gave a warm smile before she left the chamber, closing the door behind her.

Nairna said nothing, for that wasn't at all true. Although she was no longer a virgin, the idea of sharing a bed with Bram made her face flush with embarrassment. The only man whom she'd known intimately was Iver and, to be frank, there was nothing exciting about his lovemaking. She'd learned to lie still, let him do what he wished and that was that. It never lasted more than a few minutes anyway.

But last night, when Bram had kissed her, none of it was the same. He had looked upon her as though there were no other woman on this earth, as though he wanted to do nothing more than claim her, taking her body and teaching her pleasure. It made her wonder what it would be like to lie with him, to touch his warm skin and feel his body moving atop her own.

A rush of heat flooded through her and Nairna shivered, thinking of Bram's shadowed face last night. The faint moonlight had revealed a strong jawline and a slightly crooked nose.

Dark brown hair, the colour of wet earth, fell past his shoulders. A beard hid his face, but it had felt silken against her mouth. And, saints above, his kiss could tempt a woman to hand over her very soul to the Devil.

The shy boy was gone, replaced by a fierce man she didn't know. A man who had travelled through the gates of hell and emerged as a survivor.

'When were you planning to tell me that you remarried?'

She screamed, bumping her hands against the lid of the trunk. Her heartbeat clattered inside her chest and she had wild thoughts of throwing a stocking before she realised it was only Bram.

'You scared me,' she breathed, touching her chest. 'I didn't hear you come inside.'

'When did it happen?' he demanded again, moving closer. There was anger carved into his features and she sensed that she had to tread carefully.

'Three years after I thought you were dead.' She held her ground until he stood directly in front of her. Nervous energy spread over her, but she held her ground. Not a word did he speak, as though he were fighting against his anger.

'I didn't know where you went last night,' Nairna murmured. 'You left so suddenly.'

'I wasn't certain you wanted me to stay.' Bram's eyes were weary and he studied her as if he didn't quite know what to do or say. The more she studied him, the more physical needs she saw. Hunger, a few minor wounds and exhaustion permeated his bearing. Those, she could take care of. But there was something else beneath his expression, a haunted quality she couldn't understand.

'Did you care for him?' he asked quietly. 'The man you married.'

'Iver was kind enough.' She hid her shaking hands behind her back.

'I suppose you wish I hadn't come back.' A grim look passed over his face and Bram folded his arms across his chest.

'You're wrong.' Seeing him standing before her was a gift, one she'd never expected. It was as if she could blot out the years of her failures, starting over again. And the few memories she and Bram had had together had been good ones.

To change the subject, she said, 'I've sent for food and a bath.'

Bram moved to stand in front of her. It was as if he

were memorising her face, burning it into his mind. A blush warmed Nairna's cheeks when he drew his thumb over her lips, his palm cupping her cheek.

Upon his wrists, she saw striated lines and a matching band around his throat. Nairna was caught between the desire to know everything and the stoic don't-ask expression on Bram's face. She didn't know what she could say to put him at ease about the past, but it seemed best to say nothing.

He moved past her and rested his hands upon the edge of a table, his head leaning down. He looked as if he were in pain and she suspected he might need her help in the bath. Although it didn't bother her to see a man unclothed, she didn't know how Bram would feel about having her assist him.

Before she could ask, Jenny arrived with the food and clean clothing, which she set down while servants carried in the wooden tub, filling it with buckets of hot water.

'Leave us,' Bram ordered. The older woman hesitated before Nairna inclined her head and Jenny scuttled away.

When the door had closed, Bram regarded Nairna before touching the food. 'Have you eaten?'

She nodded, startled that he would ask about her first. Then he turned to look at the meal Jenny had left. Though it wasn't much—only some mutton stew and a few oat cakes—he studied it with hungry eyes, breathing in the scent as though he feared it might vanish.

'How long has it been since you've eaten?' she murmured, the truth suddenly dawning.

'Two days,' he admitted. He picked up the oat cake and dipped it in the stew, eating slowly as if to savour every mouthful. She half-expected him to attack the food, but instead he ate carefully and not nearly enough. He left most of the food unfinished, and when she started to clear it away, he stopped her. 'Leave it. I'll try to eat more later.'

He unlaced his tunic, eyeing the bath. Nairna wasn't certain whether he wanted her to go or stay, but when he lifted the garment over his head, her breath caught in her throat.

Massive scars covered his chest, hundreds of red-and-white markings, as though they'd tried to cut the flesh from his body.

Oh, sweet God above. What had they done to him? Her stomach clenched at the injustice and she feared that the simple touch of warm water would cause him pain.

Seeing him like this made her want to take care of him again, to heal the physical darkness he'd suffered. How much torment had he endured in captivity? It frightened her to think of it.

Bram offered no explanation, but when he began to remove the rest of his clothing, Nairna turned away. She waited until she heard the slight splash of water before asking, 'Do you want me to stay or go?'

He didn't answer, so she ventured a glance. His knees were drawn up in the water, his back hunched over. She took a tentative step forwards, then another.

'If you'd rather go, I wouldn't blame you,' he said at last. 'I know what I must look like.'

She bit her lip hard, her ribs tight within her. There were no words to describe the scars carved upon his skin. 'Tell me what happened.'

But again Bram gave no reply. Instead, he laid his head back against the tub and she moved towards him, offering a cake of soap.

He took it from her, seeming to understand her

reluctance to touch him. The fear of hurting him made her nervous about assisting him in the bath. She reached for a drying cloth, placing it within his reach. An awkward silence descended between them, leaving Nairna with little to say or do.

She shouldn't be this nervous. Heaven knew, she'd helped Iver in his bath dozens of times.

But this was Bram, a man she hadn't seen in seven years. She didn't know what would put him at ease, and the longer she waited, the more her apprehension attacked her self-confidence.

She reached out to touch his long dark hair, offering, 'Do you want me to cut your hair?'

He caught her fingers. 'It hasn't been cut in seven years.' His hand lingered upon hers and the wetness of his palm made her shiver.

'I'll take care of it for you, then.' At least now she had something to do. Something that wouldn't cause him pain.

His thumb rubbed slight circles against her palm. 'I'm sorry, Nairna.'

There were years' worth of apologies in those three words. She met his brown eyes with her own, and when she found herself leaning in, her heartbeat quickened. He was going to kiss her again, if she allowed it.

Her cheeks grew warm and it was hard to breathe. It had been so long since any man had given her affection. Iver had never bothered with it. She might as well have been a spare tunic instead of a wife.

Her fingers laced with his and she waited. Beneath the veiled desire in Bram's eyes, she saw an unnamed emotion. Whether it was anger that she'd remarried or frustration of another kind, she couldn't tell.

He let go of her hand and closed his eyes.

Nairna hid her disappointment and went to retrieve a sharp dagger to cut his hair. When she returned with the knife, Bram's palms gripped the sides of the wooden tub. He steeled himself when she knelt beside him, as if he couldn't bear to see the weapon.

Gently, she reached out to take a length of his hair, the locks limp against her palm. His mouth was a thin slash, his eyes staring straight ahead.

She hesitated, one hand holding his hair. 'Would you rather I left it alone?'

'No. But do it quickly.' The abrupt words spurred her into action.

Nairna cut the length to his shoulders, slicing his hair with the dagger. She tried to keep the length even, wishing she had shears to do a better job of it. Her hands moved over his scalp, and only when she'd set the dagger aside did his tension seem to dissipate.

She helped him lower his head into the water, washing his hair. With the soap, she massaged his scalp, the warmth of the water rising up against her skin.

When he sat up, his hair rinsed, Bram's eyes bored into hers. In the dark depths, she saw the same sort of hunger he'd had earlier. His bristled cheeks were wet, his mouth firm. Water slid down his face to his scarred back and the air grew heavier to breathe.

Nairna's attention was drawn to his chest and she found it difficult to think clearly when he was looking at her that way. 'Tell me what happened to you, after our wedding,' she asked, hoping to distract him. 'I know Glen Arrin was attacked.'

It had been both bewildering and humiliating. One moment, she'd been celebrating her wedding, and the next, her bridegroom had fled with his father and kinsmen.

'When we arrived home, it was under siege. The English set fire to Glen Arrin and slaughtered our clansmen. All because my father wouldn't pledge his allegiance to Longshanks,' Bram said. His mouth tightened with distaste at the English king's nickname.

He leaned closer, and she saw the wildness in his eyes. Rage was there, brimming beneath the surface. 'And they still have my brother Callum.'

He stood up from the water before she could stop him and droplets spilled over his skin, down his ribs, to his thighs. He showed no embarrassment at revealing himself to her and Nairna's cheeks burned at the sight of his manhood. It had risen slightly, as though he wanted her.

Don't stare, she warned herself. She averted her eyes, though she was curious. When she handed Bram the drying cloth, she asked, 'How are you going to free your brother?'

'I don't know yet. Perhaps we'll raise an army. Or a ransom.' He dried his face and chest before wrapping the cloth around his hips.

Ransom? Did he honestly believe that the English would accept his bribe and hand over his brother?

'A ransom won't work,' she answered honestly. 'They'll seize your coins and keep Callum a prisoner.'

'I'll get him out, Nairna.' The resolution in his voice spoke of a man who would keep his word, even if it meant his own death. He reached for his fallen clothing, retrieving something from his belongings that she couldn't see.

'I hope you do.' She turned back to busy herself with his uneaten food, while he dressed in the new clothing. She didn't know how to respond to him and it felt as if her life had been opened up and dumped upon the floor, like the spilled contents of a trunk.

She rested her hands upon the table, taking one breath, then another. Behind her, she heard Bram's footsteps before he caught her around the waist, turning her to face him. His touch penetrated the rough wool of her gown, warming her skin. He held her imprisoned, his fingers spread apart beneath her ribcage. She met his eyes with her own and in his direct gaze, she felt her thoughts scatter.

'He touched you, didn't he?' His breath moved against her cheek, sending spirals of heat through her skin. 'He consummated your marriage.'

She gave a single nod and saw the tension within his jaw. But she couldn't lie. Not about this.

She'd married Iver MacDonnell because he'd seemed like a reasonable match, even if she'd had no feelings towards him. At the age of eighteen, she'd wanted a family of her own, instead of remaining in her father's house.

'All those years,' he murmured, 'I was locked in chains and I dreamed of you. Only to find out that you wed someone else—' His words broke off, his anger palpable.

Nairna felt her own hurt rising up. 'I can't go back and change the past, Bram.' She straightened her spine, staring at him. 'But I can leave it where it belongs and start again.'

He gripped her hands and the emptiness in his face made her feel as if she'd betrayed him. There weren't any words to make it any easier.

Then his mouth came down upon hers. He kissed her to mark her as his own, as if punishing her for wedding another man.

Then, abruptly, it shifted to a softer embrace. The second kiss was as gentle as the first one he'd ever given her. With it, he reminded her of the years between them and the feelings she'd once held. He coaxed her to respond, taking her face between his hands.

Bram stared at her, his expression unreadable. 'We're leaving within a few hours, Nairna. Finish packing your belongings.' He pressed something hard and cool into her hand.

And after he left her chamber, she opened her palm. Inside lay a grey stone, with streaks of rose quartz to make it sparkle. It was the same stone she'd given him upon their wedding day.

Nairna squeezed it in her hand, letting the tears fall.

Chapter Four

'I've sent word to the MacDonnell chief,' Hamish MacPherson informed Nairna. 'Father Garrick will negotiate the settlement of your belongings.'

'What settlement?' Nairna asked, feeling uneasy about the entire situation. Although her stepson was a reasonable man, it unnerved her to think that her second marriage had not been a marriage at all. She'd made a life for herself while Bram was still alive. And though she understood, logically, that it was simply a mistake, she felt the shame of it.

'The return of your dowry,' her father replied. 'Since you will not receive a dower portion of the MacDonnell holdings, your belongings must be returned to you.' He came forwards and rested his hand upon Nairna's shoulder. 'You needn't worry about it. I'll make the arrangements so you can go home with your husband.'

Nairna nodded, but everything had changed so suddenly, she was torn between confusion and thankfulness. No longer did she have to return to Callendon. She could

walk away from that life, starting again with Bram. In
her palm, she fingered the coloured stone he'd given her,
sending up a silent wish for a good marriage.

'It will be all right, Nairna,' her father reassured her.
'But you should make your way to Glen Arrin soon, in
case more soldiers come looking for Bram.'

Nairna's heart grew cold at the thought. It disturbed
her to think that he'd nearly been murdered before her
eyes. If her father hadn't spoken up, if he hadn't bribed
the soldiers… She didn't want to think of it.

'I've ordered a wagon of supplies for you,' Hamish
continued. 'Go now, while there's light.' His expression
turned grim. 'You still have to travel past Lord Harkirk's
stronghold.'

She wished there were another way to avoid it, but the
Baron's fortress lay between the mountains, and there
was only one road to Glen Arrin.

Her father led her into the outer bailey, where Bram
was waiting. Hamish had given them a horse and wagon,
and she saw her trunk of belongings inside, along with
sacks of food and other supplies.

'I've sent you with fifty pennies,' her father added.

'No, save it for the clan. They'll need them.' She
couldn't take a single coin from him.

'The MacDonnells will return the funds to me from
the dowry I gave you before. I'll get the coins again, you
needn't worry.'

Nairna embraced him tightly, feeling her eyes blur
with tears. 'Thank you.'

'Go on, then. Send word that you've arrived safely,'
he ordered. To Bram, he directed, 'Take care of my
daughter.'

Bram met his gaze and gave a nod. He sat holding

the reins, waiting for her. Nairna looked around for her maid, but there was no sign of the elderly woman.

'Jenny is coming with us, isn't she?' Nairna asked.

Bram shook his head. 'Not yet. Perhaps later, once I've seen how Glen Arrin has fared.'

'What about escorts?' She couldn't imagine that he intended to travel alone with her, not with all the unrest in the Highlands.

'It would only attract the attention of Cairnross and his men, if they're still looking,' her father pointed out. He exchanged a look with Bram. 'And after what happened with Harkirk's men yesterday, we want nothing that will draw notice.'

Nairna didn't like it. It was dangerous, especially in enemy territory. Bram sensed her uneasiness and he touched the hilt of a claymore Nairna hadn't seen before. It was strapped to his back, hidden behind a cloak of dark wool. 'We'll be safe enough.'

He helped her climb into the back of the wagon, among the goods. And as the wagon rumbled along the road outside the gates, Nairna prayed it would be true.

The foothills rose higher as they continued further north-west, transforming into mountains. The gleaming silver of the loch brushed the stony banks, contrasting against the vast green expanse of grass. The trees grew sparser and rain spattered against the wool of her hood.

Nairna was used to the rain, but today it took on a more ghostly atmosphere with the clouds skimming the edges of the mountains.

The MacKinloch clan dwelled a two-day journey on horseback through the valley. Nairna had only been there once, and after Bram was believed dead, she'd chosen to stay with her family instead of living among strangers.

She studied Bram from her position in the wagon, noticing the lowered shoulders, the heaviness in his posture. He kept his gaze fixed upon the horizon, watching for enemies. Exhaustion weighted him down and she wondered what she could do to help ease him.

After another hour, she moved to the front of the wagon and sat beside him. His apprehensions about the journey were evident from the set of his jaw and the cast of his face.

'You haven't seen your family since you were taken captive?' she ventured, breaking the silence. Though she already knew the answer, she'd hoped to get him talking.

Bram only shook his head once.

She tried again. 'Will your other brothers be glad to see you?' He gave a shrug as if he didn't know the answer.

By the saints, this was going to be a long journey if he didn't speak a word. 'Did you leave your voice back at Ballaloch? Or are you planning to ignore me?'

Bram slowed the horses and turned to look at her. Unrest brewed in his eyes, along with unspoken frustration. 'They didn't try to free us, Nairna. My brother and I were locked away for years. Not a single person from my family came to look for us. And I don't know why.'

The vehemence in his voice made her regret pushing him. 'They sent word to my father that you were killed in the siege.' She touched his sleeve, hoping his own family hadn't truly meant to abandon him. 'I suppose no one knew the truth. I'm sorry.'

Her words did little to ease his black mood. Bram increased the pace of their horse again, the wagon bumping along the path.

The afternoon drew closer to evening, and the mist lifted just enough to see the path that lay ahead. Tucked near the side of a hill with a steep ditch on all sides lay the motte defended by Robert Fitzroy, Baron of Harkirk.

She reached for Bram's hand, fear rising up in her throat. 'The men who tried to kill you yesterday…they came from Harkirk's fortress. There.' She pointed to the structure.

Though it had once been nothing but a wooden garrison, from the looks of it Harkirk had begun transforming the enclosure into a more permanent structure with a tower. Knowing that her father's coins had gone into the construction irritated her further.

He squeezed her hand once, then released it. His eyes studied the fortress. 'How long has this been here?'

'They built the first garrison five years ago. It's changed since then.' Unfortunately, it had grown larger, as if Harkirk intended to build a castle.

'I thought the land was part of your father's holdings.'

'Not anymore.' Not since Hamish had made the peace agreement with the English. 'Lord Harkirk governs it now. He claims it's for our protection.'

Bram unsheathed the claymore from his back and set it at his feet. The weapon was a gift from her father. From tip to hilt it stood as high as Nairna's chest, and wielding the two-handed sword required strength. She wondered if he was capable of defending them with it.

Though he kept his hands upon the reins, there was

a visible shift in his demeanour. His face grew distant, his eyes searching the horizon.

When they started to pass beyond the outskirts of the fortress, two soldiers rode forwards to intercept them.

Nairna's heart sank. She'd hoped they could make it past without being noticed. Though she tried to push back the fear rising up inside, her nerves were raw. She couldn't stop thinking about the soldiers who had captured Bram, intending to murder him.

As the soldiers drew closer, Bram kept the wagon at a steady pace.

'Should we ride faster?' she ventured.

But there came no reply. He was staring straight ahead, as if caught in a trance. 'Bram?' she asked again.

'There are only two of them. And if they threaten you, they answer to me.' The flat emotionless tone frightened her as much as the soldiers, for she suspected he would kill without any remorse. Nairna prayed it wouldn't be necessary.

She risked a glance behind at the mounted soldiers. They wore chainmail armour and both carried spears. Lower-ranking soldiers, she realised. Likely sent to question them.

Bram maintained their pace and as the men came closer, her nerves wound tighter. The men surrounded them, keeping an even pace with the wagon. One sent her a slow smile that made her skin crawl.

Bram hadn't moved, not wavering from his course. If it weren't for his tight knuckles, she'd have wondered if he had even noticed the soldiers. His gaze remained focused upon the road ahead of them.

'Aren't you going to stop?' one taunted her. 'Lord Harkirk would want to offer his…hospitality.'

Nairna gave no reply, for it would only goad them on. She moved closer to Bram, not making eye contact with the soldiers. Silently, she prayed that the men would leave them alone. But instead, they continued riding, one on each side of the wagon.

'I'd like a piece of the woman,' came the voice of the other soldier. He smirked and Nairna shrank away.

At that, Bram raised up the claymore. His arm muscles strained as he pointed it at the soldier who had threatened her. In his other hand, he held a dirk.

Nairna took the reins from him and held her breath, for she hadn't known he possessed the strength to hold the weight of the claymore with only one hand.

'If you touch her, I'll remove your hand.' He sent them a dark smile. 'Or your head. And I'll enjoy doing it.'

The soldiers eyed one another, as if they weren't certain whether he would follow through with the threat. In the end, they fell back.

'Go on your way.'

Bram never tore his gaze from the men until they were far in the distance. The interaction had affected him somehow, the shadow of his past crossing over his face. Every muscle in his body was taut, like a tightly strung bow, before he lowered the claymore and dirk, taking the reins back.

Only when several miles lay between them and the garrison did Nairna start to breathe again. Too much could have gone wrong. They could have questioned Bram or taken him into custody.

Her father had been right. They needed to get far away from Ballaloch. Only at Glen Arrin, among Bram's family, would they be safe.

* * *

When the sun had begun to descend, she asked Bram, 'Where do you want to stop for the night?' Though she wasn't quite ready to sleep, she was growing hungry.

Nothing. It was as if she'd spoken to empty air.

'Bram?' she prompted again. He didn't turn, didn't move, except to keep his gaze fixated upon the road ahead. It was then that she noticed his hands were shaking. Though his posture remained perfectly upright, something wasn't right.

His eyes were unseeing, as if he were caught within a dream. Was he even aware of anything?

'What is it?'

Bram didn't speak, so she pulled against the reins, ordering the horse to stop. He didn't seem to notice that they were no longer moving. His brown eyes were vacant and she reached out to take his hands in hers. His flesh was icy cold.

'Tell me,' she whispered, suddenly frightened. The sky was darkening, the wind shifting around them. Bram appeared lost in a world of his own thoughts and she suspected he didn't hear her at all.

She reached out to touch his cheek, hoping that the gesture would awaken him from the spell he was under. Gently, she slid her fingertips down his skin to his throat. When her touch grazed against his scar, his hand shot out and grabbed her wrist. Madness brewed in his eyes and he stared hard at her, as though she were an enemy trying to slay him.

The pain made her gasp and she closed her eyes, wondering how in God's name she would break through to him. Though he'd lost a great deal of strength, she didn't doubt he could snap her wrist in half.

'Bram, it's Nairna,' she insisted. 'Look at me. It's

your—' she let out a shuddering breath '—your wife,' she managed. 'Please let go of my wrist.'

When he didn't, she fought back against the harsh pain. 'You're hurting me, Bram.'

Agonising minutes stretched on while she spoke quietly to him, praying that he would somehow see her.

And then, abruptly, he let go. He blinked at her, his eyes suddenly narrowing. When he saw her clutching at her wrist and her reddened skin, he let out a tortured breath.

'What did I do to you, Nairna?'

She shook her head, not knowing what to say. Her heart shook within her chest and she couldn't bring herself to look at him.

'I'm sorry,' he breathed, trying to examine her hand, but she kept it far away from him. 'I was dreaming. I must have fallen asleep.'

'Your eyes were open,' she insisted.

He rested his elbows on his knees, letting his face sink into his hands. His fingers were still trembling, she realised. A deep fear sank inside her, for she didn't know whether or not Bram was telling the truth. It might have been a waking dream, or it might have been madness. She didn't know.

'Let's stop here for the night,' she said quietly. 'We'll get some rest and start again in the morning.'

'Nairna.' He lifted his head and she saw the regret etched on his face. 'Never in a thousand years would I knowingly hurt you. I can't tell you how sorry I am.'

She moved away from him, stepping down from the wagon. Her thoughts were in such turmoil right now that she didn't trust herself to speak. Instead, she nodded and walked towards the stream, holding her bruised wrist.

* * *

Bram let her go, never taking his eyes from his wife. He watched as she knelt by the stream, bathing her wrist in the cool water. It felt as though someone had taken a knife and carved out his soul.

He'd done this to her. He'd let the nightmares bend him into the shape of a man he didn't know. She must have said something to him, possibly touched him. And he'd had no control over the visions that plagued him.

The encounter with the English soldiers had conjured up a darkness he didn't want to face. Seeing their armour, hearing their threats against Nairna, had brought back the past few years. Although they were no different from the countless soldiers he'd seen before, seeing them had been like pouring oil over the flames of his memory.

Because of it, he'd hurt Nairna, the innocent wife whom he'd wanted to protect. There were not enough words to apologise for what he'd done and she wouldn't understand what had happened anyway.

The years of torment had changed him, so that he no longer slept like a normal man. He remained awake for long hours, until exhaustion caught him without warning. Never did he sleep at night and never when he craved rest.

One moment, he would be standing; the next he'd have no memory of how time had passed or what had happened to him. More than once, he'd blacked out in the midst of working on one of the damned stone walls. He'd awakened to the pain of a lash striking across his back, a whip that only ceased when he returned to his labour.

You're not there anymore, he reminded himself. *It's in the past.*

But Callum was still there. And no one could shelter his brother from the English torturers.

He got down from the wagon and unhitched the horse, leading it to the water. His wife remained where she was, though he didn't miss the guarded fear in her eyes. Seeing it only intensified his self-hatred.

As the horse drank, he stared into the water, angry with himself for what he'd done. He needed to say something to her, or, better, do something to make amends. Words weren't enough.

The soft shush of her skirts against the grass told him that she'd come up behind him. 'Are you all right, Bram?'

He nodded. 'Is your wrist still hurting?'

'A little.' But in her voice he heard the tremor of worry.

He reached up to take her wrist. Gently, he caressed the skin, furious with himself.

'It's all right,' she said quietly. And in her green eyes he saw that she wasn't going to turn her back on him because of a moment of darkness. Her quiet reassurance was a forgiveness he'd never expected.

He stared at her wrist, then reached down to the hem of his tunic and rent the fabric, tearing off a long thin strip.

Nairna stared at Bram, uncertain of why he was damaging his tunic. 'What are you doing?'

He took her wrist and fumbled with the strip of cloth, wrapping it around her bruise like a bandage. His hands were trembling, but he kept winding the cloth until it covered her skin. It was loose and awkward, but she voiced no criticism. It was his way of trying to atone for his actions. Her heart stumbled, for she knew he'd never meant to hurt her.

'You don't have to do that,' she murmured. When he reached for her other wrist, she stopped him. 'I know you weren't aware of what happened. I shouldn't have touched your scar.'

For a long moment, he held on to her hand, staring at the bandage as if he were searching for the right words. 'I lost control of myself. I can't remember the last time I slept and I haven't eaten a full meal in years.'

She reached out to touch his face, bringing him up to look at her. His fingers clasped with hers, as if he needed the reassurance.

Her skin warmed beneath his and she found herself studying him. There were wounds she couldn't see, scars that went deeper than any physical wounds. And though she knew his body and mind had been damaged by the imprisonment, beneath it all, she saw a man who needed saving.

Bram moved away to gather firewood and Nairna joined him, searching for tinder. Neither spoke until he'd managed to light the fire.

She searched the supplies and brought him some food. Though he tried to eat the oat cake, he took only a bite or two before setting it aside.

'How will you regain your strength if you don't eat?' she asked, frowning at his untouched food.

He shook his head. 'It's too much, too soon.' He rested his wrists upon his knees, staring at the flames. 'Nairna, if you're weary, go on and sleep. I won't bother you tonight.' He nodded towards the wagon, in a gesture of dismissal.

But if she left him alone, he wouldn't sleep. She knew

it. Nairna moved to sit beside him. 'Come and lie down with me. I'll wager you're more tired than I am.'

In his worn face, she could see the years of exhaustion, but Bram shook his head. 'I'll stay here and keep watch.'

Another thought occurred to her. 'Are you afraid to sleep?' She wondered if nightmares plagued him, perhaps visions of the past.

She reached out for him. Bram lifted her bandaged wrist to his mouth, brushing his lips against the pulse point. She shivered slightly, the unexpected tremor sending desire spiralling through her.

'Go on and sleep in the wagon without me,' he urged, but instead she laid down beside him, resting her head in his lap. She'd come this far and she wasn't about to leave him now.

For he was her husband. And he needed her.

She felt him gently stroke her hair. As she closed her eyes, even knowing she wouldn't sleep, Bram touched her as if she were the salvation he'd craved for so long.

Chapter Five

The following evening, they arrived at Glen Arrin. The sight of his home should have filled him with relief and thankfulness, but Bram's nerves tightened with fear of what the others would say. It was his fault that Callum had been taken captive. His fault that his father had died. And though he longed to see his brothers, he was afraid of the blame he would face.

As they approached, his heart grew heavier. Glen Arrin might have been a formidable fortress years ago, but those days were long past.

Half-a-dozen thatched huts encircled the keep and the outer palisade wall revealed large open segments. Broken and frail, the fortress barely held together, like an old man too stubborn to admit his weakness.

Years ago, his father had promised to build a castle, one that could defend their clan from any attack. Those promises hadn't been fulfilled, it seemed.

'It needs a bit of fixing, doesn't it?' Nairna ventured when he'd pulled the wagon to a stop. She stared at the keep, as though she were trying to find something nice to say. 'Some thatch and new wood might help.'

He eyed her with disbelief, then glanced back at Glen Arrin. She was being far too generous. Although he'd wanted her to live with him in a place they could be proud of, the fortress was worse than he'd expected.

'A strong wind would blow it down,' he admitted. 'It's a disaster.'

'Well, I wouldn't say *that*. It just needs a few men to work on it.'

'Over the next five years,' he countered.

'It just needs a new foundation, new walls, a new roof and a new door.' She sent him a wry grin. 'Nothing much at all.'

He didn't respond to her teasing, but when she squeezed his palm, she reminded him, 'You've come home, Bram. After all this time, you'll see your family.'

Her words stopped him short. She was right. He'd been dwelling upon the appearance, rather than being grateful for his freedom.

He breathed in the clean air, heavy with moisture. And for a moment, he let the familiar sights offer him comfort. He *was* glad to be home.

He helped Nairna down from the wagon. 'Come on, then. Let's go inside. Pray God the roof doesn't fall on our heads and bury us.'

He took her hand in his, leading her forwards. As they passed the meagre huts, a few curious men raised their hands in welcome, calling out a greeting, their faces breaking into smiles. He recognised the faces of his clansmen, though he couldn't quite recall some of the names.

He led her further inside until they reached the narrow tower. At a closer glimpse, he saw how unstable the structure was. The frame was worm-eaten, the wood showing signs of decay.

Before he could think any more about it, he saw his brother standing there. Tall, with dark hair and a dark beard, Alex had grown into the image of their father Tavin.

Alex stared at him, as though he couldn't believe what he was seeing. 'My God, you're alive,' he breathed, crushing him into a hug.

Bram gripped his brother hard. Words choked up in his throat, leaving him with nothing to say. He couldn't even speak a greeting, for fear that it would loosen all the emotions he'd locked away. Seeing Alex again, grown into a man, made him aware of all the years he'd lost.

'You're taller than I remember,' he managed at last.

Alex pulled back, a smile creasing his mouth. 'I suppose you grew a beard to hide that face, so you wouldn't frighten the others.'

'I'm still better looking than you.' He managed a rough smile, and gratefulness washed through him. He did have two remaining brothers, even if Callum wasn't here.

'What happened to you, Bram?' Alex asked.

'Lord Cairnross took me as his captive.' Bram didn't make full eye contact, but he saw the discerning look in his brother's gaze. 'Callum is still imprisoned.'

Alex cursed and guilt crossed his face. 'Bram, they told me both of you were dead. I swear to you, if I'd known any differently—'

'You were four and ten when we were taken,' Bram reminded him. 'I suppose you believed what they told you.'

His brother gave a single stony nod. 'It doesn't make it right.' After an awkward pause, he added, 'Our uncle became chief of the clan after Da died.' He stared into Bram's eyes, as if trying to make excuses. 'When Donnell died two years ago, I took his place. But I know our father wanted you to be the chief.'

The last thing Bram wanted was to assume control of the clan. He shook his head, 'It belongs to you, Alex. I've no wish for the title.' Or the responsibility. Whether it was expected of him or not, he wouldn't consider taking it from his brother.

Alex remained unconvinced. 'There's time to decide on that later.' He directed his attention to Nairna then, and Bram realised he hadn't even brought her to greet his brother.

He moved to her side, touching her shoulder. 'You remember Nairna, my wife.'

She lowered her head in greeting. 'Alex. It's been a long time.'

A faint smile touched Alex's mouth, and he said, 'It has. I'm not surprised Bram stopped to bring you back with him. A bonny lass you always were.'

The compliment was meant to set her at ease, but instead it evoked a twist of jealousy within Bram. He didn't like seeing Nairna embarrassed. His hand moved about her waist, drawing her closer to his side.

Alex seemed to read his thoughts, and he reassured him, 'Peace, brother. Laren is my wife and I have daughters of my own.'

Daughters? It seemed strange to even imagine his younger brother with a wife, much less bairns. Almost as if Alex had assumed the life Bram had expected to have. Once again, he was jolted by the passage of time.

'I would like to meet your wife,' Nairna said. 'Are they inside?'

Alex shrugged. 'Possibly. Or Laren could be out walking. You can go and find her, if you wish.'

Nairna left them, and once she'd gone, Alex gestured for him to walk at his side. They moved around the perimeter of the fortress, neither speaking for a time.

The familiar walls, though worn and broken, offered a quiet peace. 'I remember climbing that wall, when we were boys,' Bram said.

'You used to run along the top edge.' Alex sent him a sly grin. 'And you dared me to join you.'

'You were too afraid.'

'No, I wasn't so foolish as you,' Alex countered. 'You lost your balance and fell into Ross MacKinloch's pig pen.'

He'd nearly forgotten about that. 'And you didn't go for help, either. You sat and laughed at me, while I was covered in dung.'

Alex grinned. 'A good memory, that day was.'

'For *you*. Mother blistered my ears, screeching about how I was going to break my neck.'

Truly, they'd been thickheaded lads. An unexpected smile pulled at his mouth.

His brother returned the smile, adding, 'It's good to have you back, Brother.' But behind the words, there was concern and he didn't miss the way Alex eyed his thin frame. 'How are you now? Do you need a healer?'

Bram shook his head. Most of his wounds were now scars. 'I'm improving each day. I just need to train, to prepare for when we rescue Callum.'

Alex shook his head. 'You'll stay here while we find Callum.'

There was no chance he'd remain behind. 'Why? You think I'm too weak?'

'Aye.' Alex didn't bother to disguise the truth. 'You've

been in a prison for seven years, and even Dougal could defeat you, as thin as you are now.'

'Dougal?' he shook his head in disgust. 'But he's only seven—' He broke off, realising what he'd said about their youngest brother.

'Four and ten,' Alex corrected.

The reminder of the lost years forced him into silence. All of them had aged, but he'd thought little about Dougal, for the boy had been off at fostering since the age of four. He hardly remembered what his brother looked like and it bothered him to think of it.

'Is he back already?'

Alex nodded. 'He's inside. I'll take you to him.'

When Bram entered the keep, trestle tables were overturned, while dogs barked, snarling at each other for bones. The stale odour of rotting rushes caught him without warning, and it was so similar to the prison conditions that he froze.

In that sudden moment, he felt the walls closing in on him and his skin crawled. If he shut his eyes, it was like being there again, trapped in chains. He stumbled back towards Nairna, who was staring at the sight in disbelief.

As soon as he reached her side, her own unique scent caught him, masking the darkness. He wanted to bury his face in her hair, blotting out the harsh memories. But he didn't dare touch her.

'I'm going to drag your legs through your arse, pudding-faced bastard!' a voice yelled. The insult had come from a young man whom he barely recognised as Dougal. Though he was tall and strong for his age, the boy was hardly able to fight off Ross MacKinloch, who appeared to be toying with him. Dougal swung a reckless punch that missed his opponent.

'Mind your temper, lad,' Ross warned. A thin smile lined the older man's face. He picked up a chair and went after Dougal.

'What are they doing?' Nairna asked, her eyes wide.

'Ross trained each of us,' Bram said. 'When we were young, he taught us how to use every weapon. He knows what he's doing. Dougal will be fine.'

'But he's just a boy,' she protested. 'He'll be hurt.'

Dougal overheard the remark, for he retorted to Nairna, 'I'm not a boy.'

'Aye, you are,' Alex interrupted. He beckoned to Dougal, 'Have you no welcome for your eldest brother?'

A shadow of resentment darkened the lad's face. 'I don't even know him. Why should I welcome him?' With that, he picked up another chair, smashing it against the stone. Holding a chair leg in his hand, he went after Ross. 'Come back and fight me, old man!'

Bram watched the pair, not letting any expression cross his face. Dougal's defiance shouldn't have surprised him. They'd hardly known each other, and it had been so long, he supposed it was to be expected that his youngest brother wouldn't remember him.

When Bram was twelve, Dougal had followed him everywhere. The young boy had tried to take Bram's weapons, dragging a bench across the room to climb up and reach the blades he wasn't supposed to touch. It bothered him to think that the boy who had once attached himself to Bram's leg was now indifferent.

Alex lowered his voice. 'Dougal's getting worse every day. Thinks he can fight the English.' Shaking his head, he directed to Nairna, 'At least when he fights with Ross, he won't be hurt. Well, aside from a few bruises and scrapes.'

Bram stared at their youngest brother. The skin upon Dougal's arms was reddened, while blood trickled from his nose. The lad fought with pure aggression, letting his rage dictate his actions. He swung his fists without thinking, his long arms and legs clumsy.

Bram watched his brother fighting, feeling a sense of unease. Was that how his father had viewed him? Had he been like Dougal, struggling to prove himself? For a moment, he imagined himself in his father's place, fighting to protect his son. If he ever had a son of his own, he hoped he could train the boy to keep a calm head.

Anger and aggression only caused clumsiness. It was better to lock away all emotions, concentrating on bringing down the enemy. He'd managed to gain his freedom by numbing himself to everything but his goal. And though he'd had to live with the guilt of leaving Callum behind, it was the only way to save them both.

A moment later, Ross tripped the lad, twisting Dougal's arms behind his back and shoving him against the floor. 'You're finished, lad. The English would have slit your throat, just like that.'

Nairna was trying hard not to look, but her face grew worried. Bram moved up behind her and started to rest his hands on her shoulders before he thought better of it. Instead, he lowered them to his sides and bent closer to her ear. 'Are you hungry? Shall I see about food before we retire for the night?'

She turned around, her clear green eyes meeting his face. 'Only if you try to eat.'

'I'll eat,' he agreed. But he couldn't resist grazing his hand against her cheek. She reddened and touched her face, shivering slightly.

Dougal stalked away after Ross released him, his tight

anger evident within his posture. He'd been humiliated before everyone and no doubt he'd want to sulk in private. Though Bram wanted to talk to him, he understood that it wasn't a good time.

When Ross came forwards, his smile was so broad, it nearly split his face. 'Bram!' He gripped him in a hug so tight, it nearly crushed his lungs.

The older man released him, pounding him on the back. 'By God, it's a miracle t'see you again.' With a gleam in his eye, he prompted, 'Alex, we'll be needing a few barrels to celebrate.' Then his gaze fell upon Nairna. 'And you've brought your lass home again.' His smile turned teasing. 'After seven years, we all know what you'll be doin' tonight.' A loud laugh erupted from the old man. 'Next summer, I suppose we'll be celebrating the birth of a bairn!'

There were resounding cheers from the other men, but Bram didn't miss the pain upon Nairna's face, though she tried to smile.

'Did you find Laren?' Alex asked Nairna, but she shook her head.

'She returned with your daughters and is preparing them for bed,' Ross interrupted. 'I imagine she'll be here soon enough.'

Frustration lined Alex's face as he gave a brief nod. But Nairna intervened, saying, 'Don't trouble yourself if she's busy with the children. I'll be glad to meet her in the morning.'

Alex gave a nod, but Bram saw the way his eyes drifted above stairs. There was something unreadable in his brother's expression, almost a sense of regret, before Alex turned back to them.

'Where is the mead?' Ross reminded the chief. 'We should drink to Bram's return!'

Alex managed a smile and gave the order. 'We'll drink tonight,' he proclaimed, 'and tomorrow, we'll have a feast.'

Though Bram understood that his brother was trying to welcome him back, the last thing he wanted was to be the centre of everyone's attention. He'd survived captivity and come home. It was enough.

'For now, I want to find a place for Nairna and I to sleep,' Bram responded. They needed shelter, and from the look of the keep, there wasn't much room. He didn't want his wife sleeping on the earthen floor amid the stench of rushes. He wanted privacy from everyone else, a place where they could retreat in solitude.

'I'll find something,' Alex agreed.

As more and more people joined them within the keep, the noise level rose higher and the mead flowed. So many of his clansmen came to welcome him, asking questions, until Bram found himself having to repeat himself time and again.

The crowds made him agitated, with so many people he hadn't seen in years. Though he tried to manage it, speaking to each one, he felt himself growing more weary and less interested in food.

'Here y'are, lad,' came a voice from behind. Ross sloshed a cup of mead into his hand. 'A long, hard drink is what you're needing.'

Some of the men snorted and another called out, 'It's not the only thing that'll be long and hard tonight!'

Nairna's mouth opened in shocked surprise and she quickly looked at the ground as if she were searching for an escape.

Bram took the drink and eyed the men. 'Go. Away.'

Ross raised a toast and drained his mug, laughing with the others. To their credit, they left him alone with Nairna.

Right now, his mood was balanced on a razor's edge. He needed to escape the crowds, to gather up the pieces of his sanity. Nairna offered him food, but he only picked at it.

'You'd better eat more than that, MacKinloch,' she ordered him. 'You need to get your strength back.'

'And what will I be needing the strength for, *a ghaoil?*' he asked, taking her fingertips.

Her face coloured and she held out a bite of fish, offering it to him. When she pushed the bite of food into his mouth, her thumb brushed against his lip.

The soft touch brought him into a deeper awareness of her. He ignored the clan members gathering and the sounds of their conversation grew muted. He looked into Nairna's worried green eyes and kept her fingers locked in his.

'Bram, are you all right?'

No. He was tired, irritated at having to be around so many people, and his mind couldn't stop thinking about the night he would spend with Nairna.

The bawdy conversation was doing nothing to alleviate the sexual hunger he felt for Nairna. He remembered the silken skin and the sweetness of her kiss. Even more, the way she'd clung to him when he'd kissed her only deepened his own arousal. He wanted to be alone with his wife right now. He wanted to explore her body, to learn the mysteries of a woman's flesh. Unless she kept her hands off him, his control was going to break apart.

When her hand came up to stroke his cheek, all semblance of reason snapped.

* * *

Nairna wondered what she'd done to provoke such a response. Bram took her arm, guiding her up and away from the others. He took her to the furthest corner, away from everyone else, and pulled her into his arms.

Behind her, she heard the sounds of cheering, the men applauding her husband.

Bram's gaze locked with hers and he looked as though he'd rather devour her, instead of the food they'd shared earlier. 'Ignore them.'

His thumbs caressed her jawline and he leaned in to rest his forehead against hers. Her body responded with a shiver, though she wasn't cold at all. Bram lowered his hands down to her shoulders, past her waist, before he brought her up against the wall.

She forgot about all the people around them, lost within the intensity of his dark eyes. His mouth moved in to take hers and she yielded to him, sensing the caged tension. He kissed her until she couldn't catch her breath, until she no longer heard the sounds of men celebrating.

Her heartbeat was racing so fast, her body responding to the desire he'd conjured. And though she knew he had the right to consummate their marriage, the flutter of nerves rose up in her stomach.

'Bram,' she interrupted, turning her face to the side. 'Not here.' Too many were watching them and she suspected he'd forgotten where they were.

His face was unyielding, his eyes turning to frost when he released her. 'You have five minutes to finish what you want to eat. After that, you're mine.'

He left her alone while he went to speak with Alex, and in the meantime Nairna sat down, trying to collect her stray thoughts.

He was going to take her body tonight. He would become her husband in flesh, as well as in name.

She steadied her breathing, letting her mind drift. It might be pleasant, if Bram's kiss was any indication. And she wasn't a maiden who would be terrified of the joining. There was nothing that should frighten her.

But something about Bram made her pulse quicken and her body ached in secret ways. She overheard more raucous jokes about sex, and though she knew the men meant no harm, it was making her more nervous. She couldn't stop wondering what it would be like with Bram.

Before she could calm herself, he returned.

'Alex has found a place for us. We'll go now and rest.'

Rest? From the hungry look in his eyes, it seemed that sleep was the last thing on his mind.

Breathe, she reminded herself. *It's nothing more than sharing his bed.* But her nerves tightened at the thought of lying naked beneath him.

As he led her through the crowd, the men cheered. When some of them tried to follow, Bram sent them a threatening look.

'If you're needing any advice, lad—'

'I don't.' He pointed for the men to return. 'Go back to your ale and leave me with my bride.'

'Give her a kiss from us!' Ross offered, making puckering noises.

Nairna wanted nothing more than to escape their teasing. Though they meant well, she needed no more reminders about what would happen tonight.

'Alex said we could sleep in one of the storage shelters,' Bram said, leading her outside. 'There's no bed, I'm afraid.'

It was better than sleeping in the keep, amid the dogs, Nairna thought.

'I brought a mattress,' she reminded him. 'We could fetch it from the wagon, along with blankets.'

'I'll get it.' Pointing to one of the wattle-and-daub huts, he told her, 'We'll stay here tonight and then find a place of our own in the morning.'

Before he left her, he slid a hand around her waist. 'Nairna, I promise it will be all right. I won't hurt you.' He leaned down and pressed a kiss to her forehead before he turned to walk back to the wagon. She held on to her waist, feeling as though his lips had burned a mark into her skin.

She was restless about the forthcoming night. To distract herself, she entered the grain hut. Inside, it smelled musty and damp. Sacks of barley and corn lay stacked in a corner, both food stores and seed for next year.

The structure was rectangular, perhaps eight feet wide. It looked more suited to horses, but Nairna supposed it was better than sleeping out in the open.

Her skin turned cold, the nervous energy rising higher. *Lie still,* she reminded herself. *Submit to him and let him do as he pleases.*

She wasn't afraid of lovemaking, only of disappointing Bram. Whenever Iver had shared her bed, her husband's thoughts were distant, his movements a cold duty. And when time went on, and she still hadn't become pregnant, there had seemed little point in the act.

But tonight could be different. She prayed that, somehow, Bram could give her the child she wanted so desperately. Her hands moved down to her stomach, the wistful longing filling her up inside.

When Bram returned, he set down her mattress,

dumping a load of blankets atop it. He stopped to look at her, his faded tunic looking pale in the moonlight.

Dark brown eyes stared into hers, leaving no doubt of his needs. And yet there was a tangible distance, almost as if he didn't want her to know him, or guess at his thoughts.

His muscles strained as he lifted several sacks of grain to block out the wind from the crevices of the shelter. As he moved, Nairna realised that, although he was thinner, there was no mistaking his strength from the hard labour he'd endured.

She studied the reddened, raised scars encircling his throat. They revealed the mark of an iron band that must have rested around his neck. Though the abrasions were starting to heal, the scar would remain.

After he'd finished moving the sacks of grain, Bram removed his tunic, baring his shoulders. Though he was thin, his lean muscles caught her eye. The urge to touch his skin came over her, though she suppressed it.

Nairna turned around, trying to loosen her gown. Bram came up behind her and helped to lift the woollen garment away, leaving her dressed in her shift. Her body grew cold from the chilled air and she hugged herself to keep warm. With one hand, she unravelled the bandage from her wrist, letting the strip of cloth fall to the floor.

With Bram so close, she couldn't help but see the massive scarring upon his body. It was monstrous to think of what they must have done to him.

'Does it hurt?' she asked, reaching to touch the whitened skin.

'It's mostly healed.'

That wasn't a no. She worried about whether or not he was in pain. He might not tell her, even if he was.

Bram's mouth rested beside her ear, his hot breath taking her thoughts apart. She could almost feel the heat of his bare skin and it both fascinated her and frightened her. She couldn't stop her intake of breath when his kiss grazed the line of her jaw.

'I'm going to sleep with you this night, Nairna. The way I should have done, these past seven years.'

Chapter Six

'Are you afraid?' he asked. He didn't want her to be. He wanted to hold her in his arms this night, to forget the years of torture and darkness.

'Yes,' she murmured. 'Not of…being with you, but—' Her words broke off and her face flushed. 'We don't really know each other. It seems strange.' Her face turned to the ground, her cheeks red with embarrassment. 'I'll try not to let that interfere.'

Her honesty was like ice water upon his desire, reminding him that she'd been with someone else before him. She knew what it was to join with a man and she spoke of it as though it were something to be endured instead of enjoyed.

It darkened his mood even more. 'Did he hurt you?'

The question came out before he could stop himself. He needed to know what had happened between them.

She shook her head slowly. But there was a sadness behind her eyes, and he sensed that her husband had not brought her pleasure within their marriage bed.

Jealousy snarled inside him. 'What was it like... with him?'

She sat on the mattress and drew her knees up, holding them to her chest. 'Bram, I don't want to talk about those years. I'd rather forget them.'

He exhaled slowly, feeling cruel for even bringing it up. She didn't appear to have enjoyed her previous marriage bed. Likely she was in no hurry to repeat the experience.

It frustrated him, because he didn't want her to lie back and endure his affections. He wanted her breathless and willing. He wanted to taste her skin, to tempt her in ways that his imagination had conjured.

His gaze drifted over her body, resting upon the full curves of her breasts, the swell of her hips. 'You're as fair as I remember, *a ghaoil*.' He sat beside her and she tried to venture a smile.

She gently touched his bared chest. At the warmth of her fingers against the scarred flesh his body responded with aching lust. She rested her cheek against his heart and he touched her hair, lifting her face to his.

He kissed her lips softly, moving down to the sensitive part of her throat. Goose flesh erupted upon her skin, and she let out a breath of air.

'Are you all right?' he murmured.

'Just nervous.'

It seemed that the more he touched her, the more uneasy she became. He tried to kiss her again, pressing her back onto the mattress. At the touch of his hands upon her legs, she shivered, suddenly turning her face away.

He knew he'd done something to bother her, but he didn't understand what it was. He stroked her long legs, moving higher. Nairna's face reddened and her shoulders trembled. She was reacting strongly to his touch and her fingers curled tightly as she felt him caress her knees.

When he reached her inner thighs, she jerked away. 'I can't. I'm sorry.' She clamped her knees together, clutching them as she shuddered. 'It tickles.'

It was the last reaction he'd expected; frankly, he didn't know what to do now. He'd broken the mood and it was clear that she wasn't at all aroused. Like a fumbling adolescent, he'd done everything wrong.

Frustration and anger boiled inside and he turned away so she wouldn't see his annoyance with himself.

'Bram,' she said, her voice filled with remorse, 'I'm sorry. I didn't mean to react that way, but my legs are sensitive.'

He felt the shift of the mattress as she lay down beside him. Nairna reached out to his shoulder. 'Will you let me touch you now?' she asked.

He rolled over, staring at her. Her deep-brown hair, like the warmth of polished walnut, fell against her linen shift. Pale milky skin held not a single freckle from the sun and he well remembered the taste of those soft lips.

Her hands moved over his chest and she directed him to turn onto his stomach. He felt the warmth of her lips upon his neck and a tremor brushed through him. She kissed his scars, tracing over the years of pain as if she could eradicate them with her fingers.

A slow heat built inside him; letting her explore his skin was a different form of torture. His body was heavy with need and he couldn't endure much more of this.

Bram rolled over and sat up, her legs straddling his waist. He took possession of her mouth, as if to show her all of the desire he'd held back over the years. The taste of her was like sunlight to his shadows and he drew her closer. She was soft, warm, and he imagined lifting her hips to impale her with his shaft.

Her tongue tangled with his, and at her unexpected response his hands started shaking. He had caressed his way down to her bottom, and between her legs his fingers encountered moisture.

He wanted to delve inside her, to tempt her into surrendering. But it was too soon for that.

He could feel the control slipping away and pulled back, afraid of losing awareness. His breathing was shallow, his body rigid with need.

Uncertain eyes met his, as though Nairna didn't know why he'd stopped. But it was too similar to the night when he'd let his mind slip into the shadows. He didn't trust himself to join with her, not when his mind was dominated by lust.

He might hurt her again, when that was the last thing he wanted. For a moment, he rested his hands upon her spine, hoping to regain command of himself. But his hands wouldn't stop shaking.

'I'm sorry for earlier,' she whispered. 'I never meant to offend you.'

She misunderstood the reason why he'd stopped, but he didn't correct her. He didn't want to reveal how close he'd come to the edge again.

He pulled her shift down lower, ignoring his body's needs, and locking away the desire he longed to quench.

'Are you all right?' she asked, reaching for him.

He could see the hurt confusion in her eyes, but there was nothing he could say to ease her embarrassment. He couldn't control his shaking hands, or his body's fierce response to her.

'It's late, Nairna. Go to sleep.' He turned away from her, wishing he could master his physical reactions.

Staring at the empty spaces between the wooden boards, he felt the warmth of her breasts pressing against his back. Her arm moved around his waist and he shoved back the instinctive need to touch her.

He couldn't make love to her until he could control himself. It wasn't safe and he didn't want to risk hurting her.

He'd never forgive himself if he lost himself in the madness again.

The rope tightened across his throat, the hemp abrading the bloody skin. Bram's vision blurred as they choked him and though he fought off the soldiers, the darkness closed in. He fought against death's summons, willing himself to stay alive. He had to, for Callum's sake. His brother hadn't spoken in several weeks and he seemed lost in a world of his own madness.

With his feet, Bram kicked hard, sending the soldier stumbling upon the ground. Air blasted through his lungs and he nearly passed out as he fought to breathe.

A quarterstaff came down upon his shoulders and he gritted his teeth as the wood reverberated through his muscles, bruising his flesh. Through it all, Callum never stopped staring. His brother was only twenty years old, held captive since the age of thirteen. Too young to have witnessed so much pain and horror.

When the soldiers stopped beating him, Bram tasted blood and he crawled through the dirt to lie at his brother's feet. He pushed away the pain, concentrating on one breath at a time. The cool dirt chilled his face, but eventually he gathered the strength to lift his head.

'I'm going to get us out, Brother. I swear it on our father's life.'

But Callum made no reply. The emptiness in his brother's eyes spoke more than any words.

The vision faded away and Bram's eyes were dry, staring into the grey morning light. Whether he'd fallen asleep or simply been caught up by the memory, he couldn't be sure. His eyes ached and his muscles were rigid and sore.

Beside him, Nairna was fast asleep, her long hair covering one shoulder. For a long time he watched her sleeping. Despite their awkward living arrangements, he was grateful to have her near.

Slowly, he eased closer until her shoulders were pressed against his chest. She stirred slightly, but then snuggled back against him. The softness of her body made a tightness gather in his chest. Simply feeling the warmth of a human touch was something he hadn't had in so long. He held her gently, for fear of waking her.

She hadn't touched him with repulsion, as he'd thought she would. Nor had she shied away from lying with him—instead, she'd held him. He breathed in the soft scent of her skin, as if drawing strength from her.

But his mind taunted him for even thinking he could have a woman like Nairna. *You don't deserve a normal life. Or a wife and family. Not after what you did to Callum.*

With reluctance, he let Nairna go and rose from his bed. Though it wasn't yet dawn, he knew he wouldn't find sleep again.

Nairna hardly saw Bram all that following morning and afternoon. She'd overheard him speaking to Alex about plans to rescue Callum, but she didn't know when they would leave.

Did they honestly believe Bram could fight the English so soon? He hadn't recovered from his imprisonment, and though there was muscle beneath his thin frame, he wasn't strong enough to defeat his enemy.

Last night, she'd slept poorly, worrying about him. He'd seemed eager to make love with her, only to stop without any explanation of why. She didn't know if she'd humiliated him with her unintended laughter. Or, worse, if she'd done something else wrong.

For a long time, she'd lain awake, her body needing his. She remembered the touch of his hands between her legs and the thought only conjured up more restless desire.

In the middle of the night, she'd awakened, only to find that Bram's eyes were open and he was staring at the ceiling.

How could anyone endure a life with so little sleep? It was no wonder his mind was still imprisoned.

She was a woman accustomed to taking care of people. At Ballaloch and Callendon, she'd ensured that everyone had enough to eat and everyone's needs were met. No one went hungry if she could help it.

But Bram's needs went beyond hunger and rest. He wasn't a man she could fix with food or a soft mattress.

He needs you, a voice inside her reminded. Bram's rough features hid a man she wanted to know. The scarring revealed his courage to survive. If she'd suffered the same imprisonment, she'd have given up within the first year.

But he hadn't. He'd endured more than any man should

have. And though the expression on his face was grim, holding years of fatigue, there was also determination.

He loved his brother and he wouldn't fail him. She understood that sort of loyalty and respected it.

But would he hold the same loyalty towards their marriage when he discovered her childlessness? It already bothered him to no end that she was not a virgin. She could see the tension in his body, the hidden jealousy in his eyes.

And Bram was nothing like Iver. He tempted her, breaking down her resolves with his mind-stealing kisses and his rough hands. Even last night when she'd slept beside him, the warmth of his body was not unwelcome. She'd felt him holding her close, his face buried against her hair.

Iver had never bothered with affection. He'd simply taken her body beneath his and accomplished his duty. With Bram, she sensed there would be far more.

She tried to shake off the tremulous feelings that prickled inside. Today, she had to learn more about the MacKinloch clan and decide how she could best help them.

She walked around Glen Arrin, surveying the grounds. The fortress showed clear signs of neglect and it bothered her that no one had lifted a hand to tidy up the mess or rebuild the rotted timbers. It was as if no one cared or had any pride remaining. Even the men had a sense of weariness about them.

As she continued back to the keep, she felt the eyes of the others boring into her skin, as though she were an oddity. Though they had been polite to her, it made her uncomfortable.

Something was wrong at Glen Arrin, but she couldn't quite determine what it was. Something beyond the poverty. Her eyes narrowed, searching for the source of her discontent.

As her gaze fell upon the different clansmen working at their tasks, tending their plots of land and going about their duties, the problem suddenly crystallised in her mind.

There were no women and children. Not anywhere.

Shock numbed Nairna from inside, though she tried to remain calm. Where could they be? Were they staying somewhere else, perhaps within a different fortress not far from here?

Or had something happened to them?

Chapter Seven

After settling the matter of where he and Nairna would live, Bram sat with Alex and Ross, listening to them discuss how they would break Callum free of the English prison. They'd debated for the past hour about whether to use stealth or force.

He didn't care. As long as they got Callum out, it didn't matter. Their words mingled together, strategies blurring, until Bram heard nothing more of what they said.

Instead, he watched Nairna. From the entrance, he could see her wandering the courtyard. There was dismay upon her face, as though she couldn't understand what had happened to Glen Arrin.

With every step she took, he saw her setting things aright. Picking up a fallen pot, finding a broom to sweep the entrance.

Over the next hour, she worked within the Hall, removing the refuse. She even located fresh rushes from

God only knew where, spreading them over the floor to mask the odours.

Her head was covered, but he could see her dark braid hanging over one shoulder. She moved with a silent grace, her face tense with worry about something.

Once she'd finished straightening the Hall, she strode forwards, as though she'd come to a sudden decision. When she reached Alex and the others, she didn't hesitate to interrupt their conversation.

'Where are all of the women and children?' she blurted out.

Bram's gaze sharpened, and he realised she was right. He'd been so preoccupied with worry over Callum, he'd hardly noticed the other MacKinlochs. But there were no women to be seen anywhere. He'd presumed they were in their homes or with Alex's wife somewhere.

He sent a questioning look to his brother, but Ross interrupted. 'Lady Laren's gone with her girls out walking. She does that each morn.'

'And the others?' Bram asked. From his brother's defensive expression, Alex appeared embarrassed, rather than worried.

'They are with our mother. She coerced them into seeking refuge with Kameron MacKinnon, the Baron of Locharr.' From the annoyance in Alex's tone, it was clear that their mother hadn't changed at all.

Brisk and steel-minded, Grizel MacKinloch had been like an unmerciful war lord when he and his brothers were growing up. With four sons, she'd had to be. While other women might have consoled their young boys with a kiss, when their sons scraped their knees, Grizel had told them that they should have minded where they were going. There was no sympathy from the matriarch, no weaknesses accepted.

And once she got an idea into her head, no one could convince her otherwise. Bram didn't doubt that she'd decided to punish the men by leading the exodus of women.

'Have you gone to visit them?' Bram ventured.

Alex's face showed his discontent. 'Once. They're safe enough, and it's only been a fortnight. They'll come back.'

Bram wasn't so certain. Their mother had never been the sort to admit when she was wrong.

Nairna's expression narrowed as she regarded his brother. She looked as though she had a thousand questions to ask, but in the end, she kept her voice cool. 'Have you told your mother that Bram has returned?'

'I sent word this morning, aye.' Alex stood up, using his height to remind Nairna of his authority.

His wife didn't back down, but instead lifted her chin, turning back to Bram. 'And are you planning to go and see her?'

'No. I'm not.' He hadn't seen Grizel since before their wedding, and he knew she'd have no wish to see him again. Because of his reckless behaviour, her husband had died. He doubted if Grizel would ever forgive him for it.

'Why?' Nairna asked. 'She's your mother. You have to go and see her.'

'Were it me, I'd enjoy the peace while I could,' Ross advised, elbowing him. To Nairna, he said, 'Grizel isn't the sort to weep and celebrate the return of a prodigal son.'

'More like to string him up and curse him for coming back,' Alex added.

Nairna gaped at them and Bram cut off any further questions, saying, 'I have to go and train with my brothers. I'll see you later.'

Alex nodded his own dismissal to Nairna. 'You might try the chapel if you cannot find Laren out walking. Sometimes she spends her time there.'

Bram overheard his wife mumble something about understanding Laren's need for prayer if she was the only woman remaining at Glen Arrin.

Before she could leave, Bram stopped her, taking her hand. 'It won't always be like this, Nairna. The other women will return.'

She gave a shrug as if it didn't matter. But he knew it did.

'I'll send for your maid, if you want.' Perhaps the female companionship would make Glen Arrin a more bearable place for her. At least, until the others returned. 'It may take a sennight until she arrives, though.'

The startled look in Nairna's eyes held gratefulness. And surprise, as if she'd never expected it from him. 'Thank you.'

In answer, Bram stroked her palm, rubbing a slight circle there. Her hands laced with his, and just the barest squeeze filled up the emptiness inside him. He held it for a moment before letting her go and rejoining his brothers.

She stood a short distance away, watching them spar. When Alex signalled for him to join them, Bram unsheathed his claymore, balancing the blade with both hands. The weapon was heavy, but he welcomed the weight. He wanted to lose himself in the sparring match, releasing his frustration.

He would regain the strength he'd lost, rebuilding himself into the fighter he wanted to be. He'd give Nairna a house of her own and all the freedom she wanted.

He wasn't good with words or courtship the way other men were. He could only hope that, in time, she would see that he would protect her and provide for her.

It was all he had left to give.

Nairna's palm was still warm. Though Bram had done nothing more than hold her hand, the gesture had made her skin grow warmer with restless needs. He'd stared at her with the intensity of a man who wanted to do far more to her. In that slight moment, she'd wanted to touch his face, to run her hand down his neck and touch his chest.

She busied herself with sweeping the entrance, although she'd already done so earlier. It was a good excuse to watch the men.

Bram and Ross faced off with swords, and it was soon clear that this match was about testing Bram's strength, not an actual fight.

'Are you certain you're wanting to do this?' Ross asked, circling Bram.

He gave a short nod, testing the weight of the claymore with a few practice swings.

Ross slashed out with his weapon, striking a blow that Bram barely defended. The ring of metal resounded in the afternoon and Nairna gripped the broomstick harder.

Despite the endless opportunities, not once did Bram counter the attack or gain the advantage against Ross. He blocked the blows, but did little else. It was defence, nothing more.

Though he continued to meet Ross's attacks, deflecting the blade, Bram's expression was grey. His eyes were glazed, his footing unstable.

He's not ready for this, Nairna thought to herself. She

kept sweeping, until the threshold was so clean she'd probably eradicated every last speck of dust. Yet she couldn't tear herself away from the fight.

Sweat gleamed upon Bram's forehead, his stare unfocused. Despite his attempts to stave off Ross's blade, the weariness burdened him until, at last, Ross stopped the fight, dissatisfied with what he'd seen.

'Let's try a different weapon.' He unsheathed his dirk, the short blade glinting in the morning sun.

At the sight of the weapon, Bram froze, his eyes growing distant. It was similar to the expression Nairna had seen before, when she'd cut his hair.

Bram's gaze paled as he stared at the dirk, seeing it, but not responding. Ross slashed the blade, adjusting his weight on the balls of his feet.

Alex moved towards them, unsheathing his own dirk and offering, 'I'll loan you mine for practice.' He flipped the weapon into the air, the blade turning edge over edge. Bram made no move to catch it and it struck the dirt at his feet.

Emptiness filled up his expression and it was as if he were no longer aware of his surroundings. Bram stared at the ground and despite Ross's prompting, he appeared lost.

To regain his attention, Ross sliced at Bram's sleeve, drawing a line of blood. The reaction was instantaneous.

Bram let out a raw cry, reaching for the blade and lunging at Ross. In his eyes, there was no sense of control, only wildness.

He lashed out at Ross, moving like a primal animal with the blade gripped in his hand. The older man's nimble footing saved him from being stabbed more than once.

Sweat dripped down Bram's brow, his movements slicing over and over. If the fight continued, Bram would either kill Ross or lose face before his brothers.

No one else knew that he wasn't aware of what he was doing. The madness had him in its vicious grip and Nairna couldn't stand aside and let it go on. Someone would be hurt.

'Enough!' she called out. 'Bram, let him go.'

But he gave the command no heed, though Ross lowered his blade. Instead, he sought to take advantage of the older man's weakness, surging forwards.

'Alex, stop him,' Nairna pleaded. The chief took up his sword and stepped between them, shoving Bram backwards until he sprawled onto his backside, his head striking against the stone wall. A trickle of blood ran down his temple and Nairna rushed to his side.

Within his brown eyes, she saw the pain and the clarity. For now, he'd regained his senses.

Nairna sent a sharp look towards the chief. They'd wanted to judge Bram's strength, and now they had their answers. He wasn't ready to fight and she saw no reason to humiliate him any further.

'We'll have another go at it later,' Ross said. But he exchanged a glance with Alex and neither looked pleased.

Nairna helped Bram rise to a standing position. His palm still gripped the dirk and he strode over to Ross, offering it back.

Afterwards, he took Nairna's hand, gripping her palm firmly. Though heavy circles lined his eyes, he appeared furious with her for stopping the fight.

Without releasing her, Bram continued walking across the fortress, through the inner bailey and towards the outer gates. Where he was taking her, Nairna didn't know, but it was evident he didn't want anyone else to be nearby for their conversation.

So be it. But she had no regrets about ending the fight.

'Where are we going?' she asked.

Bram didn't answer, but led her to a small wooded copse. Her feet crunched upon pine needles and dry leaves as they travelled away from the fortress, the land sloping uphill. By the time they reached the top of the ridge, Nairna was out of breath and lightheaded from the effort.

The view from the top was startling and she could see for miles around. Lush green hills cradled the valley and the silver reflection of the loch sparkled in the afternoon sun. From the slight altitude, mists shifted between the hills, giving it a ghostly air.

She sat down upon a large stone in the clearing to catch her breath.

'Why did you stop the training?' Bram moved forwards, his face tight with displeasure. His hand came to lift her chin up and she faltered at the blistering anger in his eyes.

'To keep you from killing Ross. You weren't in control of yourself.'

'It wasn't your right.' He glared at her, but Nairna refused to feel guilty about it.

'Do you even remember the fight?' she asked. 'Because when you went after him with your knife, you weren't even looking at him. Like the night when you grabbed my wrist.'

Bram raked a hand through his hair and he sent her a hard look. 'It was nothing like that. I remember...most of the fight.'

'Do you?' She doubted it. And from the uncertainty

on his face, it was clear that he had been caught up with pieces of the past.

'I don't think you should go after Callum,' she said bluntly. 'Let your brothers bring him back.'

'They don't know Cairnross the way I do,' he argued. 'And I left him behind once. I'll not do it again.'

She stood, walking slowly towards him. Gently, she took his wrists and raised his hands in front of his face. Bram's fingers were trembling and he had no control over the agitated movement.

'I know you want to protect him. But you need more time. You don't eat. You don't sleep. How can you possibly help him when you're like this?'

'I don't have time to waste, Nairna. With every moment I spend here, it's another second he's suffering.' His eyes were dark with fury.

He pulled his hands free, as if he had no intention of abandoning his quest. 'Don't try to stop me from fighting. It's something I have to do.'

Nairna tried a different approach. Softening her voice, she asked, 'Are you trying to punish yourself for what happened?'

The guilt in his eyes revealed it. If he died trying to free his brother, he wouldn't care.

'I gave Callum my word.' Bram moved away from her, walking to the edge of the clearing, where the valley lay below them. 'And I keep my promises.'

She took a deep breath, wondering why she was trying to convince him at all. 'Why did you bring me here?' she asked, changing the subject.

'It's where we're going to live. If it pleases you.'

A home…and land of their own? She'd never guessed they would ever possess such a valuable place. She glanced around. Though several trees needed to be cleared, the ridge was in a strategic location above the valley. From here, they could see invaders from miles away. It was beautiful and wild, but even so, it struck her as isolated.

'Did your brother grant you the land?'

'He did.' Bram's hand rested at his side, and he added, 'I refused to assume his position as chief, though it was my father's wish.'

She nearly asked why, but kept silent. It was clear that Bram had no desire to take his brother's place. And in return, Alex had granted him land worthy of his birthright.

'What sort of house will you build?' she asked. The land wasn't suited for farming, but the lush grasses were perfect for sheep or goats.

'As long as it's dry and warm, it doesn't matter to me, Nairna. You can choose whatever sort of shelter you want. My kinsmen will help us to build it.'

Bram stared out at the hills, crouching on one knee. He reached for a clump of grass, tearing out a handful. He let the grasses slip from his fingers until he held nothing in his palm. 'You truly don't believe I can get Callum back, do you?'

Heaviness weighed down his voice, and though she had no wish to hurt him, neither would she lie.

'Not the way you are now, no.' She moved towards him as he stood up.

'You don't think I'm strong enough.' He took her hands and brought them to his shoulders. She felt the tight muscles, the lean strength that could not be denied. And he wanted her to know it.

'Strength doesn't matter when you're facing arrows or swords,' she answered. A knot caught in her throat and she grew more aware of how close he stood to her.

If she moved a few inches forwards, her face would be pressed against the warmth of his chest.

'I suppose I shouldn't have come back for you, Nairna.' He turned her to face the open meadow, framed by the tall green mountains. 'I'm not much of a husband, am I?'

He removed his cloak, setting it over her shoulders. The wool still held the warmth of his skin and she drew it around her, as though it were an embrace.

'I don't suppose I'm much of a wife, either,' she admitted, the buried pain rising up again.

'Why would you say that?'

She hugged her waist and wondered how to tell him what needed to be said. He deserved the truth and it was wrong to keep it from him. She stared at the hills rising in the distance, her eyes burning with unshed tears.

'Because you'll want children and I can't give them to you.'

Bram said nothing at first. He didn't even look at her, but kept his gaze fixed upon the gleaming loch that shimmered through the trees. Her spirits lowered and she added, 'For three years we tried. And…nothing.'

His damning silence bothered her. She supposed she'd hoped he would reassure her, but he didn't. He kept staring at the valley below, and with every second that passed, her spirits sank lower. She couldn't read his thoughts to know whether he was angry or whether he simply didn't care.

Nairna turned to walk away, needing a few moments to pull her hurt feelings back together. She only got a few paces before Bram caught up to her. He pulled her into an embrace, lowering his face to her hair. She stood with him, surrounded by nothing except the misty air and the wooded hills. His strong arms held her tight, and the quiet action said more than any words ever could.

Her tears dampened his tunic, and she felt another piece of her heart beginning to crumble away.

Chapter Eight

'Laren,' Alex said, catching her by the arm as she was returning to the keep. 'Why didn't you come below stairs last night?'

Laren flinched at her husband's sharp tone. Leaning down to her children, she murmured, 'Go on to your chamber, girls. I'll join you in a moment.'

Her four-year-old daughter Mairin stared at them with a troubled gaze, but she obeyed, holding Adaira's chubby arm in her hand.

In her husband's eyes, she saw the embarrassment and frustration that she hadn't greeted the visitors to Glen Arrin. But he didn't know the truth.

Last night, she'd sat upon the spiral stone stairs, watching the festivities from above. She couldn't bear being surrounded by so many people drinking and laughing. It was easier to remain back in the shadows where no one would notice her.

She'd seen Alex's brother Bram and the way he'd looked at his wife with such intense longing. It had been years since Alex had looked at her that way.

Right now, there was only disappointment on his face.

'I was with the girls,' she lied. 'I couldn't leave them.'

'He's my brother, Laren. You should have come.'

She didn't deny it, for Alex was right. But he didn't understand how out of place she felt among the MacKinlochs. She'd never felt welcome as their Lady, and more than a few whispered about her behind her back. They didn't understand how awful it was for her.

'Where are Bram and his wife now?' she asked.

'I gave them the land on top of the ridge to build a house. Last night, I had to put them in the grain shed, because there was no place else for them to sleep.'

She didn't miss the subtle chastisement, but even their own quarters were just as bad. The roof leaked and it was cold at night. Likely the grain shed was more comfortable.

'I want to have a welcoming celebration tonight,' Alex added. 'Could you arrange it?'

The idea made her slightly panicked, for she had no other women to help her. The MacKinloch men, though strong fighters, wouldn't dream of setting foot in the kitchens. As only one woman, with her girls, it would be next to impossible.

'I don't know,' she admitted. There was food enough, but the preparations would take a great deal of time.

'Brodie has some geese you could roast,' Alex suggested. 'And I'll send Dougal to help you.'

With the women gone, the task would be nearly impossible. Laren didn't know how to feed so many men, and if she failed in this, it would only give her husband another reason to be frustrated with her.

Their marriage hadn't been the same in the two years since he'd become the MacKinloch chief. He hardly ever talked to her anymore, and he slept on the far side of the bed. They'd grown apart, despite five years of marriage.

But then Alex rested a hand upon her shoulder. The touch of his palm warmed her, and as she looked into his dark eyes, the sudden ache of longing came over her.

'I'll do what I can,' she whispered, even knowing that she likely couldn't succeed.

Alex let his hand fall back to his side. 'We're leaving in the morning for Cairnross. If you hadn't heard, our brother Callum is a prisoner there.' He stared at the outdoors, adding, 'I'd rather leave Bram here, but he's too damned stubborn. If we're not careful, he'll get himself killed.'

'Be careful,' she urged. The bleak fear in her heart threatened to crack apart the tight control over her feelings. But when she took a step closer, Alex moved aside, his gaze and thoughts focused elsewhere.

As her husband left the keep, she wondered if there would ever come a time when he would look at her with love again.

Bram worked for the next few hours, sweat rolling down his tunic as he lifted stones for the foundation of their house. The punishing work made his arms ache, but he was accustomed to the labour. Nairna wasn't.

His wife struggled to lift stones that were too heavy for her and he could see the over-exertion in her face. 'Leave them,' he advised. 'You can help me with the framing later.'

She pushed a strand of brown hair out of her face, looking frustrated. 'I wish I were stronger. You shouldn't have to do this by yourself.'

'I don't mind. And we won't be working much longer. The sun will set soon.' He hefted another stone and laid it into the trench he'd dug, aligning it with the previous stone until they were level.

When he stood, Nairna was in front of him. Worry twisted in her face and she touched his shoulder. 'I should have told you before, about not being able to have children.'

In her eyes he saw the guilt. And he knew he ought to tell her words of comfort, saying something to make her feel better. But he lacked the right words. Instead, he simply shook his head. 'Don't let it trouble you.'

'It does.' Her voice was heavy with tears. 'I hope things will be different…with us. But I thought you should know, it probably won't be.'

She looked so upset, he didn't know what in the name of the saints she expected him to say. If he told her he didn't care, she'd believe he was lying. Did she expect him to blame her? He was glad she hadn't become pregnant. If she'd borne a son to another man, it would have eaten him up inside. Even now, it felt like a knife twisting in his flesh, just to think of Iver MacDonnell touching her.

He gave a shrug, trying not to make too much of her distress. Right now, he wanted to build a shelter for them, a place where they could be alone from everyone else. But as he reached for another stone, his lack of response seemed to flare up Nairna's anger.

'Doesn't it matter to you at all?' she demanded. Her green eyes were fiery, her skin flushed.

Bram set the stone aside when Nairna moved closer. She was saying something about how he ought to care more about whether or not they had a family, but he didn't pay much heed to her words. He was watching the way her mouth moved and the way her gown was damp from her earlier exertion.

'Bram.' Nairna frowned. 'Aren't you listening?'

'Not really.' He led her across the clearing to a small waterfall that spilled in a rivulet down the hillside into a stream. 'You're worrying about something that hasn't happened yet.' He reached into the clear water and scooped up a handful. 'Have a drink. You look thirsty.'

She looked at him in disbelief. 'I don't understand you. I thought you'd be angry.'

'Why would I be angry over something that's in God's hands anyway?' He held up the water to her lips and she bent to drink from his hands. 'If we're meant to have a child, then we will.' He touched his damp fingers to her face. 'We haven't even tried yet.'

Her face coloured, but it seemed he'd softened her anger. She lifted a handful of water to him in return and Bram sipped from her fingers. He held her fingers a moment, before Nairna pulled them away.

She bent down and collected a smooth stone from the stream bed. 'Do you remember when we used to skip stones?'

He did. They'd spent hours talking together, wagering over who could skip stones the furthest. 'You were never any good at it,' he said, picking up a stone of his own. 'Or has that changed?'

She tossed the stone into the air and caught it. 'I don't know if it has or not.' When she flicked her wrist, trying to send the stone across the water, it sank to the bottom. 'Clearly not.'

Bram tossed his own stone and it skipped the water three times. He kept his satisfaction hidden and reached for another stone.

'I suppose you're going to boast now.'

'No boasting.' But he had another idea. Moving

behind her, he pressed his second stone into her right hand. 'I'll teach you how.'

His left arm curled around her waist, his right hand showing her how to move her wrist. 'It's all a matter of timing.' His voice rumbled against her ear and Nairna shivered.

'You have to hold it gently.' His left hand moved up to her ribcage, caressing her. 'Not too firm.'

He brought his hips up against her and she sent him a suspicious look. 'From where I'm standing, it feels rather firm to me.'

He tightened his grasp, his arousal moving against her bottom. 'Sometimes firm can be a good thing.'

An unexpected smile broke over her face. 'Show me.'

He released her and reached for the ties at his trews. 'If you insist.'

'No,' she laughed, clutching at his tunic. 'Skipping stones, I meant.'

'Oh. That.' He didn't hide his wickedness this time and took her back in his arms. Holding her hand, he demonstrated how to send the stone across the water, but when Nairna tried, she kept using too much force.

'You're not trying to stone the water, Nairna. Go softer.'

After several practice attempts, she started to improve. The sixth try resulted in a stone that skipped twice before it sank.

She beamed at him and he was caught by the warmth in her smile. He wanted to kiss her, to reclaim the lost years between them. But the sound of approaching horses interrupted the moment.

'I suppose you'll have to show me later,' she said with regret, as Ross and Alex arrived. Bram tossed the stone into the water as his brother dismounted and walked towards them.

'We're hosting a feast tonight to celebrate your return home,' Alex said.

'There's no need for that.' Bram hated crowds of people and a feast would only pinpoint their attention on him.

'Everyone is wanting a reason to celebrate. You've given them a good excuse to drink too much ale and forget their troubles.'

Bram made no response and he wished he had an excuse not to go. But he could see from Nairna's face that she wanted to.

'Come as soon as you're able,' Alex offered and raised a hand in farewell, as he and Ross departed.

When they'd gone, Nairna reached for her mantle. 'I should go and help with the preparations.'

'I don't want a feast, Nairna.' He'd rather remain here, away from his kinsmen who would ask questions he didn't want to answer.

'They're your family,' she said. 'You have to attend.'

He stared at her, shaking his head. 'I came home without Callum. It's nothing worth celebrating.' If they knew the terrible price he'd paid for his freedom, a feast would be the last thing on their mind.

'Go on without me,' he urged. 'Help Laren if that's your wish. I'll continue to work on our house.'

'Your brother will expect you to be there,' she said, reaching up to touch his face. 'Don't disappoint him.'

Bram let his hands linger upon her, wishing Nairna weren't so intent upon returning to the keep. But he let her go, knowing that a woman like his wife thrived around people and gatherings. She would want to be there, lending a hand with the food and the people.

He didn't know if he could stand to see their pitying looks. Nor could he answer, when they asked what he'd done to escape.

All around the fortress torches flickered. Nairna stopped to wash her face and hands; to her surprise, she smelled fish and…was that roasted goose? Her stomach rumbled, and she wondered what preparations remained.

When she entered the Hall, Alex stood at the far end, speaking to his kinsmen. A woman hung back in the shadows, her long red hair gleaming in the firelight. Beautiful and serene, the woman remained in the background, shying away from the men who argued over the food and drink at the trestle tables below.

It had to be the Lady of Glen Arrin, Nairna guessed. As she walked forwards, several of the men fought over the platters of food, even coming to blows. She winced when one man went sprawling on the floor after another punched him in the jaw.

But no one made a move to stop them. Nairna looked up at the dais, but the fighting seemed to have no effect upon the chief of Glen Arrin.

When she reached them, Alex rose in greeting. He glanced behind her, as if searching for Bram. He introduced her to the woman, saying, 'Nairna, this is my wife Laren.'

Laren ventured a timid smile and Nairna returned it. Alex's wife might be her only female ally in this place and she was grateful to meet her at last.

'Where is Bram?' Alex demanded. 'Didn't he come with you?'

'He was finishing up some of the work on our house,' she explained. And though she knew Bram didn't want a feast in his honour, she supposed he would come eventually. 'He'll be here soon enough.'

Laren nodded, but said nothing. She looked painfully uncomfortable beside her husband, as if she wanted to be anywhere but here. At Alex's suggestion, Nairna came and sat beside the Lady of Glen Arrin.

It was then that she noticed Laren was wearing gloves at the table. It struck her as odd, but no one else made any comment about it. Perhaps that was simply her habit.

'I am glad to meet you,' Nairna said. 'It's good to see another woman here.'

She'd hoped Laren would start a conversation, but the woman's cheeks flushed and again she only nodded. It was as if she were too afraid to speak in front of her husband.

One of the men brought out baked trout, served on a wooden plank. Nairna tried a little of the fish, wondering where Bram was. She stared into the crowd of men, searching for any sign of him.

Over an hour had passed since she'd left his side and she worried about him being alone. He didn't appear comfortable around so many people, even when they'd first arrived. She needed to find him, to understand what was going on.

She excused herself from the table. 'I'm going to find Bram,' she told Alex.

'I'll come with you.'

He stood up, but Nairna shook her head. 'No, let me do this alone. I promise I'll return with him.'

She skirted her way through the crowd until she reached the entrance to the keep. Torches flared against the darkness and the faint reflection of the loch lay silver against the moonlight. Nairna clutched her wrap around her shoulders, her eyes searching.

Outside the gates, she had started along the path leading to their house when she saw a shadowed figure sitting against the hillside.

Her heart steadied when she realised it was Bram. He was reclining against the hill, his arms propped up beneath his head. Unrest brewed in his eyes and she sat beside him.

He didn't speak, made no excuses for his absence. She didn't push for answers, for she suspected that he had his reasons for not entering the fortress.

Instead, she stretched out beside him. Several stars dotted the sky and she reached out to take his hand. 'It's a nice night.'

He didn't respond. Had he not laced his fingers with hers, she'd have thought he hadn't heard her. In the cool air, her breath formed clouds. As time drew on, at last he asked, 'Did you eat with them?'

'A little. I wanted to wait for you.'

He sat up then, resting his hands upon his knees. 'Nairna, you should go back without me.'

She didn't know if it was his aversion to crowds or another reason that kept him away. 'What is it, Bram? Why can't you join them?'

He shook his head. 'There is no reason at all they should be glad of my return. I should have died in prison.' His eyes glittered in the darkness. 'Sometimes I wish I had.'

She reached up and touched the scar upon his throat, not knowing what to say to him.

His hand covered hers and he answered her unspoken question. 'They took a knife and slashed my throat, when I was seventeen. Not deep enough to kill, but enough to make me afraid.'

His expression grew distant. 'Some of the others did

die. I didn't know then that they kept the strongest of us to be used as slaves. They kept Callum alive because I worked twice as hard to fight for his life.'

His voice roughened as he relived the nightmares. 'I did everything they asked me to do—sometimes the work of several men. If I failed in my task, they punished Callum. Then me.'

He pushed her hands away from his throat, rising to his feet. 'Can you imagine what they did to him, when I took my freedom?' Guilt radiated through his posture, even though he began walking towards the fortress. 'If he's still alive, I have to get him out.' When he reached the entrance to the keep, she saw the raw pain in his eyes. 'There's nothing at all for me to celebrate.'

'It's not only for you,' she whispered. 'It's for the men, too.' She touched his face, needing him to understand the truth. 'They're lost, Bram. Their wives and children are gone. They need the distraction, even if it's only for a single night.'

He hesitated, but she could see that she was starting to break through to him. 'You should go for their sake. Not for yourself.'

The weariness in his expression broke her heart, but she took his hand, leading him forwards. 'Joining your family can't be any worse than what you've already endured.'

He didn't look pleased about it, but he relented at last. Nairna took his hand and he escorted her inside.

A breath of relief filled her up and she remained at his side while his clansmen welcomed him, raising their cups. Bram's expression remained sombre, but he nodded to them, accepting a cup of mead as he passed.

'What took you so *long,* Bram?' his kinsman Brodie teased.

Though her cheeks were furiously red, Nairna knew that the jesting would only get worse if Bram said nothing. Already she could see the grim cast to his face and the desire to be anywhere but here.

'He was *hard* at work,' she said, lifting her own cup in a silent toast.

The others roared with good-natured humour, several of the men raising their own cups in response. Her remark had the intended effect—it softened the banter and after a few minutes more, the men turned back to the feasting. But although it was meant to be a celebration, the atmosphere was fraught with tension. More than a few eyed Bram with envy when his arm came around her waist, as if they were missing their own wives.

When she stole a glance at her husband, Bram moved in, his breath warm against her cheek. 'Hard at work, was I?'

'It seemed that way to me.' She was finding it difficult to concentrate with his body so near.

To distract herself, she took another sip of mead. Bram pulled the cup away and drank from the same place where her mouth had rested. The look in his eyes had transformed into something more alive. She'd managed to take his mind off his sorrows, and now, he was eyeing her as though he had every intention of seducing her.

When they sat down with Alex and Laren, she noticed that the Lady of Glen Arrin had hardly touched her food. If it were possible, Laren looked even more uncomfortable than Bram.

Though Alex talked with his kinsmen, seeming to enjoy the food and drink, he hardly spoke to his wife. But as Nairna watched them a little longer, she saw the way Alex stole glances at Laren from time to time. He was looking at her with a blend of longing and frustration, as though he didn't know how to make things right between them.

'Thank you for such wonderful food,' Nairna said to Laren. With a chagrined smile, she added, 'Next time, I'll help you. I feel terrible that you had to do this alone.'

'It was good,' Alex said softly.

Laren's attention jerked to her husband and she dropped her gaze, looking embarrassed. She toyed with her food for a few moments longer, then said to Alex, 'I'm going to go and make sure the girls have gone to bed.'

The chief didn't reply as she slipped away silently, but Nairna saw the way he never took his eyes off Laren.

Nairna leaned closer to Bram. 'Why wouldn't their children have eaten with us?'

'I don't know. I suppose they must have eaten earlier.'

'Has it always been this way between them?' she whispered.

He shrugged, and she took that to mean he didn't know. After all, his brother had married during Bram's imprisonment.

'Would you mind if I went to speak with Laren?' she asked. 'I'd like to meet her daughters.'

'Go, if you like. But I'm not staying here much longer. You can meet me in the grain hut.'

He lifted her hand to his mouth, pressing a kiss upon her palm. The warmth of his breath made her flesh rise up and a ripple of anxiety flowed through her as she wondered if Bram would find her pleasing as a wife.

Nairna followed the winding stairs to the second floor where there were only two chambers. Voices came from inside the first room and she listened a moment to the sounds of girls chattering.

She pushed the door open slightly and saw two girls, one hardly more than four, and a chubby baby girl, perhaps a little over a year old. Each had hair as red as an autumn leaf, with sweet faces and bright blue eyes.

A pang of envy struck Nairna hard, seeing the beautiful children. *One day,* she reminded herself. She had to hold faith that God would answer her prayers.

Laren was brushing the older girl's hair, while the child whined, 'Mama, that hurts!'

'Mairin, stand still and let me get the tangles out,' Laren said. No longer did the chief's wife appear timid and overwhelmed. Instead, she seemed relaxed and in command of her children.

But as soon as she caught sight of Nairna, the brush stilled. 'Was there something you needed?'

'I wanted to meet your children,' Nairna said, smiling at the girls. The youngest daughter ran over and grasped Laren's skirts before burying her face to hide. Her wispy red hair stuck out around her ears in wild curls and Nairna had the urge to kiss the soft little cheeks.

'This is Adaira.' Laren extricated her daughter from her skirts. 'Mairin is my eldest.'

The child gave a slight curtsy, but looked suspicious. She strode forwards and studied Nairna. 'I don't like your gown.'

'Mairin,' her mother warned. 'Don't be rude.'

Nairna pulled a stool over and sat down. 'That's all right. I don't really like it, either, but I don't have many gowns.'

'Me, either.' Mairin sighed. 'I wish we'd gone away with the others.'

'Why didn't you?' Though Nairna spoke to the young girl, her eyes met Laren's.

'Our da needs us,' Mairin pronounced. 'He'd cry if we left.'

Laren's face softened at her daughter's prediction. 'It's time that both of you were in bed. Come now, and say good night.'

She leaned down to kiss each of them and Nairna studied the gloves that Laren still wore. Though it was cold enough, true, she couldn't imagine why the woman kept them on unless it was to hide something.

As each child was tucked into bed, Laren sent Nairna a nod of dismissal.

'Wait. I wanted to speak with you.' If there were any answers to be had, the Lady of Glen Arrin would know them. 'Please.'

Reluctance coloured Laren's expression, but she finally acquiesced. 'For a moment.' She led Nairna down the small corridor to the other chamber.

Inside, a stunning tapestry hung from the walls. The bold colours were captivating and something about the design struck Nairna as unusual. It was a common scene of Saint John the Baptist, yet the colours were vibrant.

'Did you make that?' Nairna asked. It was artistry such as she'd never seen before. Worthy of hanging within a palace, if the truth be known.

Laren nodded. 'What did you wish to ask me?' From her dull tone, it appeared that she was uncomfortable with having to converse.

'Why did the women leave?' Nairna asked.

'Because of the English raids,' Laren said. 'Lady Grizel, Alex's mother, led them to take refuge with Lord Locharr. There was too much fighting and she thought they would be safer there.'

'And you chose not to go with them?' Nairna prompted. Though it was only curiosity, she hadn't expected the look of hurt that crossed Laren's face.

'They left without me. And for almost a sennight I didn't know where they'd gone.' Laren gripped her elbows, taking a breath. 'I would be lying if I said I didn't want to join them. But my chance is gone. Alex won't ever let us leave.'

'But the fighting has stopped, hasn't it?'

Laren's expression tightened. 'Oh, I've no doubt it will start up again. It always does.' Murmuring a farewell, she returned to her girls.

Nairna was left to wonder what she meant by that.

Bram wasn't inside the grain hut when she first arrived, but he returned within minutes. Nairna didn't know if he'd spent the time talking with Alex, but his hair was wet, as though he'd washed in the stream. The dark strands hung against his neck, contrasting against his face.

When he reached her, she saw that his beard had grown ragged. It appeared that he'd tried to cut it, but had failed to do a good job of it. Nairna reached out to touch his face. 'Do you want me to shave you?'

He hesitated, rubbing the rough surface. Then he nodded.

'Let me get some warmed water,' she offered. 'Sit and wait a moment.'

When she went to fetch the shaving soap and blade, she wondered if tonight would be the night when they consummated their marriage at last. She took a deep breath, reminding herself that there was no reason to be afraid. It was simply a matter of lying still, accepting his attentions and praying that their union would result in a child.

But the more she thought of it, the more her nerves tightened. What if she didn't please him? The other night, he'd stopped when she'd reacted badly to his touch.

Stop worrying, she warned herself. It might be for nothing anyway. After all the training Bram had done earlier and the time he'd spent constructing the house foundation, he had to be exhausted. He might prefer to sleep instead.

When she returned with the shaving supplies, Bram was sitting upon a large sack of grain. Weariness was evident in his lowered shoulders and in his eyes. She unwrapped the cloth bundle and when he stiffened at the sight of the sharp blade in her hand, she finally understood his reaction. The weapon disturbed him; no doubt it evoked memories of the soldier cutting his throat.

'Do you trust me?' she asked quietly, setting the blade down within reach.

'I don't know,' he admitted. A dangerous smile played at his mouth and Nairna wet a piece of linen in the hot water.

'I'll stop, any time you ask me to.' She lifted the linen to his cheeks, wetting the surface. The faint wisps of steam rose against his face and she let the warmth penetrate his skin.

'Close your eyes,' she murmured. When Bram obeyed, she took the soap and lathered her hands, bringing them to his cheeks. Gently, she soaped his face, letting her fingers move across the beard and down his neck. It was strange that such a common touch evoked feelings inside her own body. It was as if she were touching herself instead of him.

Though Bram kept his eyes closed, his hands moved

around her waist, bringing her to stand between his knees. Nairna used the dagger to shave him, and at the first touch of the blade his thumbs dug into her side.

Instinct still ruled his mind, so it seemed.

'It's all right,' she whispered. 'Just remain still.'

He obeyed and she spoke of mindless matters while she shaved him, revealing the smooth masculine skin. She didn't know if he even heard a word of it, but not once did he relax. His expression was grim, as though she were torturing him. Then her blade slipped and his eyes flew open.

'I'm sorry,' she said, wiping at the tiny nick on his skin. 'I didn't mean for that to happen.'

His gaze had gone cold, as he stared at the weapon. His eyes were like glass, hardly seeing her at all. The way he was looking at her, she wasn't certain she should touch him again.

When there came no answer, she repeated, 'Bram?'

Bram took a deep breath, then another. He didn't want to feel the kiss of the blade against his skin. The scars upon his back itched in memory, though he knew Nairna meant him no harm.

'Finish it,' he ordered, steeling himself. He didn't want to look like a half-shorn animal, just because he couldn't control his response to a knife.

Nairna's fingers moved over the shaven skin, as if searching for any other cuts. Her light touch seared him, setting his senses on edge.

He wanted to remove her gown, seeing every part of her. Having her stand so close and not being able to do as he wished was honing the edge of his frustration.

Her green eyes regarded him with apprehension, as if she could read his thoughts. A shaky breath released from her lungs, but she raised the dagger to the curve beneath his chin, gently cutting away at the ragged surface.

The glint of the knife entranced him and he found it hard to keep his gaze fixed upon her. He hadn't realised he'd been holding his breath until she moved the knife away and he expelled a sharp exhale.

'I'm almost finished,' she whispered, soaping the underside of his throat. Her gentle fingers moved to touch one cheek while her hand brought the blade against his skin, removing the last bits of beard growth.

He endured the scrape of the dagger, every muscle clenching at the touch of metal against his skin. And when she'd finished, he seized the blade and tossed it across the storage shed. His arms captured her, bringing her up against the back wall. He kissed her hard, unleashing the dark needs that possessed him.

Chapter Nine

Nairna couldn't grasp a clear thought as Bram conquered her mouth. The heat of his lips, the way his tongue stroked hers, made her knees go soft.

He drew his fingers over the rise of her pulse, down the exposed flesh at her bodice. Nairna shivered, unable to understand the feelings he'd aroused.

With the shadow of his beard gone, Bram appeared even more handsome. The planes of his face, the slant of his jaw, held the appearance of an ancient warrior.

His hands moved to the laces of her gown, loosening them. The wool was heavy, a barrier between them. He waited a moment to see if she would voice a protest, but she couldn't have spoken a single word if she'd wanted to.

He slid the fabric away from her shoulder, lowering his mouth to the bared skin. He exposed her breasts in the cool night air and cupped the fullness of them, running his thumbs over the softness of her hardened nipples.

A tremulous, swollen desire tightened inside her. She bit the inside of her cheek as he abraded her sensitive skin with his roughened palms. The vein of desire seemed to run from her taut breasts down to the wet centre of her womanhood. Her fingers dug into his shoulders when his mouth trailed a path down her throat, resting upon her heart.

And when his lips curved over her breasts, it was as if she'd been struck senseless. His hot mouth teased her nipples, his tongue swirling and sucking. Nairna tried to pull away, but he held her trapped. He kissed every part of her breast, all the way to the sensitive tip. With every fierce suckle, she felt an answering throb between her legs.

'I love the taste of you,' he murmured upon her skin. His mouth descended on hers in a possessive kiss. Sleek and hot, he invaded, mercilessly taking her mouth for his own. She tasted his need and trembled beneath the onslaught.

He took her back against the wall, supporting her weight with one knee. 'I want you, Nairna,' he murmured against her cheek. 'More than anything in this world.' Wild and tempting, his tongue teased hers.

The length of his erection rested between the juncture of her thighs and Nairna could hardly breathe.

The wildness in him was barely beneath the surface, held by a single thread of control. But right now, Nairna was starting to edge that control away from him.

Bram wanted to draw her down upon the mattress, stripping away her clothing until her bare skin rested beneath him. He wanted to fill her with himself, invading her softness until she cried out with release.

But he'd never taken a woman before and didn't know

what he should do. When his hand moved up her skirt, he sensed the sudden change within her. Nairna's hands rested against his chest, and though she kissed him back, she appeared nervous about it.

He released her, stepping back. 'Do you want to do this?'

The uncertainty in her eyes made him pause. 'I won't deny you, Bram.'

Something didn't seem right about her acceptance. She covered her breasts, adjusting her clothing until the outer gown fell onto the ground and she wore only her shift. The creamy linen clung to her and her nipples were taut against the fabric.

Nairna lay down upon the mattress, no longer looking at him. 'I'm ready.'

Ready for what? Bram stared at her undergarment, trying to make sense of it. He removed his tunic, kneeling down beside her. Nairna inched the hem of her shift higher, until it bunched near her thighs, just below the curve of her bottom.

Understanding suddenly dawned upon him. 'Did your husband take you like this?'

She nodded, her face bright with colour. 'It's your right, as my...' she looked at the ground as though she were uncomfortable with the words '...my husband. And I do want children, so...' Her voice trailed off, but he detected the anxiety beneath her veil of calm.

He'd heard of men taking a serving wench in that manner, simply lifting her skirts and driving deep inside. But it wasn't what he'd imagined. He wanted her naked beneath him and it was sobering to learn that her experience wasn't at all what he'd expected.

Bram ran his hand across her hair, moving down to her face. 'Was it always this way?'

She nodded. 'Bram, if you're planning to—' She stared up at the ceiling again. 'It's all right.'

'Did he ever give you pleasure?' he asked. 'Or was it simply a duty?'

'It didn't hurt me.' She looked worried, as if she were afraid she wasn't giving the right answers.

'That's not what I asked.'

And when he saw the confusion in her eyes, he understood the truth. Though Iver MacDonnell had taken Nairna's virginity, he'd taught her nothing about enjoying the marriage bed.

Bram stretched out beside her, forcing her to look at him. 'I don't want it to be that way.' He didn't want her to lie like a stone while he took her. He knew women could be pleasured, that sex was meant to be enjoyed by both of them.

How he wished he knew what to do. Nairna huddled on the edge of the mattress and it didn't seem that she understood what he was talking about.

'Nairna,' he said quietly, 'look at me.'

Clearly embarrassed, she blurted out, 'I know I never pleased Iver. I thought there ought to be more, but I couldn't feel things the way he could.'

'There's nothing wrong with you. Only with him.'

Even as he spoke the words, he felt his own apprehensions worsening. If her previous experience hadn't been good, what made him think he'd be any better? He wanted to touch her, to explore her body and learn how to bring her to fulfilment. But she appeared so upset, he didn't know how he would ever calm her anxiety.

He pulled her into his embrace and Nairna rested her cheek against his chest. The tension in her body was unspoken, in the way she curled up, half-shielding herself.

If he'd had any experience with lovemaking, he might have been able to coax away her fears. But he didn't. And it seemed wrong to push her when she was nearly in tears, thinking that she'd been a poor wife.

His hands moved over her nape, softly soothing away the knots. He wanted to distract her, to take her mind off her fears.

'Alex wants to leave in the morning to go after Callum,' he said.

Nairna looked up at him for a long moment, worry lurking in her green eyes. 'I didn't realise it would be so soon.' She caught his hand in hers. 'I wish you would stay.'

'You know I can't.' Though his fighting skills were weakened, he held the knowledge that would get them safely inside and out again.

The Earl of Cairnross, Gilbert de Bouche, had kept the prisoners chained belowground, bringing them out to construct thicker walls or to expand the fortress.

What Cairnross didn't know was that Bram and the other prisoners had created weaknesses in the structure at various points. They'd even left one hidden portion of the outer curtain wall with loose stones. Bram knew exactly where the unmortared segment was, and that weakness would allow them to slip inside the fortress to free the prisoners.

'I can get the men inside to rescue Callum,' he said. 'And if they follow my lead, they can take him out before the English even know we're there.'

Nairna rested her hands behind her head. 'Do you really want to go back to Cairnross, after what they did to you?' Her eyes met his, holding a thousand questions he didn't want to answer.

He blocked out the memories, refusing to let the past

interfere with what he had to do. Getting Callum out was all that mattered. 'I've no choice.'

'How long will you be gone?' she asked.

'It will take four days to reach Lord Cairnross's fortress, if we ride hard. Then four days back again.'

He rolled onto his back, staring up at the ceiling. His head pounded with an oncoming ache, and he felt his hands beginning to shake again. He took one breath, then another, trying to still the tremor.

But he could no more control his trembling hands than he could stop his heart from beating. It slashed at his pride and he hated that she was seeing him like this.

Nairna touched a cool hand to his forehead. 'It's all right, Bram,' she whispered. 'If you're to make this journey, you need rest.'

'I don't sleep, Nairna. It's not something I can do anymore.'

'Try.' She brought her fingers over his eyelids and he shut them, breathing in the soft fragrance of her skin. Though his mind refused to remain still, troubled with thoughts of Callum, his wife's touch brought him comfort.

And though he wished, more than anything, that Nairna's presence could take away the nightmares, he doubted if it would ever happen.

'I never thought I'd be sending you off to fight again,' she said, her hand resting over his eyes as if she could will him to sleep.

As he lay unmoving beneath the butterfly touch of her fingers, a slight note of uneasiness pulled at him. There was always a risk involved with any fight. Before he'd brought Nairna back with him, he hadn't cared about his own fate. If he died in the battle, so be it.

But now he had a reason to come back.

* * *

Though he kept his eyes closed, Nairna knew Bram wasn't sleeping. She shivered, remembering the tales she'd heard of Lord Cairnross. It was rumoured that he had been sent by the English King Edward, not to ally with the Scots, but to execute them.

Some believed Cairnross had used the black arts to build his fortresses, for no one knew how he'd accomplished so much, so quickly. It was clear now that he'd done so with the blood and sweat of his captives.

And Bram had been one of his slaves.

Though she tried to distance herself, she worried about her husband's quest to find Callum. She didn't want to watch him ride away, or relive the anguish if he never came back. She gripped the coverlet, her eyes burning. Tonight, he'd touched her intimately, evoking such feelings that she'd found it impossible to remain unaffected. She wanted to take care of him again, to push back the years to the bride she'd been long ago.

But the man had grown away from the boy. There were needs he held now that went beyond food or sleep. It was as if he needed her, more than nourishment or water.

His body was so close to hers, she could feel the warmth. Nairna shifted upon the mattress, her gown bunched up between her thighs. She couldn't stop herself from thinking of Bram's mouth on her skin and the rush of sensation that had flooded through her, moistening the secret place between her legs.

Aye, it was different between them now. But instead of the shy, stolen moments, she craved something else from him. Something to calm the restlessness rising up within.

Slowly, she eased backwards, until their bodies

touched. Bram reached for her waist, pulling her close. He rested his face against her hair, and upon the back of her neck she could feel his breath. His touch penetrated her skin, awakening her to strange, pulling needs. A part of her wanted to turn her mouth to his and experience the forgetfulness that he could grant.

Temptation beckoned to her and she longed to feel his body filling up the emptiness inside. She turned to him and her nose brushed against his, her mouth only a few inches away.

'What is it, *a ghaoil?*' Bram asked, reaching out to slide her hair behind her ear. The tender gesture made her hesitate, for she didn't know if he would even want to make love to her. She had no experience in seduction and didn't know what would please him.

When she embraced him closer, her breasts pressed against his chest. She lifted her knee over his and the moment her bare skin touched his, he froze.

He didn't move, nor did he give any indication that he'd changed his mind about joining with her. All of her courage fled and Nairna felt her face flood with embarrassment.

She untangled her leg from his and rolled away, closing her eyes. 'Be safe tomorrow,' was all she could utter before turning away.

The following morning, Bram rose at dawn to prepare for the journey. In sleep, Nairna's face was soft, her lips tempting him to steal a kiss. But if he dared to taste her, he'd never stop. Only by the grace of God had he managed to keep his hands off her last night.

When she'd embraced him, he hadn't known what she'd wanted. Was she merely bidding him good night? Or was she trying to show him affection?

Before he could decide, she'd told him to be safe and turned her back. He'd spent a painful remainder of the night, his groin raging with need. He hardly trusted himself to sleep so close to her, for fear that he'd lose sight of himself and take her without any finesse.

Marriage was killing him in a slow, sexually frustrating death.

Though he wanted to tell her goodbye, he didn't want to awaken her, preferring to remember her like this. Bram found one of her riding gloves and held it a moment, slipping a small token inside.

He closed the door behind him and saw that Alex and Ross were already preparing the horses and supplies. Bram continued walking across the courtyard until he reached them.

There, he found his younger brother Dougal glaring at them like a sulking child. 'I want to go with you.'

'Not while I breathe.' A lad of four and ten was too young to venture into a fight such as this one. Bram studied Dougal, seeing traces of himself in the young man's eyes. Once, he'd been every bit as hotheaded and determined.

He softened his voice, adding, 'I need you to guard Nairna and Laren, as well as the others.'

'You're not leaving me behind,' Dougal insisted. 'I can fight better than you. Besides, Alex thinks you don't have the strength for the journey. I heard him talking about it last night.'

Bram showed no reaction. 'You're still not going.'

'I will. Once you've gone, I'll follow.' The stubborn slant to the boy's face made it clear that he intended to do just that. 'You can't stop me if you're already gone.'

Bram grasped Dougal by the wrist. The boy yelped

as he dragged him past the others, seizing a length of rope from near the stables. While the boy cursed and struggled, Bram tied him up, securing the end of the rope to a post. 'You're going nowhere, lad.'

He didn't care that what he was doing would humiliate his brother. What mattered most was keeping him safe. The ropes weren't tight enough to hurt him, only to prevent him from following. He also left enough slack in the rope where Dougal could enter the stables for shelter, if it rained.

'I hate you,' Dougal raged, struggling against his bonds. 'I wish you'd never come back.'

Bram returned to his horse, knowing that it was the boy's anger speaking. But the barbed words had their intended effect. It bothered him that his youngest brother didn't know him anymore. And Dougal couldn't understand that Bram only meant to protect him.

Alex raised an eyebrow at the sight of their brother fighting to tear off the ropes, struggling to escape. 'You think that will stop Dougal?'

'Do you have a better idea?'

Alex shrugged. 'Not really.'

When they returned, Bram supposed he'd have to do something to atone for his actions. But it was better for Dougal's pride to suffer than for him to become Lord Cairnross's captive.

'Nairna or Laren can cut him free tomorrow,' Bram said. 'By then, we'll be far from here.'

'I don't envy them, having to live with Dougal while we're gone.' Alex grimaced. 'He changed after our father died. He's angry all the time.'

'What about our mother?' Bram ventured. 'Was he better when she was here?'

Alex shook his head. 'No. Grizel ignored him in her grief and he became a hellion. She wanted nothing to do with either of us.' With a nod towards their brother, he added, 'Leave him be. That's the only solution.'

Bram cast a look towards Dougal, who was raging at the others around him. Some of the older men teased him, which only provoked the boy's temper further.

He saw Nairna approaching, carrying a bit of food. When she caught sight of Dougal, her face grew troubled.

She made the mistake of going to speak to the lad, and when she offered him the food, Dougal snarled at her, kicking at her ankles.

Bram's temper erupted and he crossed the space until he reached the boy. He ignored Nairna's protests and caught Dougal by the scruff of his tunic. 'You don't touch my wife. You don't speak unkindly to her or dare to harm her in any way.'

His hands exerted a light pressure, and when Dougal tried to bite him, Bram tightened the force.

Without looking at his wife, he added, 'Nairna, he's not to be released until tomorrow morning.'

'But—'

'He can't follow us.' Looking deep into the boy's eyes, he lowered his voice. 'You don't know what kind of hell Callum is enduring right now. But I do. And I won't let you or anyone else become their captive.' Raising the boy's chin, he added, 'While I'm gone, you'll treat Nairna with respect. Or you'll answer to me for it.'

Bram released the boy, letting Dougal see his scarred wrists. At the sight of his mauled skin, the boy quieted.

Nairna looked upset, but Bram took her hand, leading her away.

'It's not right,' she protested. 'He's too young to be tied up like that.'

'He's four and ten. And he knows better than to behave like a stubborn fool.' With a squeeze to her hand, he ordered, 'Don't let your compassion get the best of you, Nairna. Don't believe a word that passes his lips. He'll try to find us if you free him.'

He had no doubt that Dougal would do anything possible to escape. 'Swear to me,' Bram urged. 'Don't let him follow us.'

Nairna gave a slight nod, worry creasing her lips. 'Do I truly need to wait until tomorrow?'

'If he behaves himself, you can cut him free late tonight.' He stopped walking when they were a few paces away from Alex and the others. 'It's for his safety.'

Reluctance lined her face, but she agreed with a nod. He could see that she didn't like what she had to do, but she understood his reasons.

He stopped walking, taking a moment to study her. In her eyes he saw worry and regretted that they'd had no time together.

'I'll return in just over a sennight, if all goes well,' he said.

She embraced him. 'God be with you on your journey.' Into his hands she pressed a bundle of food.

She'd known he wouldn't take the time to break his fast, and the gesture made him tighten his arms around her.

A hollow feeling unfurled within him, for he didn't know if he'd see her again. If the worst happened…

It's different this time, he reminded himself. Instead of Nairna remaining in his shadowed memory, she would be here, waiting for him. He had a flesh-and-blood reason to return, a woman who had already driven out so many of the demons.

Until then, he had to concentrate on finding Callum. And coming back alive.

'You're not going to leave me here,' Dougal growled as Nairna drew close.

'Have you broken your fast this morn?' she asked, ignoring his fury.

'Why would you care?' He spat at her feet.

Nairna continued past him, returning to the Hall to fetch some bread, before she came back. Her brothers had always been in worse tempers when they were hungry. No doubt Dougal had been so eager to follow Bram and the others, he'd neglected a morning meal.

When she reached him once more, she held out the bread. 'Do you want this?'

'What I *want* is for you to cut me free.' He glared at her, fighting against the ropes that held him bound to one of the palisade posts.

'And what I want is for the women to come back,' she countered.

'They don't matter. Good riddance to them.'

'Even your own mother?' She broke off a piece of the bread, setting it on the ground within reach.

He snatched it up, shoving it into his mouth to avoid answering. Behind his brown eyes, she saw the shadow of hurt. 'I don't care if I see any of them again.'

The lie slipped from his mouth and he didn't meet her gaze. Nairna left the remainder of the bread at his feet.

'I'm going to bring them back,' she promised. 'But first, I need to learn more about what happened with the attacks.'

'I've nothing to say to you.' Dougal ate the bread, his

gaze fixated upon the horizon where his brothers were disappearing over the ridge. The intense longing on his face and the adolescent sense of unfairness possessed him.

Bram was right, Nairna realised. If she dared to loosen the ropes, the boy would be gone within a few minutes. Though she hated the thought of keeping him tied up, there seemed to be no alternative.

'I'll bring you food and drink later,' she promised. With a reluctant glance back at Dougal, she left him behind.

Inside the Hall, the MacKinloch men had left the evidence of their own meal from the night before, with bits of bread, discarded meat and refuse strewn everywhere.

The chief's wife Laren crossed the Hall, seeming to recognise the dismay on her face. 'It's a waste of time to let it bother you.' She lowered her voice and leaned in. 'The men here don't bother to think of living any differently. In all the time I've lived here, nothing has changed.'

'What about Alex? Doesn't he care?'

Laren's mouth tightened. 'He's occupied with other matters. Table manners are the least of his concerns.'

'The women,' Nairna guessed. 'Is he trying to bring them back?'

Laren shook her head, disappointment crossing her face. 'Not really. He says they'll come back when they've learned their lesson. He's more interested in defending Glen Arrin against the English.'

'And what if you'd gone with them?'

Laren only shrugged. Her silence suggested that her husband wouldn't even miss them. Nairna almost reached out to take Laren's hand, but realised the woman didn't want her sympathy. Whatever sort of marriage she and Alex had, it was not a happy one.

'I can't see why the English would want this place,' Nairna said. Most of the fortress was in a deplorable state.

'The location would give them a garrison closer to the Highlands. With the mountains, you can see any invaders from miles around.'

'Is that why Bram wants to build our house up on the ridge? So he can see the English before they get here?'

Laren gave a nod. 'He and Alex thought it would be a strategic location.' She reached out and adjusted her gloved hands, lifting her mantle to cover her hair. 'I only hope the English leave us alone until Alex and Bram return.' She nodded towards the far end of the room. 'There's an underground storage chamber beneath the Hall. I usually take the girls belowground when we're under siege.'

Nairna didn't care for the sound of that. 'Does it happen often?'

But the Lady only shrugged. 'From time to time. Unfortunately, the MacKinloch men love any opportunity to fight.' A shadow of melancholy passed over her, and her blue eyes turned wistful. 'They'll never surrender their freedom. They're too proud.'

Nairna couldn't help comparing the two clans. Her father hadn't cared about pride or freedom. Hamish had pledged his loyalty to the English king, to save their lands and protect the people. He'd made his choice, to turn his back on the rebellion. And though his cowardice bothered her, eventually he would be forced to confront the English. In contrast, the MacKinlochs lived in the shadow of constant battles. She didn't know which was worse.

'My girls and I are going for a walk,' Laren said, her face reddening slightly. 'We should be back in a few hours.' From the guilty expression on her face, it was clear the Lady of Glen Arrin had no desire for Nairna to accompany them.

'While you're gone, might I have a look at the household accounts?' Nairna blurted out. 'At my father's fortress, I helped them to increase their earnings. It might be that I could do the same here.'

Laren shrugged. 'If you wish.' She gave instructions as to where Nairna could find them and then excused herself from Nairna's side, ignoring the mess within the Hall.

As Laren crossed the room, it seemed that there was no light left within her, as if she'd abandoned hope. Her girls emerged from the narrow staircase and joined their mother, holding hands in their quiet retreat.

Where were they going? Along the edge of the loch for their walk? It struck her as unusual for the Lady to abandon the keep for hours on end. Something wasn't right. Nairna thought about following them, but decided against it. She had her chance now to learn more about Glen Arrin, without Alex or Bram to interfere. Perhaps she could determine ways to rebuild their holdings.

Earning money was something she understood. Numbers and coins could be multiplied and increased. And if there was a way to improve their living circumstances at Glen Arrin, she would find it.

Nairna leaned up against the outer curtain wall, her mind mulling over the problems of the clan. Her mind was filled up with ideas. Sheep could bring in the profit of wool, or perhaps they could increase their cattle herds. There was a little space for farming, but only enough to provide grain.

As her brain spun off dreams of increasing the wealth, her heart worried about Bram. She remembered his heated mouth seizing hers, the way he'd cupped her breasts, running his thumbs over the nipples. Nairna turned her burning face to the wall, her skin growing more sensitive. Though he wasn't here, she imagined him removing the clothing from her body, baring her skin to his touch. His lips would kiss her and she wondered if his hungry mouth would move over her breasts, down to her thighs.

The air in her lungs grew heavier, and Nairna pressed her hand against the wooden enclosure, trying to shut off the vision.

Bram had said he would return with Callum in a little over a sennight. She wanted to believe that he would return safely with his brother, but her greater fear was that once again, she'd lose him.

She pushed back the fear gathering inside. Right now, she had to be strong, to wait for his return. But once he did come back, what then?

Would she finally become his wife in body, rekindling what was lost between them? Would her womb finally bear a child of their union? Or would she become bitter and angry at herself, their marriage weakening as Laren's had?

Her gaze moved across the inner bailey, taking note of every man and adolescent who remained. There were about twenty younger men and ten elder. Though the men worked in their daily tasks, the air of neglect hung heavily.

As stubborn as their chief was, she doubted if Alex would go after the women, despite what his men needed.

But perhaps there was something she could do.

* * *

At dawn, Nairna cut Dougal free. The boy's eyes were bloodshot, as though he hadn't slept at all. She'd given him food and drink at several intervals, as well as a blanket last night, but hatred darkened Dougal's face. As he passed by her, he deliberately walked into her shoulder, knocking her aside. Nairna was so startled by his aggressive behaviour that she had no time to respond until he was already past her.

She rubbed her shoulder and one of the other adolescent boys came forwards. 'He didna hurt you, did he?'

Nairna shook her head. 'I suppose he blames me for following Bram's orders.'

'He doesn't like anyone. No one likes him, either.' The young man shrugged. 'He'll get himself killed in a fight one day.'

Nairna blinked at the nonchalant assessment. 'I hope not.' Never had she seen anyone with that much fury locked inside. It was unsettling and she wondered if anyone had ever attempted to talk with Dougal.

'Don't let it bother you.' The young man, whose name she learned was Monroe, started to walk away.

But Nairna caught up to him, wanting more answers. 'Was he always this way?'

'He got worse after the women left,' Monroe admitted.

'They need to return. The clan is lost without them.' It occurred to her that she was in a better position than the men to ask them to come back. She could find out the true reasons why they'd left and do what she could to bring them home.

'I'm going to go after them,' she said suddenly. 'And bring them back.'

'They might not come,' Monroe said. 'Lady Grizel,

Alex's mother, won't set foot upon Glen Arrin again. She said so. And if she doesna come, the others won't either.'

'It can't hurt to ask.'

Monroe sent her look of disbelief. 'You don't know Lady Grizel well, do you?' He didn't bother to hide his shudder.

Nairna ignored his cynicism. 'I'll need escorts and supplies. Can you gather some men together for me and we'll leave on the morrow?'

'I can ask, but it's safer if the women and bairns stay with Lord Locharr,' Monroe argued. 'His castle is stronger than Glen Arrin will ever be.'

'Don't you think Alex is trying to change that?' The chief of the MacKinlochs struck her as an ambitious man. 'Glen Arrin can be more than it is.'

'It'll ne'er happen,' Monroe said. 'The clan's too divided. Bram was meant to be chief, but he doesna want it anymore. He's too weak, anyhow.'

'He is *not* too weak,' Nairna shot back. 'In a few weeks, he'll be as strong as any of them.'

'If he comes back.' With that, Monroe nodded his head in farewell and walked away.

Nairna's skin turned cold. *He'll come back,* she reassured herself.

He had to.

Chapter Ten

Bram remained in the shadows, watching the English soldiers who patrolled the garrison. He knew their faces, especially the men who had guarded the prisoners. Some had been impassive, merely obeying orders. Others had enjoyed tormenting those in chains.

He gripped the crossbow Alex had given him. Though he would have preferred hand-to-hand combat, given his physical weakness it was likely the better choice to remain here.

He'd led Alex and Ross to the loose section of the palisade wall near the back of the fortress. Vines and underbrush had grown over the wall, and the greenery kept the loose stones hidden from the rest of the soldiers. They'd spent the last half-hour removing the stones in silence, until the opening was large enough for a man to fit through.

Bram chose his position behind the veil of vines, keeping his crossbow loaded. With any luck, they could free all of the prisoners and get Callum out, using the chaos to make their escape.

As his brother and Ross entered the fortress with stealth, time crept onwards. Bram stared at the limestone, remembering how, day after day, he'd stacked the stones atop one another. The backbreaking work was done in silence, occasionally interrupted by a soldier issuing a command or smashing a quarterstaff against a captive's shoulders.

He lost sight of Alex and Ross as they disappeared with the others, keeping to the shadows. The remnants of a stone wall lay unfinished near the inner curtain. The Earl had several garrisons across Scotland, and Bram had worked upon many of the structures before they'd been moved to Cairnross.

Had they arrived a few hours earlier, the prisoners might have been working on the wall. As it was, the men were likely belowground, trying to steal an hour or two of sleep. The underground cellar wasn't tall enough to stand in, and remembering the interior brought a phantom ache to his neck and shoulders.

Bram's gaze grew fixated upon the opening within the ground; it was as if he were looking through water, with blurred images and muffled sounds. Though he kept a bolt fitted to the crossbow, he felt himself slipping away from the present into the past.

The scars upon his neck itched, a bead of sweat rolling down to his collarbone. The scents of the garrison stung, bringing him back to the years of imprisonment. When a soldier passed by him, he held his breath.

He could almost feel the slash of the dagger against his flesh once again. Taste the blood in his mouth from where they'd struck him across the jaw, yelling taunts about his weakness.

Where was Callum? He craned his neck, searching for a glimpse of his brother. Right now, he wanted to leave his position, to free the others from captivity and bring his brother out of the darkness.

Broken memories assaulted him, and as minutes transformed into an hour, there was still no sign of Callum. It was as if he'd vanished. Bram's fingers trembled upon the trigger of the crossbow. With the slightest pressure, he could kill one of the English soldiers who'd threatened them.

One of the soldiers lifted a torch and headed to the underground entrance where the prisoners were held. What was he planning to do?

Without waiting to find out, Bram released the bolt. It struck the stone wall beside the soldier, bouncing away in a clear miss. Seconds later, the man dropped the torch. He unsheathed his sword and charged at Bram, his voice crying out a warning to the others.

The crossbow fell from his fingers onto the ground. Bram reached for the claymore he'd worn strapped to his back, but his hands froze upon the hilt. His arms felt as though they were weighted down with stones, unable to move.

He saw the eyes of the man who had tortured his brother and himself. Nausea swam in his stomach, and when the soldier's blade raised high for the killing blow Bram managed to unsheathe his weapon. He barely defended the blow that slashed at him, stumbling like a child.

His mind roared at him to strike back, to fight for his brother's life. But his arms moved too slowly, his body broken down. It infuriated him that he'd come so far, only to lose his strength.

Move, damn you, he ordered himself. But his strength

wasn't enough to counter his lack of co-ordination. He'd truly fallen hard. God above, what had happened to him? After all this time, his fighting had worsened. Shame burned through him when Alex stepped in to cut down the soldier.

His brother stared at him, as if he no longer knew him. 'It was a mistake for you to come.'

Bram knew it, though he said nothing. He locked glances with Alex, furious with himself for his weakness. He'd foolishly believed that his anger would carry him when raw skill would not.

He reached for his crossbow, but Alex stopped him, handing him a shield instead. 'Get back to the horses and wait for us. Ross went below to free the others, but Callum wasn't there. He's gone.'

The words took the air from his lungs. Had they been too late? Was his brother already dead?

The roar of the other prisoners resounded in the night air as they fought for their freedom. One seized a torch and used it to set a shelter on fire. Flames and black smoke soared into the sky, while they ran for the gates, some with their hands and ankles still chained.

On the opposite end of the garrison, Bram saw a woman huddled against the other end, cowering against the wall. If she didn't move, she'd be caught in the violence. All around her, prisoners cut down their captors, slaughtering the English with any weapons they could find.

Seeing her fear reminded Bram of his wife. He couldn't leave this woman here, any more than he'd want Nairna to be trapped in such a place. As he crossed the garrison, slipping through the shadows, his thoughts drifted back to her. Though he supposed his wife was safe enough at Glen Arrin, he hadn't liked leaving her behind.

It reminded him too much of the night he'd left her after their wedding. He'd kissed her goodbye, never realising that it would be the last touch between them for seven years.

And tonight, if he didn't get out of this burning fortress, it might well be the last time he saw his wife.

Bram stared at the woman, who kept her face to the stones, quaking with fear. Interfering with her fate was a mistake. He knew it, yet he couldn't stop himself from approaching her.

He avoided the men around him, keeping his shield up, until he reached her side. 'Are you a hostage?' he demanded.

She gripped her arms, as if she hadn't heard him. Lowering her hood, he realised that she was only a little younger than Nairna. With veiled hair and terrified eyes, her gaze darted about as if she didn't know where to flee.

'If you want to leave this place, my brother can grant you sanctuary,' Bram offered. 'My wife will look after you, and I promise, you'll face no harm.'

The woman stared at him as if fighting her own indecision. There was distrust on her face, but an even greater fear of staying behind. In the end, she picked up her skirts and ran towards him. 'Please,' she begged, in heavily accented Gaelic, 'help me get home to my father.'

Bram caught her hand and drew her outside the broken wall. He spied Alex and Ross starting to make their own escape and he led the woman to their horses.

When Alex and Ross arrived with the others, the chief

lost his temper. 'Bram, what in God's name have you done? She's not coming with us.'

'We can't leave her there,' he argued.

'She's one of them,' Alex snapped. 'And if you bring her, Cairnross's men will follow her to Glen Arrin.'

'No,' the woman interrupted. 'If you send word to my father, he'll come for me and you will be rewarded.'

'And just who is your father?' Alex demanded.

The woman's face turned cool. 'Guy de Montpierre, the Duc D'Avignois.'

Alex's face grew intrigued. Bram could read his brother's thoughts without words. Rescuing the daughter of a French duke might result in a reward for their clan.

'I am Marguerite de Montpierre,' the woman continued, offering them a regal nod. 'I was betrothed to Lord Cairnross.' From the distaste upon her face, it was evident that she had not wanted to marry the man.

Bram wasn't certain why the duke would want his daughter to wed an English lord instead of a French nobleman, but he didn't ask. Perhaps she was a bastard.

'You may have our protection until your father arrives,' Alex agreed. 'But you'd best pray that Cairnross doesn't find you.'

The woman pulled the hood of her cloak over her veil and Bram boosted her onto the saddle. In the distance, the garrison was in flames and he saw it crumbling to the ground.

'I'm glad to see it destroyed,' Marguerite remarked.

'How long were you there?' Bram asked, as he climbed up behind her, urging the horse faster.

'Only a sennight. But the prisoners…' She shuddered at the memory.

Bram said nothing, not wanting to know what had happened since he'd escaped. He knew well enough the sorts of tortures that the soldiers used. His chest tightened at the memory.

'Did you ever see a man called Callum MacKinloch?' Bram asked, though it was likely a fruitless hope. 'Younger than me, one of our brothers?'

'He was sent away a few days ago,' Lady Marguerite admitted. '*Oui,* I saw him.'

'Where?'

She shook her head, keeping her gaze fixed forwards. 'To the south. That's all I know.'

'But he was alive and unharmed?'

'Alive, yes.'

But she didn't say unharmed. Within her voice he heard a note of worry and wondered what they'd done to his brother.

Don't think of it now, he urged himself. At least he had a place to begin searching. And in the meantime, until they found his brother, he would spend every minute training.

Never again would he find himself too frozen to move, letting the nightmares of the past dominate him. He would rebuild the skills he'd lost over the years, no matter how long it took.

And he wouldn't give up until Callum was found.

Four days later

'You've gone brainless,' Dougal told Nairna.

She shrugged. 'If you're too frightened to escort me, I'll find someone else.'

Her barb struck its mark and Dougal stiffened. 'And what if I don't want to? I don't even like you.'

Nairna tilted her head as though it were no matter.

'I'm leaving for Locharr now. Monroe is going with me. I suspect he's strong enough to protect me.'

'Monroe is afraid of horses.' Dougal sent a disgusted look towards the adolescent, who was indeed looking nervous about the prospect of riding.

Nairna rested her hands on her hips. 'He'll do well enough, if you won't help.' She'd not received an offer of any additional escorts from the MacKinloch men. They'd claimed that they couldn't leave Glen Arrin unattended. Since it was only a few hours' ride, she saw no choice but to use Monroe and Dougal as her guides. At least there was no need to bring supplies or food. They could return tonight, if the women agreed to it.

She confronted Dougal and demanded, 'Are you coming or not?'

He mounted the horse Monroe gave him and started off through the valley. Though he kept a sour expression on his face, his posture showed his eagerness for an escape from Glen Arrin.

Nairna reached for her riding gloves, but her right palm wouldn't slide into the leather. When she reached inside the glove, she found a scrap of linen. She unfolded it and found a dried sprig of purple heather inside.

It must have been from Bram. Nairna blinked, for it had been over a sennight since she'd seen her husband last. The simple gift caught at her heart, and in that moment, the loneliness swelled up inside.

Last night when she'd slept alone, the mattress had seemed larger, the space empty. She'd touched the space where he'd laid his head, praying for his safe return.

It was easier to sleep with his warm body pressed against hers. She wondered what it would be like to roll over and feel his kiss claiming her mouth, his hands moving over her skin.

Nairna stroked the heather, closing her eyes for a moment. Bram had conjured up the past with a single flower, of the days when they'd exchanged gifts with one another. As she tucked the flower away, the shaky emotions started to well up.

Quickly she pretended to check the bridle to hide the foolish tears pricking at her eyes. Despite all the years between them, she still cared about Bram. She touched the heather, promising herself that if he returned, she would be a good wife to him.

As she spurred her mare onwards to catch up to Dougal, Monroe hung behind. Though his own mount seemed gentle enough, the boy's face had gone white as he gripped the horse's mane for balance.

Once she was certain he wouldn't fall, Nairna rode up beside Dougal. He rode as if he'd been born a part of the horse. The natural gait seemed to flow between them and he appeared to revel in the freedom. No longer was he the angry, frustrated young man. Instead, there was a peace upon his expression.

'Is this your horse?' she prompted, trying to open a conversation. 'He's beautiful.'

'He belongs to Alex,' Dougal said. But his hand passed over the stallion's neck with an air of possession. He quickened his pace, as if to avoid further conversation.

Nairna rode faster, determined not to be left behind. The wind slashed at her face, her hair whipping free of its braid. When he saw that she'd kept up with his pace, surprise transformed his mood. On impulse, Nairna smiled at him. 'Want to race?' Without waiting for his reply, she urged her mare into a full gallop.

'You don't know where you're going!' Dougal shouted.

'Then you'd best keep up and show me!' she called back. It had been years since she'd ridden so fast and the exhilaration of speed intensified her enjoyment of the ride.

As she'd predicted, Dougal caught up and overtook her. Nairna tried to increase her mare's gait, but she knew that the animal would tire too soon. Instead, she kept a slight pace back, letting Dougal have the advantage. He led them towards an enormous castle in the distance, one she'd never seen before. Tall square towers were surrounded by strong walls, perhaps eight feet high.

It must have been built by the Normans, she guessed. Possibly twenty years earlier. It must have taken thousands of pounds to build such a place. Along one of the towers, she saw climbing vines, trailing up the stones.

A small stream flowed across the land ahead, and Dougal slowed his mount in front of it. Nairna judged the distance, took careful aim and jumped the stream with her mare. They landed safely and she turned to smile at Dougal. 'I win.'

'You shouldn't have jumped her,' the young man argued. 'She's not used to jumping. She might have broken her leg.' Dougal dismounted and sloshed through the stream, moving forwards to inspect the mare.

Nairna dismounted to allow him a better look, then asked gently, 'It was a good race, Dougal. You're one of the best riders I've ever seen.'

He flushed, but he didn't acknowledge the praise. 'She'll be all right. But don't jump her again.'

Nairna rubbed the mare's back. 'Do your brothers know you ride this well?'

He shook his head. 'All they care about is teaching me to fight.'

'How did you learn?'

Dougal returned to his own stallion, inspecting the

animal and speaking softly to him. 'I sneaked out at dawn and taught myself.'

'Why wouldn't you ask your brother for a horse of your own?' she began. 'Alex might—'

'He won't.' Dougal cut off the conversation and nodded towards the castle. 'Now, if you're wanting to talk to Grizel, you'll find her inside.'

Not 'my mother,' but 'Grizel,' as if the woman were a stranger. Casting her gaze back to Monroe, who had finally caught up, Nairna suddenly spied several riders behind him. The sun hid their faces from view, and when Dougal saw the direction of her gaze, he drew closer to her, resting his hand upon the hilt of his dirk.

'Who are they?' Nairna murmured, half-afraid to wonder. Her question was answered a moment later, when Bram came riding over the crest of the hill.

Bram hung on to his horse, the green hills blurring as he raced towards his wife. Though he'd longed to see Nairna again, he'd never expected to find her at Locharr. He didn't know what had driven his wife to come here, but he intended to find out.

When he pulled his horse up short, he directed the worst of his anger at Dougal. 'Why in the name of the bloody saints would you bring Nairna here?'

Fury incensed him, at the thought of the horse stumbling and throwing Nairna off to break her neck. The race had been reckless and dangerous. But before he could speak another word, Nairna moved close to him and threw her arms around his waist.

He gripped her hard, as if he could bring her within his skin. Even when her hands relaxed around his neck, he wouldn't release his tight grip. She smelled earthy, of wildflowers and herbs, and, God above, he'd missed her.

'I asked Dougal to bring me here,' she explained. Lifting her face to his, she said, 'I'm glad you made it home safely. Did you find Callum?'

'No. They moved him to one of the other garrisons.' He drank in the sight of her, from her tangled brown hair to the soft green of her eyes. When his gaze settled upon her mouth, he considered whether or not to kiss her.

'Was anyone hurt?' she asked.

'None of our men. And we freed the remaining prisoners.'

She gave a nod, but her face appeared troubled. 'What will you do now?'

'We need to find Callum while he's still alive.' Bram released her, striding towards the horses. Though he'd wanted to pursue Callum immediately, Alex had refused. Instead, his brother planned to send clansmen to each of the outlying fortresses until they discovered which one held Callum.

He understood that his brother's calm, rational plan would work. But it didn't diminish his need to see this through. Remaining behind, waiting for someone to find Callum, made him feel helpless. Useless.

'Alex sent men to search the other garrisons. When they've found Callum, I'll go after him.' His gaze flicked over the large stone wall in the distance surrounding Locharr. 'We brought back a woman from Cairnross. I left her with Alex.'

'A woman?'

He saw his wife blink at his pronouncement, as though she weren't certain what to think. 'Why was she there? What happened to her?'

Bram shrugged. 'She was betrothed to Lord Cairn-ross. I wasn't about to leave her there.'

Nairna stepped back, staring at him with dismay. 'You stole Lord Cairnross's betrothed?'

'No. It was her choice to come.' He didn't regret it for a moment and his temper started to push at the edges of his control. 'I wouldn't have left a dog with Cairnross, Nairna. Much less a woman.' He reached the horses, adding, 'Her father is a French duke.'

'Duke or not, Cairnross will bring an army to attack us.' She rubbed at her arms, as if she'd grown cold think-ing of it. 'Couldn't you have taken her to the kirk for sanctuary?'

'There wasn't time. And she'll be safe enough for now.' At least until they sent word to her father. He'd leave that in Alex's hands.

'Or Lord Cairnross will burn Glen Arrin to the ground because we took her,' Nairna dared to say.

He didn't deny that the English would retaliate. 'We can defend ourselves.'

'Not well enough.'

He bit back the urge to argue, for words wouldn't dem-onstrate anything. 'We should go back to Glen Arrin,' he said, guiding her by the arm. He didn't know why she'd come to Locharr, but he didn't want her to join the other women here. An emptiness centred through him as he wondered whether she'd planned to leave him.

'I can't go back until I've finished what I came here to do.' She withdrew her arm from his, trying to walk back to the castle. 'I want to talk with your mother and the women. You should visit her, now that you're here.'

He'd rather be eaten alive by insects than spend an hour with Grizel MacKinloch. 'I'd rather not.' He kept his tone emotionless, for she didn't understand what she was suggesting.

He supposed that Nairna was missing her own mother, who had died years ago. But Grizel wasn't at all gentle or kind.

'All right. If you want to return to Glen Arrin, go on without me. I'll see her for myself.' The glint in her eyes told him that she wasn't about to abandon this idea.

'Grizel hasn't changed, Bram,' came Dougal's voice.

The young man drew closer, leading the stallion alongside him. Beneath his tone, there was still resentment and Bram couldn't blame him for it.

'I don't suppose she's forgiven me.' Bram came up beside his brother, wanting to make amends. 'And I doubt that you have, either.' He rested his hand on Dougal's shoulder. 'I know you're angry that I ordered you bound when we left. But I didn't want you hurt.'

'I'm old enough to fight,' his younger brother insisted. In his eyes, Bram saw the frustration of being left behind. Dougal leaned his cheek against the stallion's face and the animal gave a light nicker.

It was like looking at a younger version of himself, when he'd claimed to his father that he was old enough to defend the clan. Nothing he said would make any difference to Dougal. The only thing that would help his brother was the right preparation.

'Train with me,' Bram suggested, 'and when we've located Callum, we'll make the decision then. If you're strong enough.'

The light of determination blazed across the boy's face, but he gave a silent nod.

'You'll have to prove yourself,' Bram said. 'But if you're not ready to travel with us, there's no shame in defending our home.'

His brother's brown eyes met his own. Though it was clear Dougal was itching to voice all the protests rising inside, he held his tongue.

'Shall we go inside?' Nairna ventured, nodding towards the castle walls. His wife appeared anxious, despite her outward eagerness.

'If you want to visit the other women, I'll take you to the gates.' And perhaps, once she'd met Grizel, she would be satisfied to leave his mother where she was.

'I want to bring them home,' Nairna said. 'It's not right for them to be living within these walls, not when they could be home with their husbands.'

Dougal and Bram exchanged looks. 'One night,' Bram said, meeting his brother's gaze. 'No more.'

'Even that might be too long.' Dougal winced.

His wife eyed them as though she thought they were being unreasonable. 'No one could be that bad, Bram.'

She let him assist her onto her mare and he let his hand linger upon her calf. Her bare skin was warm and when she held still, he envisioned sliding his palm up her leg. He wanted to take her off the horse, pulling her to him, to show her how much he'd missed her.

Her hand touched his and she leaned down. 'Thank you for the flower,' she said, raising her gloved hand. There was a softness in her face, as if he'd done something right.

Bram mounted his own horse and took the lead. 'Let's get this over with.'

Chapter Eleven

Grizel MacKinloch awaited them inside the inner bailey. Tall and slender, she held herself as though she expected the world to grovel at her feet. Her dark brown hair was tightly braided, pulling the wrinkles taut from her face. As soon as she saw Bram, her expression slid through an array of emotions—shock, sadness and fury.

Dougal took the horses, not even bothering with a greeting before he retreated to the stables.

Nairna took Bram's hand in hers. Though she'd wanted to believe that his mother would be glad to see him, there was no love on the woman's face. The atmosphere around them felt colder, and Nairna was beginning to sense what Dougal and Bram had tried to tell her.

'My lady mother,' Bram greeted Grizel, bowing slightly.

She stared at him, as though he'd crawled out of a grave. 'Bram.'

There was no embrace of welcome, no tears shed over his return. Instead, there was an air of impatience, as if she had somewhere else she wanted to be.

He's your son, Nairna wanted to point out. Hadn't Grizel missed him at all? Was there no warmth in her heart?

An indignant feeling started to gather in Nairna's chest as Bram turned to introduce her. 'You might remember my wife Nairna, of the MacPherson clan. You met her once when we were betrothed.'

His mother hadn't attended their wedding, though Nairna didn't recall why. She'd been so caught up in her happiness of marrying Bram, she'd hardly noticed anyone or anything else.

Grizel's glance was cool. 'I see.' Her eyes flicked over Nairna in disdain.

Even so, Nairna remembered her own manners, dropping into a light curtsy. 'I am glad to see you again, my lady.'

The woman gave a slight nod, then turned to Bram. 'Why did you come here?'

'It wasn't my idea,' he replied.

The bluntness of his tone made Nairna interrupt. 'Would it not be better to speak inside? I would like to meet Lord Locharr and we can rest from our journey while we talk.'

If Lady Grizel and Bram began fighting before she had the chance to smooth things over with the others, there was little hope of convincing the women to return.

'There's no reason for you to stay,' Grizel remarked, wasting no time in making her point. 'If you came to ask us to return, the answer is no. I'll not go back to Glen Arrin, so long as breath remains in my body. And certainly not if *he* is there.' She nodded to Bram.

There was no reaction at all on Bram's face, only calm acceptance. Nairna's temper flared up, and she couldn't stop herself from demanding, 'Why would you say such a thing to the son you've not seen in seven years?'

Was the woman that heartless?

Grizel drew up her posture, her eyes hardened. 'Would you want anything to do with the one who caused your husband's death?' Without waiting for a reply, she swept past them, striding into the castle.

The clench in Bram's jaw revealed that Grizel had struck a raw spot. Nairna saw the fury that lingered there, but he held it back.

'Bram, I—'

'It's true, if that's what you're wanting to know.' He headed for the stables, as if he could release his anger with the rapid pace.

Nairna struggled to keep up and nearly stumbled when Bram stopped suddenly.

'My father died when he took a sword that was meant for me. Grizel blames me for it.'

'She's wrong.' Nairna raised her eyes to her husband's, and in them, she saw the shadow of the boy he'd been. A boy who had been close to his father and no doubt lived with the cross of Tavin's death. She couldn't stop herself from moving into his arms, trying to bring him comfort without words.

But this time, Bram's hand only touched her back, as if he were too angry to hold her. Whether it was his frustration towards Grizel or whether he simply didn't want to embrace her, it was the first time she'd experienced hesitation from him. It bothered her more than she'd thought it would. Awkwardly, she removed her arms from his waist.

'Do you want to leave?' Bram asked.

She couldn't—not until she'd spoken with the others. 'I haven't finished what I came here to do.' She held back a moment, thinking to herself. 'And I want to have words with your mother.'

'Don't be bothered by what she said. It's simply her way.' Bram continued inside the stables, where Dougal had led the animals. The boy spoke quietly to his stallion, absorbed by the horse.

'I'll see to your horses,' Dougal offered, nodding to both of them.

Bram handed over the reins and went to stand by one of the stalls. His gaze settled off into the distance, and as the minutes passed, Nairna felt him slipping further away.

'What happened at Cairnross?' she murmured, coming to stand beside him. There was more that he hadn't told her, something that bothered him still. His fists tightened as if squeezing an invisible enemy.

'As I told you, Callum wasn't there.' His clipped response clearly said he didn't want to talk about it.

She hadn't meant to bother him, but something else must have happened. The frustration on his face went deeper and she sensed him pushing her further away.

'Bram—?' She reached out to touch his shoulder, but he moved back.

'I'm in no mood to discuss it, Nairna.'

Beneath his irritated demeanour she sensed that something had unnerved him. Had he fallen into another spell, losing himself in the battle? Or had someone been hurt?

He wasn't going to talk about it; that was clear. No amount of gentle questioning would break through the wall of guarded pride.

It hurt to see him like this, knowing there was nothing she could do. But she wanted to make the offer, none the less. 'If there's anything I can help you with, I'll do my best.'

He turned to stare at her and the emptiness in his brown eyes made her take a step back. 'I'm not something you can fix, Nairna. Leave it be.'

Brittle hurt bloomed inside and she didn't know what to do. One moment, her husband was holding her as though he'd never let her go. The next, he'd cut her off, refusing to talk to her.

Confusion gathered around her like a cold gust of air. Risking another glance, she saw her husband watching her. Though Bram didn't speak, nor reveal any of his thoughts, he hadn't taken his eyes off her.

Her troubled thoughts were interrupted by the appearance of a middle-aged man, short of stature, wearing a dark-green silk tunic, hose and a matching mantle. A heavy gold chain rested around his neck, denoting the Baron's rank.

'I heard that we had visitors,' the man said, his smile broad. 'I am Kameron MacKinnon, Baron of Locharr.'

Though his fair hair was thinning and his midsection had grown plump, the man emanated warmth and friendliness. Nairna curtsied, introducing herself and Bram, who came closer.

Standing just behind Lord Locharr was an older woman and an adolescent girl. Bram leaned in close, his warm breath against her ear as he whispered, 'That's Ross's wife Vanora and their eldest daughter Nessa.'

The sensation of her husband's breath sent a shiver through her skin. When he stepped back, she couldn't suppress the feeling of disappointment.

'Forgive Lady Grizel for what she said earlier,' Lord Locharr said quietly. 'She's been through some difficult times and her grief has hardened her.'

It was the man's attempt to smooth over the uncomfortable atmosphere and Nairna managed a nod. 'I hope it was all right that we came to pay a visit. The MacKinloch men are missing their wives and children and I came on their behalf.'

Lord Locharr glanced to the women beside him, as if gauging their responses. Vanora stiffened, reaching out to take her daughter's hand. She looked uncomfortable about the question, as though she were undecided on the matter.

'Come inside,' Lord Locharr offered, sending her a kindly smile. 'You should stay the night with us and we'll talk it over.'

Though the invitation was not unexpected, Nairna saw the tension in Bram's face. Her husband's hands came to rest upon her shoulders, as if he wanted the Baron to know of his prior claim.

Bram's fingers pressed into her shoulders, his thumbs stroking the tension from her skin. The possessive motion took her unawares and the sensation was so soothing that she wanted to lean her head back, closing her eyes.

'I'll see to it that you have a chamber to yourselves,' the Baron said. He nodded the request to Vanora, who disappeared with her daughter. 'If you would both like to sit and enjoy a cup of mead or wine, we can talk while your chamber is readied.'

The older man gestured for them to join him upon the dais at the long wooden table. Nairna did, out of politeness, but she didn't miss Bram's reluctance. 'You have a lovely home,' she began. 'I'm certain the women and children are grateful for your hospitality.'

Lord Locharr poured them each a cup of mead. 'It was my pleasure. I enjoy having the little ones around.'

He filled his own cup and added, 'But what you really want to know is when they're returning.'

Nairna nodded. 'It's not right for families to be split apart.'

'And neither is it right for women and children to be attacked by the English every few weeks.' His eyes turned to Bram. 'They came to me for sanctuary, for an end to the violence. I was only too happy to grant it.'

'How many were killed?' Bram asked.

'Not so many. The MacKinlochs were always good fighters,' the Baron admitted, 'but one of the younger girls was killed in the last incident. After they buried her, Lady Grizel gathered up everyone and brought them here.'

Not the actions of an embittered old woman, Nairna realised, but one who wanted the safety of those who could not defend themselves. Were she in Grizel's place, she might have done the same.

'I would like to speak with her again,' she told Lord Locharr. 'Where might I find her?'

'You're wasting your breath,' Bram responded. 'Nothing you say will make any difference.'

She supposed that could be true. 'I still want to try. I've nothing to lose.' From what she'd seen of Grizel, the woman appeared to have little sympathy or kindness in her. But she'd managed to bring half the clan to safety, keeping them protected from danger. Not an easy task at all.

'I'll wait for you in our chamber, then.' Bram stood and nodded a cursory thanks to the Baron. 'If you're determined to speak with her again, I won't stand in your way.' Without another word, he returned outside. Nairna tried not to let her husband's cynicism weaken her resolve.

'Grizel isn't an easy woman to speak to,' the Baron admitted, when Bram was gone. 'But there is more to her than most people realise.'

Nairna believed so, too, but she wouldn't know for certain until she spoke to Grizel alone. 'Where can I find her?'

'Why are you here?' Lady Grizel knelt beside a wooden tub, her fingers covered in soap bubbles as she scrubbed the hair of a red-haired boy. Nairna guessed the child was two years of age and he sat within a large wooden bucket, whining as the matron rubbed his scalp.

'I thought without Bram present, we could talk about what happened with the women and children.'

She wanted to understand whether Grizel was truly filled with such hatred, or whether it was nothing but empty words.

The older woman used her hands to scoop handfuls of water to rinse the boy's head. When he started to cry, she sent the boy a grim look. 'Quiet, now. You're fine.'

'I know that you left Glen Arrin after the last attack,' Nairna ventured.

Grizel lifted the boy out and wrapped him in a drying cloth. She hardly looked at the boy as she tended him. It was efficiency, nothing more. And it was starting to chafe at Nairna's patience. Without asking permission, she reached out and took the child from Grizel. She sat down, pulling him onto her lap.

After Nairna dressed him in a clean garment, the boy snuggled against her. At the feeling of his warm body nestled close, Nairna fought back the ache of longing.

Grizel hardly appeared to care. 'We were attacked

nearly every sennight,' she said, 'because our men refused to pay bribes to the English.'

Nairna rubbed the child's back, shushing him as he fussed. She tucked his head beneath her chin, holding him close.

'The men didn't care what happened—all they wanted to do was fight.' Grizel nodded towards the boy. 'His parents were killed in the battle.'

An uneasy sense of understanding crossed over Nairna as she pressed a kiss against the child's hair.

The lives of men are worth more than coins, her father had said. And now she was beginning to understand that.

Nairna took a breath and rocked the boy in her arms, watching as his eyelids grew heavy in sleep. 'And what if the fighting were to stop? Would you return, then?'

'They won't stop. They're stubborn and hotheaded, every one of them.'

'Not all of them,' Nairna said, thinking of Bram. He kept to himself, isolated from his brothers. 'Bram and Alex are doing everything they can to get Callum back.'

A flash of pain slipped over Grizel's face before she looked away. 'Leave me now. I've no wish to speak of them again.'

'And what about Dougal? He needs you, too.'

Grizel let out a sigh. 'Ever since he returned from fostering and found Tavin gone, he does nothing but fight all the time.'

'You're his mother,' Nairna insisted. 'And he's not a grown man yet.'

'Dougal hasn't spoken to me in months.' Angry hurt bloomed within Grizel's voice as she wiped her hands upon her gown. 'He doesn't need me.'

'So you'll turn your back on your sons, after all they've suffered?'

'Every time I see Bram's face, I remember that Tavin died because of him.' Grizel's eyes grew wild, her temper spilling over. 'Bram was foolish and believed he was strong enough to fight the English. Callum followed him when we tried to keep the boys away.'

She rose to her feet. 'You don't know what it's like to have your heart ripped away, losing your husband and two sons.'

'I know what it's like to lose a husband.' The soul-wrenching grief had hurt so badly when she'd lost Bram, Nairna knew exactly how Grizel had felt. But a sixteen-year-old boy could not be blamed for it.

'Bram suffered for seven years,' Nairna continued. 'He blames himself for the losses.'

'And well he should.'

'He was nothing but a boy.' Nairna felt her own anger rising. 'A boy who loved his father and wanted to fight at his side. To prove himself worthy.'

'But he wasn't,' Grizel said softly. 'He let his temper rule his head. I watched him run to face the enemy and Tavin stepped in to take the sword. He bled to death in my arms while the English took my sons.'

Grizel stared hard at her. 'He might be your husband now. But I've no wish to speak to him or see his face again.'

Chapter Twelve

The chamber door opened and Bram saw his wife standing there, looking utterly defeated. It didn't surprise him that Grizel had cut her down. His mother had no sympathy in her at all, nor kindness.

He wanted to draw Nairna into his arms, telling her it didn't matter. But he didn't move, uncertain of his wife's mood right now.

'You were right,' Nairna said, her voice heavy. She sat down upon the edge of the bed, staring at the stone wall. 'You needn't say it.'

'It's my fault,' Bram heard himself saying. 'She's angry with me and you bore the brunt of it.'

'No.' Nairna's hands dug into her skirts, and he heard the anger in her voice. 'It wasn't your fault she chose to shut everyone else out.'

Bram came to sit beside her, not knowing what to say, but his wife looked angrier that he'd ever seen her.

'You're her son,' Nairna said. 'She has no right to

blame you for an accident. It was the English who killed your father, not you.'

'He wouldn't have been caught in the fight, if I hadn't run towards them.'

'You don't know that.' Nairna drew her feet up, tucking them beneath the frayed skirt. 'She should be grateful you're alive, not angry.'

Bram rested his arm across her shoulders and Nairna came to him, burying her face in his chest. The warmth of her body permeated his, and against his better judgement, he pressed her back on the bed until she lay on her side facing him.

Only a hand's distance separated them as they lay together. A lock of brown hair curled over her shoulder and he tucked it back, staring at her face. Nairna stilled, watching him with wariness. But he made no move to touch her; he simply absorbed her features.

'I'm glad you're alive,' she whispered, reaching out to touch the scar upon his throat. At the softness of her fingers upon his skin, he closed his eyes.

She traced the mark of the shackle that had chained him. 'Does this hurt you?'

He shook his head. It was only the sensation of her touch that was starting to have a different impact. Heat rushed through his veins and he rolled onto his stomach to hide the physical response to her.

'Bram,' Nairna whispered. 'I'm sorry I forced you to come here.'

'You didn't know.'

Her hand moved against his hair, fingering the edges. 'We'll leave in the morning. If any of the other women want to come back with us, I'll ask—'

He caught her hand, bringing her palm to his mouth. With his lips, he reverenced her skin, bringing it over his roughened cheeks. He heard her slight gasp of air; immediately he released her hand and sat up.

He didn't want to push her too quickly or frighten her. To distract both of them, he pointed out a gown draped over one of the chairs.

'Lord Locharr left that for you,' he remarked. 'He bought it for my mother, but she refused to wear it.'

Made of silk in the Norman style, the kirtle was deep purple, with narrow sleeves and a sleeveless surcoat to be worn over it.

'I don't need a gown—' Nairna started to protest, but Bram cut her off.

'I haven't seen you wear any colours since we came from your father's house. I'd like to see you in it.'

Nairna didn't speak for a long time. When she did, she asked, 'Do my clothes bother you?'

Jesu, he wasn't intending to criticise her. 'It doesn't matter to me what you wear. But you used to wear colours and I thought you might like it. That's all.'

She sat up, as if considering it. When she looked back at him, her face was crimson. 'I have no ladies' maid to help me dress. But if you'll help me, I'll…try it on.'

Nairna turned her back, reaching for the silk gown. The fabric felt smooth, and the weave was so fine she knew instantly how costly it was.

She loosened the laces of her gown, only to feel Bram's hands upon her. He stood behind her, and when she lifted her outer woollen gown away there was nothing but a thin shift to cover her bare skin. His fingers stroked over her shoulders, down her bared arms.

The length of his manhood pressed against her backside, as he kissed her neck. His arm slid around her, then he brought it higher to rest over the mounds of her breasts. Her nipples tightened against his forearm and the needs rose up inside, clouding her mind.

Bram turned her to face him. The hunger on his face was undeniable, as if he were holding back by a mere thread. Upon his face she saw the strained control and it bothered her, knowing she was the cause of it.

Hotheaded, Grizel had called Bram. Undisciplined and rebellious, ruled by his temper.

But that wasn't Bram at all, she realised. Not anymore. If anything, he'd reined in his emotions, locking them away. He wouldn't release anything and the tension was taking its pound of flesh from him.

He'd imprisoned his spirit, as surely as the chains had imprisoned his body. A dark loneliness seemed to dwell inside him, after his own family had abandoned him.

Grizel's accusations infuriated Nairna, that she would blame her son for the unfortunate turn of fate. Bram wasn't responsible for Tavin's death, or Callum's imprisonment. And until he could accept the truth of it, he would be caught in shackles of his own making.

His hands moved back up to her shoulders, while his mouth explored the skin of her neck. Nairna held herself motionless, unsure of what her husband had started.

He turned her to face him and his eyes were heated with need. She stood on her tiptoes, wondering if she dared to kiss him. When she did, his reaction was immediate, his mouth claiming hers in a frenzy, as though he wanted to absorb her into his skin.

The more she tried to satiate the desire, the worse it grew. He caressed her bottom, and as his tongue delved inside her mouth, she felt the heat building inside her.

He seized the hem of her shift, pulling it up until he bared her womanhood. Embarrassment pooled inside her, but it dissipated a moment later when his hands moved to part her legs. He cupped her intimately, as if learning the shape of her body.

With his fingers, he traced the seam that led to her entrance, and she moaned as his finger passed over a sensitive spot.

She tried to move his hand away, but he explored further, dipping his fingers against her opening. With his thumb, he pressed inside, and she felt the gentle invasion.

'I want you, Nairna,' he murmured against her mouth. 'I want to claim you. As your husband.'

She shuddered as he withdrew his thumb and pressed it inside again in silent imitation of the way he would join their bodies together, if she yielded to him.

Though her body was ready to accept him, her mind tangled up with apprehension. Bram was so different from Iver, and she was afraid of the feelings he'd stirred within her. To grant herself a little more time, she whispered, 'Tonight.'

His dark eyes grew heated and he stroked her one more time before withdrawing his hand. 'Tonight,' he agreed.

Nairna eased her shift down to cover her nakedness. Her body ached with frustration while Bram helped her to don the purple gown. The soft fabric felt good against her skin, just as Bram's hands had felt sensual upon her body.

With every touch as he dressed her, she felt herself falling a little deeper into the spell of his arousal. Her breathing was unsteady when he laced the gown and she tried to calm her heartbeat.

She found herself thinking about the man Bram had become. Though his exterior was guarded against any emotions, there were traces of the boy he'd been. The flower he'd left inside her glove…the way he'd held her so tightly upon his return. She believed that there was more he felt for her, though he wouldn't say it.

Nerves skittered within her stomach as she considered what would happen later, when they shared a bed. Beneath his façade of control, did any of their past feelings remain? Or was it merely wishful imaginings?

As they joined Lord Locharr and the other women for a light evening meal, Nairna wished she'd ignored her fears and succumbed to his touch. For now, she couldn't stop thinking of it.

The night blurred with a sea of faces. Bram would have preferred to take his meal alone, in his room, but Nairna had wanted to speak with the women and children.

He watched her talk to them, moving from one person to the next. She listened to each of them, asking questions that he couldn't hear from his position. When it was clear that she intended to speak with everyone, he excused himself from the table and retreated outside.

Noises and sounds overwhelmed him and he needed the calm silence of the night. Overhead, the sky brewed heavy clouds that threatened to spill out with rain. He found Dougal curled up asleep in the stables, as if he were trying to guard the horses.

Grizel had hardly spared her youngest son a glance. It was as if all of them were dead to her. He didn't understand why she would turn her back on Dougal. Though the lad was hot-tempered, it was only immaturity. He could see Dougal's fierce craving for attention, even if Grizel couldn't.

Bram continued past the inner curtain wall, walking

without thought. The minutes dragged on and he settled back, sitting against the wall to stare at the moonlight.

He couldn't stop thinking about Nairna. He wanted to strip away her clothing and lay her upon their bed, learning every part of her body.

Earlier, when he'd touched her intimately, he'd been heavily aroused by her wetness. To know that she desired him, that her body was ready for him to sink deep within her moist depths, was a startling discovery.

His mind had filled up with images of penetrating her, feeling the wetness enclosing him like a smooth sheath. Nothing in his life could have prepared him for the instinctive needs that were claiming control of his mind. And then, as if to torment his mind further, he saw her walking towards him.

'There you are,' she said, reaching down a hand to him. He supposed she'd come to lead him back to their chamber.

But instead of taking her hand and rising, he didn't move. If he touched her at all, he'd pull her into his lap and kiss her with all the pent-up savagery that lurked beneath.

Nairna lowered her hand, her face growing concerned. He took a deep breath. First one, then another, until he steadied his racing heart. The cold stone wall pressed against his spine, and with his eyes closed his senses grew calmer.

'Bram?' Confusion misted her features and she lowered her hand when he didn't take it. 'Is everything all right?'

He inclined his head, saying nothing more. He needed to seize control of his thoughts, to force the past back into the shadows.

'Some of the women have agreed to return,' Nairna

told him. 'Not everyone, but it's a start.' Twisting her hands together, she added, 'Grizel isn't among them, if that's what you're wondering.'

'I wasn't.' He knew his mother had made her choice and nothing would soften her heart. He didn't care what she thought of him, but it irritated him that she would also cut off Dougal.

The rain started to pour down at that moment and Nairna reached for him again. This time, her hand closed over his, and she pleaded, 'Come inside. Take shelter with me.'

The sky had turned the colour of a dark bruise, while the rain intensified. It spattered upon her flesh and gown, giving him little choice but to follow her

As they entered the keep, he imagined peeling off her gown from her body, tasting the droplets of rain from her skin. He wanted to drink from her, to satiate the thirst that grew within him.

They crossed over to the spiral staircase, avoiding the crowd of women and children. He let Nairna lead him above stairs, and as she walked, he stared at her slender figure and the way her body moved with grace.

When they reached the bedchamber, he closed the door behind them and lowered the bar. Outside, the rain poured down upon the roof, the sound strangely comforting.

Nairna was saying something about Lord Locharr and the women, but damned if he had any idea what words had just come out of her mouth. He stared at her, mutely aware that she'd unfastened her hair and the wet strands rested upon her shoulders. She backed up to him, pulling her hair over one shoulder while she continued talking.

'Will you help me with this?' she asked.

Bram stared at her bared neck, and the urge to kiss the exposed skin grew stronger. Nairna struggled to lift away the sodden surcoat.

The damp silk was like a fire to his arousal, burning away his defences as he unlaced her. Beneath her gown, the wet shift revealed the dusky rose of her nipples. Lust speared him—God above, he wanted her. But he was afraid that if he dared to touch her, he would forget himself and behave like an animal.

Nairna went to search among her belongings and withdrew the smooth stone he'd given her before. 'I kept this with me when you left to go after Callum. Like a charm to bring you back to me.'

She pressed it into his hand to hold, then unfolded something else. It was a faded crimson ribbon, ragged at the edges. She reached up to her wet hair and tied it back with the ribbon. 'And you gave this to me when we were young.'

'You kept it.' He never imagined she would, after all these years.

'It was the only thing I had left of you.'

Within her voice, he heard the unspoken longing and it fired his desire. He took the stone, bringing its smooth surface down the column of her throat. Wet from the rain upon her skin, he slid it further, until it rested upon her heart. 'I remember when you used to bring me water, while I was training.'

Nairna covered his palm with hers and he slid the stone lower, beneath the curve of her breast, tracing around it. His wife's breath sharpened, but she didn't stop him.

'I remember that I slept alone on my wedding night, when you should have been there beside me.'

'I was sixteen and thoughtless.' He brought the stone

over her wet shift, using the gentle pressure to arouse her. Her nipple grew taut, straining through the fabric for his touch. He used the flat stone to caress her, before he brought her to sit upon a chair.

Kneeling before her, he remembered how sensitive her legs were. He touched her ankles and brought his mouth to her knees. He kissed the rounded skin as he caressed her calves. Immediately, tingles swept through her in response.

Her breathing grew unsteady, and her knuckles tightened upon the arms of the chair. He flicked his tongue behind her knee and she exhaled, reaching for his hair.

But he wouldn't let her go. His hands moved over the softness of her legs while his mouth moved between her thighs.

Her womanhood lay bared before him, and when he spread her legs apart he could see the moist rose flesh. Though he was tempted to touch her there, he waited, letting the anticipation fill her as he kissed the soft skin leading towards it.

She closed her eyes, lifting up her face as if she couldn't bear the intensity of his touch. Her cheeks were flushed, her body trembling.

His own hands began to shake and the room suddenly blurred before his eyes. Hell's teeth, not this. Not now. He blinked, trying to clear away the dizziness.

'Bram, what is it?'

He took a deep breath, but the chamber shifted again, the floor seeming to move beneath his feet. He couldn't seem to regain control of his vision.

'I need a moment.' He turned away from her, striding to the window. He rested his hands against the stones, as if he could gain steadiness from them. The exhaustion of being without sleep for so long was making it harder for him to stand upright. The weakness infuriated him.

Behind him, he heard Nairna's soft footsteps. She touched his arm, but he didn't turn around. His hands dug into the limestone, trying to reclaim his hold upon the moment between them. But his body wouldn't cooperate with the desires of his mind.

For a long moment Nairna said nothing, but merely rested her hand upon him. When he continued his silence, at last, he heard her retreating towards the bed.

'It's all right,' he heard Nairna say. 'Come and rest beside me. I won't ask anything of you.'

Hearing the sadness in her voice made him even angrier at himself. He wanted to touch her, to satiate this reckless craving inside him. But he didn't trust himself, not when his vision and senses were failing him.

'Wait for me in the bed and I'll join you later.' Leaning against the hard back of the chair, he closed his eyes. The darkness enfolded him in its suffocating arms and he struggled to find control over his body and mind.

The rainstorm raged outside, but Nairna felt as if she might as well be caught in it. The shelter didn't seem to matter, for her husband was slumped in a chair, his posture awkward.

What had gone wrong? One moment, he'd treated her like a desirable woman, while the next, he'd seemed unaware of his surroundings. Now, his eyes were closed, as if he were suffering in some way.

The wind battered the wooden shutters; the eerie sound seemed to disturb Bram within his sleep. He was mumbling something she couldn't understand.

Nairna didn't know what was happening, but she couldn't simply remain in bed and wait. Bram's eyes remained closed, but he sat up when another howl of the wind penetrated the space.

The shutter rattled against the window, grinding wood against stone. Bram's eyes flew open at the sound.

'It's nothing,' she reassured him. 'Just the storm.'

But it was as if he hadn't heard her at all. His face was pale, his mouth set in a firm line. Nairna reached out a hand to take his palm, but he didn't return the faint squeeze. His skin was cold, as if he'd been sleeping outside.

'Are you awake?' she whispered, already knowing the answer.

He stared right through her. What nightmares tormented him, she didn't know. But he wasn't aware of their surroundings, nor even of her.

'Come and lie down,' she murmured, hoping to coax him back to sleep. When she reached for his waist, she struggled to draw him to his feet, and thankfully it was only a few paces before she pushed him back to the bed.

He sat down and she helped him to undress. The darkness hid his body, but she eased him beside her.

When she started to cover him with the blanket, she didn't know if he had regained awareness or was still asleep. Her answer came when he seized her, holding her in a tight embrace. He held her as if gaining warmth and comfort. She rested her cheek against his bare chest and heard the rapid heartbeat.

Though his hands were cold, his body was far warmer than she'd imagined. In his embrace, her skin grew heated, warming the damp shift. She tried to move beneath the coverlet and the motion pulled at her linen shift, baring her breasts.

Though likely he couldn't see her in the darkness, she

felt awkward and vulnerable with her bare skin against his. Bram lay on top of her with his mouth against her throat, his breath intensifying her pulse beat. The thickness of his manhood rested between her thighs.

She felt herself go liquid at the thought of him claiming her.

'Don't hurt him,' he whispered against her skin. 'Not Callum. Let me take his place.'

Nairna saw that her husband's eyes were closed. He wasn't aware of anything that was happening. 'It's a dream,' she told him. 'You're safe now.' She touched his forehead, smoothing his hair over.

'Nairna,' he murmured.

'I'm here.' She stroked his bristled cheek, trying to soothe him. His grip relaxed as she touched his face, silently easing the nightmare.

As his embrace softened, she saw the desperate need inside him, for peace. And he'd found it within her arms.

She leaned down and pressed a kiss upon his mouth. He answered it, taking her lips with his own. The years turned back and she remembered what it was to kiss the shy young man she'd agreed to marry.

As his kiss deepened, she found herself opening to him. She wanted to reclaim the past, to become the wife she'd never been.

Bram rolled over, bringing her on top of him. Nairna's legs opened, cradling his heavy thighs. Her bare breasts pressed against his chest, while she could feel his hardened erection against her womanhood. Her shift was bunched up, bringing them together intimately. The touch of his shaft against her wet entrance was so very tempting.

Slowly, clarity transformed Bram's expression until he no longer appeared lost in a dream.

'Did I hurt you?' he asked. 'I don't remember what happened.'

'You were talking about Callum.' She traced her fingertips over his chest, and as she touched him his length shifted against her. The desire to take him inside her body was provoking erotic thoughts. She wanted to feel the sensation of him deep within, and when he moved a second time, the blunt head of him evoked a sensual pleasure she hadn't expected to feel.

Before she could realise what he was doing, Bram wrenched her shift free of her thighs and pulled it over her head. He lifted her hips, guiding her higher until he was poised against her wetness. The firm length seemed to tease at her secret flesh, and she gasped when he eased her up, sliding her against his shaft.

She moaned when he stroked over the soft hair above her woman's flesh, the ache intensifying into a shaking desire she couldn't control. Her body shifted against his erection and she needed to take him deep inside.

She was wet and aching, and in the darkness she didn't know where he would touch her next. His hands slid over her waist, up her ribcage, to tease at her nipples. Without warning, a hot mouth covered one of them, and as he suckled her she felt his length probing inside.

Nairna tried to relax against the invasion, but it had been a long time since she'd taken a man. In spite of the restless needs, she grew tense.

Bram brought her onto her back, only partially inside her. He pulled back again, slowly moving deeper, until their bodies were joined. For a moment, he held still and she struggled to adjust. When he pulled back, a primal instinct made her arch to receive him. The friction when he entered caused another surge of wetness and she waited for something to happen.

Beneath her palms, she could feel his racing heartbeat. Though she tried to adjust her hips to take him in a little further, she started to forget what she was doing when he began to move in rhythm.

The pulsing motion surged against her, and as he filled her she sensed something building inside. There was a rising pleasure that she'd never felt before. Her breathing quickened and she started pressing back in counter pressure to his thrusts.

But then when she gave a slight cry, Bram slowed down. He pumped a few more times inside her and gripped her hips as he shuddered with release.

Nairna lay beneath him, unmoving. Bram rested atop her, his weight fully relaxed. Confused, she reached up to touch his hips, hoping he would start up again. It seemed incomplete somehow.

'Bram?' she whispered, running her hands up to his neck. But the only answer from her husband was silence and a deep breathing that told her he'd fallen asleep at long last. He didn't even notice when she extricated herself from him, rolling over to sleep.

Her body was still unbearably aroused, despite the soreness, and she wished she knew what it was she needed.

She nestled closer to him, trying to find the elusive sleep. And though Bram never once let her free of his embrace, it was a long time before her body calmed down enough to find slumber.

Chapter Thirteen

When Bram awakened, his wife was gone. He sat up, feeling dazed, as if he could have slept for hours longer. It was the first time he'd had a single night without restless dreams.

He stretched, wincing at the stiffness in his shoulders. When he rose from the bed, he realised he was naked.

Images flashed through his mind of claiming Nairna. She'd tried to calm him after a nightmare, and her touch had driven him past reason, until he'd finally joined her body with his.

Christ's bones, he didn't know what he'd done. Had she agreed to the lovemaking, or had he been so caught up in his visions that he'd taken her without any care?

His shaft tightened with the memory of being inside her and plunging into her wetness. The thought made him restless, wanting her back within his bed. He wanted to spend the entire morning in her arms, tasting her skin, touching her until he learned what aroused her.

No doubt she'd be less than eager to share his bed

again. A dull feeling settled inside him. He needed to make amends, perhaps with a gift of some sort. But he didn't know what would please her.

Uneasy, he rose and dressed quickly. The gown Lord Locharr had given her lay discarded upon the chair and Nairna's grey gown was missing.

He reached down to touch the fallen garment, fingering the silk. Nairna wasn't a woman who bothered much with fabric or gowns, but he ought to take better care of her.

His gaze settled upon the fallen stone and he leaned down to pick it up off the floor. The rough texture had been worn smooth by his fingers, after seven years of clenching it within his grasp.

When he'd first courted his wife, words hadn't been necessary. He'd shown Nairna that he cared and she'd understood what he lacked the words to say. Right now, he needed to atone for the way he'd treated her, but with actions, not words.

He went below stairs, and stopped when he saw Nairna seated among the women, talking to them while Grizel glowered in the corner. His wife spoke words of encouragement, inviting them to return home.

'It will be different,' Nairna promised them. 'But only if you make it so.' Her eyes shifted, as if she sensed his presence. When she saw him, her face coloured, but she didn't look away. 'Leave the past where it belongs and start again.'

He studied her, even as he walked closer. Her brown hair was covered beneath a barbette, several strands resting upon her shoulders. It made her look younger, more innocent.

But no less desirable. Her mouth had softened, and

even though she answered one woman's question, she kept her gaze fixed upon him.

Bram ignored the other women, stepping his way around over-curious toddlers who tugged at him. Reaching down, he took Nairna's hand in his and bade her rise.

His wife's face blushed and she murmured an excuse, even as she let him take her away. He was grateful she'd trusted him enough to follow without question.

'Is something wrong?' she asked when he took her past the inner curtain wall, leading her to the stables.

He leaned in, resting his face against hers. He could smell the light scent of grass and flowers, as if she'd been sitting within the pasture earlier. Earthy and fragrant, he wanted to breathe in her scent and take it with him.

Every instinct ordered him to kiss her, to touch her the way he wanted to. But within his embrace, he sensed her tension. She wasn't holding him in return. Her arms remained at her sides and he felt the light tremble of her nervous hands.

Was she now afraid of him? He hoped he hadn't hurt her. Though the words wouldn't change what had happened, he wanted her to hear the apology.

He rested his hand against the wall, forcing himself to meet her eyes openly. 'Nairna, I didn't mean to take you that way last night. I wasn't myself.'

She didn't quite meet his gaze. 'You haven't been yourself for a long time.'

He knew it, but there was nothing he could do to change it. He could only ask, 'Are you all right?'

She nodded. 'I'm fine.'

She spoke as if it were of no consequence, like an accident to be dismissed. Hearing it made him only angrier at himself. Making love to Nairna was something he'd imagined since he was a boy. He'd wanted her to desire him, to welcome him into her bed. But he didn't know how to coax the right response from her.

'You look better,' she ventured, when the awkward silence continued between them.

'I slept last night,' he admitted. 'For the first time in many years.'

He wished she could understand what that meant. In thanksgiving, he lowered his mouth to hers, drinking from her lips as though she were a precious chalice. He was trying to make amends, to soothe her fears. But once again, all the things he wanted to say were muted.

Instead, he rested his hands upon her back, but he didn't pressure her. And though he wanted to share her bed a second time, he thought it best to leave her alone. At least until he'd reclaimed the control he needed.

They rode home within the gates, but throughout the journey, Nairna worried about the forthcoming night. The vision of Bram touching her again, using his mouth and hands to evoke the pleasures she'd only glimpsed last night, brought a swift reaction of moisture between her thighs.

She was both afraid and interested, if she were honest with herself. Somehow, last night, he'd released all the pent-up emotions and desires. He'd clung to her as if she were the rock that held him steady in the midst of a sea storm. And the lovemaking hadn't been unpleasant, not at all. There had been desperate moments, when she'd been consumed by need for him. She'd felt a sense of building anticipation, falling beneath the spell of desire.

In the end, it had happened so fast, she'd been left wanting. It had taken over an hour for her to fall asleep, and even then, she was afraid of what had changed between them.

There was a chance, however slight, that their shared night would result in a child. She prayed that it might happen. But even if it didn't, she wanted to be with Bram again.

Her husband had slept hard last night, not even waking when she'd risen from the bed. It was the first time she'd ever seen him that relaxed. And it was because of her, from the peace he'd gained in her embrace.

She thought of his bare skin warming hers and shivered at the thought of joining with him tonight. She wanted to believe that their lovemaking would be better this time. Questions burned in her mind about the intimacies of marriage, but she didn't know who to ask.

The very idea of voicing such questions made her nervous. She couldn't ask the chief's wife Laren, for she hardly knew the woman. And heaven knew, she couldn't ask the men.

Throughout the ride back to Glen Arrin, Bram had kept himself apart. He'd ridden ahead of their small travelling party, with Dougal bringing up the rear. About a dozen women had joined them, along with their children.

Though Nairna was glad of it, she hadn't found the friendly companionship she'd been hoping for. The air was charged with tension from over-excited children and women who appeared to question their decision to come home.

Bram helped Nairna down from her horse, and held on to her waist a few moments longer. He looked as though he had a thousand things he wanted to say to her, and the fierce intensity in his eyes made her skin tingle.

He released her when Ross's wife drew closer. Although

Vanora had agreed to return, the older woman appeared wary, as if she didn't believe the fighting had ceased.

'Well, now,' Vanora said with a sigh. 'Shall we see how bad it is?'

Nairna bristled at the negative comment, though the keep did need a great deal of work. She pointed at the tower, offering, 'It's not so bad, really. We may need to scatter fresh rushes and sweep again, but—'

She broke off, studying Vanora and the others when she saw their gaze fixed upon the guards who stood at intervals around the outer curtain wall. 'You're afraid they're going to fight again.'

Vanora's expression twisted. 'Not afraid. I know they will. The MacKinlochs will use any excuse to fight with the English. The foreigners haven't conquered us yet, but it's not for lack of trying.' Vanora leaned in, lowering her voice. 'It's not right, not with our wee ones about.'

'We'll do what we can to keep the peace,' Nairna said. Even so, she knew it might not be possible. Not if Bram and the others had taken Lord Cairnross's bride.

At the entrance to the keep, Nairna saw a young maiden awaiting them. She was dressed like a queen, in embroidered blue silk and jewels, and Nairna guessed she was eighteen or nineteen years of age. Her hair was veiled, but golden strands escaped from beneath it, lifting with the wind. A silver band rested around the crown of her head.

'Who is that?' Vanora demanded.

'Lady Marguerite de Montpierre,' came Bram's answer from behind them.

Nairna's hopes plummeted when she mentally added up the cost of the girl's wardrobe. If they had taken a woman like this from Lord Cairnross, there was no hope of peace. An army of English would pursue a woman of such wealth and status.

Vanora made the sign of the cross. 'The Virgin Mary protect us. If you stole a princess from the English, we're all going to die.'

'Not a princess,' Bram admitted, 'but her father is a French duke.'

'Oh, well, that's all right, then.' Vanora rolled her eyes in disgust. 'Have you lost your wits? Don't you think he'll want her back?'

'He might,' a male voice answered. Ross MacKinloch stood before his wife, his hand resting upon the hilt of a sheathed claymore. 'But we're not going to let them take her. Alex has sent word to the Lady Marguerite's father, and I don't doubt he will arrive soon.'

'Or murder us all for kidnapping her,' Vanora shot back. The acidic words held a deep fear and Nairna took a step away from the married couple.

They began to argue with one another, their voices rising with anger.

'Don't let them bother you,' Bram said, resting his hand upon one shoulder. 'They've always been at each other's throats, for as long as I can remember.'

'Then why do they stay together?' she whispered.

Bram shook his head and shrugged. 'They've been married so long, perhaps they're used to it.'

He took her hand in his, and lifted it to his cheek. She felt the soft bristles of his stubble and suddenly remembered the feeling of his warm mouth over her flesh, the prickles abrading her skin.

Her breath formed misted clouds in the afternoon air and Nairna raised her woollen hood to guard against the cold. 'I'll go and welcome Lady Marguerite,' she managed, when he released her hand.

'I'll see you tonight,' Bram told her, before he departed to speak with a group of men.

Nairna couldn't answer, for the very thought of the intimacy made her skin rise up with shivers of longing. She needed a diversion to pull her mind away. As she walked towards the keep, she hoped to hide away with the household accounts, letting the numbers pull her restless mind back to something tangible.

But first, she had to keep her word to Bram and speak to Lady Marguerite. Like an ethereal maiden, the young woman was tall and slender, her walk graceful and elegant.

Seeing the woman's beauty, even as young as she was, made Nairna feel like a clump of mud amidst spring flowers. Still, there was nothing to be done for it. Squaring her shoulders, Nairna greeted the lady and introduced herself.

'Bram told me that they brought you back from Cairnross,' she ventured, hoping that Marguerite would explain what had happened.

The young maiden nodded quietly. 'I was thankful to leave.' Although she had a deep French accent, the woman spoke the Gaelic tongue well enough to be understood. A shudder passed over her, and she gripped the edges of her silk gown. 'And grateful to your husband for rescuing me.'

Nairna brought the woman food to break her fast. 'When you were at Cairnross, did you happen to see any of the prisoners?'

Marguerite inclined her head, closing her eyes in memory. 'I learned of them on the second day.' Her eyes opened and her fingers stilled together for a moment. 'I could hear them screaming.'

She closed her eyes again for a moment, her lips

pressed together. 'I know what you wish to ask me. Your husband asked about his brother Callum when he agreed to take me back.'

Nairna nodded, waiting for the woman to continue. 'Go on.'

'They chained Callum in the centre of the fortress, for all to see. Lord Cairnross planned to make an example of him.' Marguerite shuddered at the memory. 'They whipped him until his blood ran into the stones. Then they left him there, as night was falling.

'I waited until nearly everyone was gone, and I tried to help stop the bleeding. I gave him water and stayed with him for a while.

'I suppose Lord Cairnross learned of it, for the next morn, Callum was gone. He was sent to another fortress, to the south.'

Marguerite raised her eyes to Nairna's. 'It was probably my fault that they moved him. I shouldn't have interfered, I suppose. But I couldn't stand back and watch him suffer.'

Nairna took a breath, sickened by the thought of Bram's younger brother tormented in that way. 'I would have done the same,' she admitted.

'I pray that they didn't kill him.' Marguerite finished her meal and looked around. 'Thank heaven, your husband and the chief freed the other prisoners. And me.'

'Will your betrothed husband come after you?' Nairna asked. She was certain Lord Cairnross wouldn't allow his bride to be abducted without seeking retribution.

Marguerite shrugged. 'Even if he does, I won't wed him.' A ruthless expression swept over her face, transforming her regal demeanour into that of a warrior. 'I wish he'd been killed in the fight. He deserved it, for what he did to those men.'

Changing the subject, Marguerite continued, 'The chief has sent word to my father, to bring me home again.'

'Where is your father now?'

'In Edinburgh.' Marguerite's expression dimmed. 'I fear it will take some time before he can be here. But I know he'll come for me.'

In the meantime, Nairna fully expected Lord Cairnross to attack Glen Arrin. By freeing the prisoners and seizing his bride, Bram and Alex had struck a blow against the man's pride. Nerves twisted within her stomach, and she wondered whether Bram and the others would be ready for the fight.

Marguerite rose and offered, 'I fear I'm not good with household matters, but I will do what I can to help you until my father arrives.' The woman's furtive glance around showed her dismay at the broken-down keep.

Nairna no longer worried about all the work to be done. With the women returning from Locharr, they could accomplish a great deal. She looked around for Alex's wife Laren, but saw no sign of her.

Before she could ask Marguerite anything, her attention was drawn to three riders approaching on horseback. Nairna shielded her eyes against the sun, and a fierce joy broke over her when she saw her maid Jenny arriving with two of her father's men.

She ran to the older woman, embracing her after one of the escorts helped Jenny down from her mount. 'I'm so glad to see you,' she wept.

She felt like a foolish little girl, but seeing her maid again was something she hadn't expected. Aye, Bram had told her he would send for Jenny, but a part of her hadn't really believed it. He'd kept his word and this was a gift that meant everything to her.

The older woman patted Nairna's shoulders, 'Now, now. No tears, Nairna.'

When she drew back, Jenny's wrinkled face pulled back in a smile. 'These old bones need a bit of rest after such a journey.'

'Come inside.' Nairna supported the woman as she walked within the keep.

Jenny's eyes narrowed at the sight of the unkempt Hall. 'I see we've work ahead of us, haven't we?'

'Not for you,' Nairna corrected. 'Rest yourself and have something to eat and drink.' She nodded at Lady Marguerite to follow her. 'Before we do anything else, we're going to find Alex's wife, Lady Laren. Do you know where she is?'

'Oui,' Marguerite confirmed. 'She went with her daughters to the loch, early this morn.'

Nairna wasn't surprised to hear it. But Laren had been avoiding Glen Arrin long enough.

Today, she intended to find out exactly what secrets the chief's wife was hiding.

Chapter Fourteen

The heavy weight of the axe was welcome, as Bram swung to cut down a fir tree. The physical labour demanded more energy than he had, but he ignored the pain and toiled through it. He wanted to finish the house for Nairna and live beneath their own roof, as soon as possible.

Seven other clansmen worked alongside him, and there was a noticeable difference in their demeanour, now that some of the women and children had returned. They seemed preoccupied, their glances slipping towards the keep in the valley.

'So Vanora returned, did she?' Alex said to Ross. The two men worked to build a frame around the house and Ross gave a shrug.

'She did. Though I'm not certain why. It might've been better had she stayed.'

'You won't be saying that tonight,' one of the other men teased, 'when she's sharing your bed.'

A gleam brightened in Ross's expression. 'Aye. Even

if she's a sharp-tongued woman, she knows how to use her tongue in the right way.'

Bram didn't join in with the roar of laughter from the other men. The conversation grew bawdy, with the men boasting about how long their shaft was, when they lifted the support beams into place.

'I know you've been enjoying marriage, haven't ye, lad?' Ross laughed, wiping his forehead with his hat. 'You're hoping we can finish this house tonight, aren't you? Have a bit of privacy with your bride.'

'I don't want her to have to sleep in the grain shed much longer,' Bram agreed, 'and, aye, I want it finished.'

'We'll get the walls up,' Alex said. 'That I can promise, Brother.'

'And when Nairna comes back, Bram will get the rest up.' Ross wheezed with laughter, but Bram couldn't smile at the revelry.

He returned to the fir trees he'd cut and began stripping away the smaller branches. While they meant no harm with their teasing, it only reminded him of how he'd lost control of himself that night. He'd taken his wife with hardly any thought or care, and though she claimed he hadn't hurt her, neither had he pleasured her.

The rough bark splintered his hands, and in the distance he spied one of the women bringing a drink of water to her husband. The water dripped over the man's neck as he drank, then he gave his wife a kiss of thanks.

Watching them together was like seeing himself with Nairna, seven years ago. And when the man reached down and lifted his toddling son into the air, ruffling the boy's hair, Bram wondered if he would ever have children with Nairna.

The fierce need made him turn away to hide his envy. There was only one way he could have such a life. He had to keep a tight rein over his desires and thoughts, so that he would never again lose control or awareness.

Only then would Nairna want a man like himself.

It was nearing sunset when Nairna and Marguerite reached the edge of the loch. Birds soared overhead, swooping down in search of fish. The women dismounted and let the horses graze while Nairna took the narrow path along the rocky shore. There she saw Laren's younger girls, Adaira and Mairin, playing in the sand, decorating with seashells.

Marguerite's face softened when she saw the girls. Nairna introduced them, and Mairin's eyes widened at the lady's gown. 'Where did you get that dress, Lady Marguerite? From the queen?'

Marguerite smiled. 'From my belongings. Your father allowed me to bring a few of my things with me from Cairnross.'

A wistful smile slid over the young girl's face. 'I would like to have a gown like that one.'

'Perhaps one day you shall,' Marguerite said, reaching out to smooth Mairin's hair.

'Where is your mother?' Nairna asked the girls.

'She's in the cave, working,' Mairin answered. 'I have to keep Adaira here when the fires are hot.'

'The fires?' Nairna sniffed the air and, sure enough, caught a whiff of smoke. 'What is she burning?'

'She's making her glass.' Mairin picked up a seashell and set it on top of a pile of sand.

Making her glass? Intrigued, Nairna followed the scent until she saw a wide-mouthed cave facing the loch. Inside, she saw Laren labouring over a hot clay furnace. She was adding beechwood ash to a crucible, while another container was heating in a different part of the furnace.

Nairna drew close, not interrupting, but she caught her breath when she saw bits of coloured glass lying upon a slab of stone. The glass was cut into intricate shapes and vivid blues and reds gleamed in the morning sun, like sapphires and rubies. It was clear that the smaller pieces were forming an intricate picture, meant for a window.

'It's the most beautiful thing I've ever seen,' Marguerite breathed.

Laren jerked with surprise. 'What are you doing here?' she demanded to Nairna. 'Has something happened?'

Nairna ignored the question and moved closer. 'Does Alex know that this is what you do each day?'

Laren shook her head, her expression growing sharp. 'And I don't want him to know. He wouldn't understand.' She sent a suspicious look towards Marguerite. 'You're not going to tell him, are you?'

Marguerite shook her head. 'I would not. And I meant to thank you for giving me a place to sleep with your daughters while I await my father.' She sent Laren a soft smile. 'It is kind of you.'

'How long have you been making this glass?' Nairna couldn't believe that Alex wouldn't already know of Laren's talent. When she looked closer, she saw the burn marks that marred Laren's hands and forearms. It explained the gloves she always wore.

'Two years,' Laren admitted. 'Father Nolan was apprenticed to a glassmaker who escaped from Murano, many years ago. His hands were too weak to make the glass anymore, but he taught me everything he knew.' Her face dimmed slightly. 'He died last winter, but under his teaching, I learned a great deal.'

'Where are the pieces you've made?' Nairna asked.

Laren pointed to the back of the cave, where there were many leather-wrapped bundles. From an initial count, there seemed to be at least a dozen.

Nairna's mind tallied up figures and estimates, her thoughts racing. 'Do you realise how much this could be worth to Glen Arrin?' If they could sell the pieces to the nearby parishes, it meant wealth and prosperity for all of them.

'They're not good enough. And even if they were, Alex would never allow it.' Laren picked up the piece of cooled glass with her gloved hands and set it upon the stone. From a leather bag she withdrew a cutting implement and began heating it over the fire.

'I would think he'd be proud of this,' Nairna said. Unable to stop her curiosity, she unwrapped one of the glass panes to reveal a circle fitted with green, crimson and blue bits of glass. 'Why won't you tell him?'

A sad look transformed Laren's expression. 'We've had some…difficult times these past two years. Alex and I don't talk often.'

Nairna didn't ask what had happened in their marriage. The wrenching pain on Laren's face made her reluctant to ask. Instead, she wrapped up the glass and exchanged a glance with Marguerite.

'I could arrange for these to be sold, without Alex learning of it,' Nairna offered. It wouldn't be difficult to find buyers interested in the glass, particularly the kirks and monasteries nearby.

But Laren didn't appear interested at the prospect of selling the pieces. 'Some of them were my early attempts and I don't think—'

'They are still fine enough to sell to some of the

smaller kirks,' Nairna interrupted. 'The larger pieces could go to a cathedral. Perhaps even to Rome.'

Marguerite moved between them. 'You have a talent, Lady Laren. It is a gift that should be shared with others.'

But Laren shook her head. 'I know that I'm a disappointment as Lady of Glen Arrin.' Her eyes glittered with unshed tears, even as she turned her attention back to the glass. 'Alex and I were wed for three years before he became chief.' A softness came over her face at the memory. 'He loved me then. And we were happy.'

Laren's gaze drifted to the ground. 'I never wanted to be the wife of a leader. It terrifies me when I see them staring. I've heard what they say about me behind my back and I know it hurts Alex.'

A lonely tear escaped from her blue eyes. 'Though I might be a failure at everything else, this is something that belongs to me. It's all I have.' She lifted the red-hot cutting implement from the fire, as though it were a glowing weapon.

'And I'll break every last piece before I'll let anyone take this away from me.'

The rough outline of their house stood at the top of the ridge, nearly completed except for the roof. Bram had stayed behind to work longer than the others, needing the time alone.

On the walk down to Glen Arrin, his thoughts were as heavy as the stones that lined the hills. He'd lifted thousands of them over the years when he'd been in captivity.

Bram closed his eyes, stopping near Ross's house. His shoulders were stiff from exertion, his neck aching. He envisioned Nairna working out the knots in his muscles and the image made him hunger for more than food.

The scent of her body, the touch of her hands upon him, would be his undoing. Even now, he raged to be close to her, to merge into the comfort of her embrace.

As he passed Ross's house, he stopped short at the sound of dogs barking. Mingled with the noise, he heard the unmistakable yipping of puppies.

Around the gate, he saw the animals playing and tumbling with one another. He started to walk by, but then it occurred to him that Nairna might welcome a dog of her own.

But as he took a step towards the puppies, he heard the whimper of an older dog lagging in the shadows.

'If you're wanting a pup, you can have your choice,' Ross offered, stepping outside, 'or you can have the cur if you want him. He'll probably die in a few years, but he's not bad for herding sheep.'

The older man opened the door wider in silent welcome. 'Would you and Nairna like to join us for a meal this night?'

The scent of lamb stew filled the air and Bram pushed away the hunger. 'Thank you, but we'll be eating with Alex and Laren.'

He eyed the dog, a mixed breed of collie, terrier and who knew what else. The dog rose up on his haunches and trotted over. When he reached Bram's side, the cur began sniffing his ankle.

'Lift your leg on me and I'm leaving you here,' Bram warned. In answer, the dog sat and eyed him with deep sorrowful eyes.

He exchanged a glance with Ross, who only shrugged. 'If it were me, I'd give Nairna one of the pups.'

Bram agreed with him, but as soon as he moved, the dog stood up and followed him.

When he stopped, so did the dog. Bram leaned down to scratch the beast's ears and was rewarded with a lick to his hand.

He sighed. It might not be the best form of atonement for what he'd done to Nairna last night, but it was all he could do.

He only hoped his wife could see past the animal's unsightly appearance to see the affection beneath the surface. 'Come on, then, dog. Let's find Nairna.'

Nairna and the other women worked to prepare a meal for the men that night. Though Jenny's hands were too old to slice meat, the woman busied herself with collecting flasks of mead and loaves of bread.

Nairna was setting aside food for Bram, when her maid came closer and murmured, 'Has he been good to you, my Nairna?' A gnarled hand closed over hers, and Jenny gave it a gentle squeeze. 'Are ye enjoying being a wife?'

Her face must have revealed her uncertainty, even though she nodded. Jenny came closer to look at her. 'Now, sweeting, what is it that you're needing? He hasna hurt you, has he?'

'No, but I don't know how to be a better wife to him.'

Jenny patted her arm. 'Oh, surely that's not true. Has he pleased you in bed, then?'

Nairna glanced around and saw that both Marguerite and Laren had found excuses to move closer. Both of them were leaning in, eavesdropping.

'Bram has pleased me a little,' she admitted, 'but I

worry that he'll be disappointed when I can't bear him a child.'

'Nonsense. You were married to an old man with old seed. This young, virile husband of yours will plant a babe in your womb soon enough. And you'll enjoy the ploughing, see if you don't.'

Knowing that Laren and Marguerite were hearing every word was enough to make Nairna's cheeks flame hotter. She wanted to have a strong marriage with Bram, one where he would look at her the way he used to, when they'd first been betrothed. And perhaps grow to love her.

'But how can I please him?' she asked. 'I don't know what I should do.'

The older woman reached out and touched her cheek. 'Sweeting, if you're wanting to satisfy your husband in bed, there's nothing easier.'

Now that the other women made no effort to hide their prying, Nairna supposed there was no point in trying to whisper.

'Nairna, you simply don't know the power you hold, as a woman.' Jenny's wrinkled face split into a wide smile. 'There's not a man alive who would turn down a naked woman who asked him to make love with her.' The old woman patted her hand again, adding, 'You'll bring him to his knees.'

Marguerite and Laren leaned in, their faces fully interested, though neither would admit it.

Jenny sent them a conspiratorial smile. 'And there's a great deal more I can tell you.'

Nairna worked alongside the other women, giving orders for the trestle tables and benches to be set out for the clansmen. When she'd finished, she spied Bram walking inside the keep.

Her husband didn't smile, but there was an intensity in his expression that made her nervous—as if she were about to become his conquest. Her hands started shaking, and when he drew nearer, all the physical memories of last night came flooding back.

She remembered the feeling of his firm body moving atop hers, the carnal sensation of him filling her. And when she thought of Jenny's advice, her imagination spun off more ways of spending this night with Bram.

The hair around Bram's face was wet, his tunic damp as though he'd stopped to wash. The reddish scar around his throat was matched by the two bands around his wrists. Beside him trotted the homeliest excuse for a dog that she'd ever seen.

'Here,' Bram said, pointing to the dog. 'He's not much to look at, but he seems friendly enough.'

'A dog?' Nairna studied the animal, unsure of whether the animal was a gift or an apology, from Bram's guarded expression.

The animal glanced up at Bram, as though asking permission. When Bram gave a nod, the dog walked forwards and sat down, cocking his head to study her.

Then he nudged her knees. Nairna bent down and rubbed his ears. The dog rolled onto his stomach, raising his feet into the air as if begging for affection.

'Do you want him?'

When the animal started licking at her fingers, something warmed inside her heart. She'd never had a dog that belonged entirely to her. Her brothers, yes. And though there had been many dogs in Ballaloch, never had she held any connection with them. As she rubbed at the dog's belly, the animal arched with delight.

'Ross warned me that he's old. You might want a younger dog who won't die in a few years.'

Nairna shook her head. There was a calmness in the dog's eyes, as if he would follow her anywhere she asked him to. 'I'll keep him.'

'You're certain?'

She nodded, and when he started to walk away Nairna stopped him. 'Bram, he's a sweet dog. Thank you.'

He gave her a slight nod and she felt her heart softening. 'If it's all right with you,' she said, 'I've already arranged for our meal in the grain hut.'

She wanted to talk to him about Laren's glass, without Alex knowing about it. But Bram stopped in place, staring at her over his shoulder. The heated look in his eyes suggested a very different reason of why they ought to be alone.

Nairna dropped her gaze to the floor, her cheeks burning. 'Or if you'd rather eat with Alex and the others, that's fine. It's no matter to me.'

'I'd rather be with you,' he said quietly.

'All right. I'll meet you there with the food.'

After Bram had gone, she went to see Laren about the bundle of food and wine she'd arranged earlier. The dog trotted along behind her, clearly interested in the contents of the bundle from the way he sniffed at it.

Nairna walked slowly, feeling anxious about the night ahead. Though she knew exactly what to do, it didn't mean she was confident in herself.

Use your mouth, Jenny had said. *And especially your tongue.*

Nairna's face blazed with colour, but she couldn't let her embarrassment triumph over the task of seducing her husband. The more he made love to her, the greater her chances of having a bairn of her own.

She opened the door and saw Bram standing on the far side of the hut, watching her. Nairna's mouth went dry when he came close and shut the door behind her.

'I should get the dog some water,' she blurted out, suddenly needing the distraction of caring for the animal. 'Go on and eat.'

Before she could leave, Bram caught her hand. He held it, his fingers caressing the bare side of her palm. Nairna froze in place, her heart stuttering in her chest. But all her husband did was raise her hand to his mouth.

'I'll wait for you.'

When he'd gone, Nairna took her time finding water and food for the dog, whom she'd decided to name Caen. Minutes passed, and though she was hungry, she was afraid to return to Bram.

She would have to bare herself before him, letting him see every part of her. The thought of revealing her naked body sent prickles of nervous energy racing through her skin. The other night, there had been darkness to hide her flaws. What if he didn't like what he saw?

The sky threatened rain again, so she brought the dog's food and water inside. She stroked his head, ensuring Caen had what he needed before she turned back to her husband.

Bram was seated against one of the barley sacks. Before him lay the food she'd set aside: some baked trout that one of the men had caught in the loch earlier, along with oat cakes and a cup of mead.

'Aren't you going to eat?' she asked.

He leaned forwards, resting his wrists upon his knees. 'Aye.'

But when he reached for the oat cake, he broke it in half, handing her the other. She ate alongside him;

though his appetite had improved, there was a rigid air to Bram, as though he were fighting against himself.

She noticed the scraped skin upon his knuckles and the calluses upon his hands from the axe. 'When did this happen?'

'Today, when I was building our house.' He shrugged it off, pulling his hands back. 'It's nothing.'

He rose up and drew her to stand. 'Nairna, when you said I didn't hurt you last night, were you telling me the truth?'

She managed a nod, but her cheeks felt feverish from the admission. Though she knew there was no reason to fear him, she involuntarily took a step back.

Bram drew nearer until the wood of the chamber pressed up against her back. He stood a breath away from her and rested his hands upon her hips.

'There are many things I want to say to you,' he murmured. 'But I've never been good with words.'

Heated and fierce, he claimed her lips, his tongue sliding within her mouth. At the invasion, Nairna's knees went soft. She could feel his rigid desire, but despite her fears, Bram was melting her resistance.

His breath heated the softness of her throat and shivers overtook her body, making her more aware of him. The primal look upon her husband's face flustered her. He looked as though he had no intention of sleeping this night and every intention of joining with her.

Nairna swallowed hard, keeping her eyes shut tight. It was time to obey Jenny's suggestion. After loosening the laces of the grey gown she'd worn, she lifted it away. The air was cold, but she forced herself to remove her shift until she stood naked before him.

Bram stared at her as if he were fighting himself. His

gaze moved down over her curves, but he didn't say a word.

She felt exposed and vulnerable, not at all comfortable with his detached manner. When she covered her breasts with her arm, he moved it away.

'No. I've been wanting to see you in the light. Don't ever hide yourself from me, *a ghaoil.*' He led her forwards to the mattress on the ground. Nairna's knees were shaking, but Bram lowered her down. She shut her eyes tightly, curling up onto her side.

Behind her, the warmth of Bram's body filled up the empty space. 'What are you afraid of?' he asked.

She shook her head, for there were no coherent words to voice what she was feeling. When he cupped her cheek, she couldn't stop the shiver. His hands moved over her body, down her waist. A warmth of unexpected desire flooded through her.

Her thoughts fled when he began exploring her skin. He caressed her as though he intended to learn every part of her. She felt her nipples rising and a mysterious ache echoed between her thighs.

His mouth travelled from her shoulder to the top of her breast, but when she looked into his eyes, they were devoid of emotion. He was tightly locked away, in complete command of every action.

Nairna tried to reach out to him, but he took her arms and held them still.

'No,' he bade her. 'I lost myself last night and took you without any thought of your needs.' His touch skimmed down the dip of her waist and over her hips, then down to the sensitive skin of her bare calves. Though he touched nothing but her leg, she caught her breath at the caress. When she felt his hand between her thighs, Nairna couldn't stop the startled gasp that escaped.

'I want you to feel good this night,' he swore, bringing his mouth to her stomach, moving even lower. As if she were a holy offering, he worshipped her flesh.

He stroked the soft inside of her thigh and she struggled to calm the shivers that he'd provoked.

'Close your eyes,' he whispered. She did and his breath warmed the intimate skin that guarded her womanhood.

'Bram,' she breathed, reaching to grasp the back of his head. When he raised up to look at her, she confessed, 'It doesn't seem right, not to touch you.'

She wanted to open up the guarded side to him, so that it would be a shared moment between them.

The scarred flesh on his back was rough, mingled with smooth, unmarred surfaces. Bram's brown eyes seared into her own as she explored the texture of his shoulders.

'Don't, Nairna. It's better this way.' He removed her hands from him and confusion clouded her mind. Jenny had told her that a man liked to be touched, that if she kissed him on any part of his body, he would enjoy it.

She almost asked him why, but when his fingers moved to touch the folds of her womanhood, the sudden flare of heat took her without warning.

Against his fingers, she grew embarrassed as her flesh grew wet and aroused. He touched her intimately, changing the pressure as he learned what pleased her. And when he lowered his mouth to her entrance, the unexpected tenderness sent her body into a pool of sensations she didn't understand. Her fists gripped the coverlet as he feasted upon her with mouth and tongue.

He tasted her secret flesh and the gentle pressure rose hotter. She was nearly sobbing with frustration, arching against him in search of the fulfilment that lay just out of reach.

'I need you inside me,' she begged. 'Please, Bram.' But she couldn't seem to break past the mask of control he wore. She reached out and tried to loosen his clothing, but the moment she touched him, he slid a finger inside her.

Her body trembled and she bit back a gasp. When his thumb pressed hard, rubbing against her centre, she found herself panting for breath. He kept up the relentless rhythm, watching her as she arched to receive him. She was drowning in his touch, and when he leaned in to kiss her the needs cracked apart, sending a wave of heated delirium throughout her body. She shuddered, crying out when the release pulled her under.

He stroked her again and Nairna convulsed in the aftershocks. She understood that he was trying to please her, but she needed more from him now. Her hands moved up to unfasten his trews.

Bram stopped her, shaking his head. 'Not tonight, Nairna.'

He'd meant only to touch her, taking nothing for himself, but it made the act meaningless. Did he truly believe that she would want to experience lovemaking without him? She couldn't understand why he was punishing himself, but it seemed he intended to leave her alone now.

'I want a child, Bram,' she murmured. 'And I need you inside me for that.'

He said nothing, so she reached up to touch his hair. She stroked the side of his face, running down to his neck. 'Look at me, Bram.'

He did, and in his eyes she saw the raging needs locked away beneath the surface. Right now, she wasn't about to let him push her away. Not if she had the power to seduce him.

The first night they'd shared had been his first. And she wanted his second time to be even better. Stubborn, was he? She'd show him stubborn.

'You're going to let me see you naked now,' she ordered, reaching for the tunic that covered his chest.

'Nairna—'

'No,' she cut him off. She walked over to her belongings, moving slowly to catch his eyes. After digging around, she found a dagger and brought it towards him. 'I'm a reasonable wife. But you're not behaving like a reasonable husband. So you're going to take off your clothing for me now or I'll be cutting it off you.'

She brandished the knife, asking, 'Which will it be?'

He propped his head up, leaning against his elbow as he stared at her. His eyes flared with interest. 'You wouldn't dare.'

She moved over to him and straddled his waist, bringing the tip of the dagger to his tunic. Holding the fabric firm, she put a slight cut in the linen. 'Wouldn't I?'

He eyed the dagger, but he didn't look as uncomfortable around the blade as he once had. Instead, he looked interested in what she planned to do.

Nairna took both sides of the fabric and tore it apart. The edges fell to the sides, revealing his chest. She leaned against him, pressing her bare breasts to his skin. The darkness in his eyes turned hooded with even more desire.

'You've ruined my tunic.'

She shrugged. 'And I'll ruin your trews as well, unless you stop denying me.'

He raised his hands behind his head. 'What are you planning to do?'

She didn't really know, but he'd given her permission to lower his trews, so she did. His erection was thick and long, springing to rest against his stomach. When she'd removed his clothing, she took her hand and explored the velvety texture of his manhood.

Bram looked intrigued as she stroked him. She rather thought she could bring him to his own pleasure in this way, but there was something else she wanted to try.

Though she was slightly embarrassed about it, she lowered her mouth to him. Bram's reaction was instantaneous, as he let out a growl.

'Nairna, I… What are you doing?'

She suckled against the head of him, using her tongue to stroke his length. 'Seducing you.'

He dragged his hands through her hair, and as she took him into her mouth he let out a rigid groan. 'Nairna, I don't think I can hold back if you do that.'

She released him and straddled his waist. Jenny had been right, she realised. She could indeed bring her husband a great deal of pleasure.

Bram guided her up and lifted his shaft to her wet entrance. She lowered her body atop him and a tremor seized her at the sensation.

Bram let out a slight hiss when she adjusted herself, rising up and down. His fists were clenched, his muscles taut.

'Am I hurting you?' she ventured. She kept her movements slow and smooth, rising and falling as she took his length inside her.

He looked as though she were torturing him, and with every penetration his body grew tighter.

She remembered that her previous husband would

sometimes increase the pace, so she experimented with taking Bram faster, bouncing against him as she sheathed him.

Strangely, the motion began to conjure up the startling warmth she'd experienced earlier, the shimmering tremors that echoed inside her womb.

Abruptly, Bram took her waist and started driving inside her, in counterpoint to her own thrusts. Her breathing grew shaky and she felt herself building tighter, her body shifting and reaching for something.

Then she felt it, the pulsing of her body melting against him, shuddering with wetness as he forced her to ride him. His palms filled up with her breasts and he suddenly let out a shout of his own, lifting her a few more times until she collapsed upon him.

She couldn't put into words her own feelings right now. Neither did he. Instead, she lay over him, with his body still joined with hers.

And wondered if she'd done anything at all to break through to him.

Chapter Fifteen

The next morning, Bram lifted the heavy claymore with both hands, swinging the sword in a wide arc. The blade glinted in the morning sun and he faced off against Ross, trying to lose himself in the training. Though he'd grown stronger in the past few weeks, it wasn't fast enough to suit him.

His blade met Ross's shield; no longer did he feel the weakness of his early days. The weight of the weapon was balanced in his hands, the punishing pace welcome.

There was still no word from the messengers Alex had sent. They were no closer to learning the whereabouts of Callum, and Bram's impatience had reached the edge of reason. He wanted to be among the men searching.

But after the disastrous fight at Cairnross, he knew that his time was better spent here, preparing for the next English garrison he might face. The unnerving silence from Cairnross made him all the more suspicious.

He swung the claymore again and the metal struck hard against Ross's shield.

'You're improving,' the older man commented. 'But you're too stiff, lad. Relax your movements. Move with the claymore and let it become a part of you.'

Bram tried to loosen his stance, but the tension was what kept his grip firm upon the iron weapon. As he trained, he kept his control tight, his movements focused upon precision.

Perspiration slid over his forehead, but he never wavered in his attack. The minutes slipped by and he answered Ross's own blows by lifting his claymore with both hands. His mind began to drift, and when he saw his wife walking past the training field his thoughts wandered just long enough for Ross's blade to slice into his forearm.

The pain was swift, the blood rising up upon his skin. Nairna rushed over to him, but Bram hardly heard her words of concern, or Ross's curse about his lack of attention. He stared at the redness flowing over his arm, and he set the claymore aside.

He removed his tunic and swabbed at the blood, forcing himself to walk to the edge of the loch.

'Bram.' Nairna caught up to him, her gaze focused upon his arm. 'Are you all right?'

He gave a nod, never ceasing his stride. The blood flow had already slowed, and though it might take a few days to heal, it was nothing serious. 'It's fine.'

It irritated him that he'd let his concentration slip. Though his fighting had improved, he wasn't satisfied yet. He needed to be ready for the fight against the English, as soon as Callum was found.

'Do you need me to stitch the cut for you?' Nairna asked.

'No. It's shallow.' He knelt before the stream, bathing his arm in the wetness and washing away the blood. The morning sun warmed his skin; too late he realised he'd bared his back to Nairna.

Her fingers moved across the scars and she spoke not a word. With infinite gentleness, she traced the years of his past, as if she could smooth away the mark of his imprisonment.

He didn't want her touching that part of him. Rising to his feet, he hid his scarred back and kept the tunic pressed to his wound.

When he regarded her, he saw the blush rise upon her cheeks. Her deep brown hair was working its way free of the braid she'd woven, and the strands framed her face. He wanted to kiss her, to pull her body close and fill her with himself.

'We'll finish the house today,' he told her. 'I'm going back to the ridge.'

'I'll come and help,' she offered. Her gaze centred upon his wounded arm. 'Are you truly all right, or are you just saying that?'

'I've experienced worse,' was all he would tell her.

She lowered her chin and took a step closer to him. 'Some day, I hope you'll trust me enough to tell me about it.'

He didn't intend to. What good would talking about his imprisonment do? Dwelling upon it wouldn't change what had happened. It was over and finished. No need to reopen the past.

Behind Nairna, he spied the dog he'd given her. The animal was seated, calmly waiting for his mistress. For a long moment, Nairna waited, as if to see whether or not Bram would change his mind.

'There's something else I want to ask you,' she

ventured. 'I've some goods that I…want to sell to the parish of Inveriston, not five miles from here. I would like to journey there with an escort. I could be back by nightfall.'

She bit her lip, as though she were hiding something. Whether or not she was telling the entire truth, he didn't know, but he didn't want her going anywhere, not with the English threat. 'We've no need for the money right now, Nairna. I'd rather you stayed here.'

'Dougal could escort me,' she said. 'He did well enough when we went to Locharr.'

'I don't want you leaving Glen Arrin,' he said. 'Not yet.'

She reached for his hand. 'I could find someone else to go in my stead. It would mean a great deal of money for us.'

'Why is it so important to you?'

She met his gaze squarely. 'Because money gives us power. And if we're to face the English again, we shouldn't be struggling at every turn. I've had a look at the accounts and there are ways we could improve—'

'Don't.' He cut off her arguments, soothing the harsh tone by kissing her. 'Alex is the chief. The funds of Glen Arrin are nothing for you to worry about.'

'But they are,' she insisted. He was about to cut her off again, but there was anger flashing in her eyes. 'You don't understand. I'm not skilled at weaving or spinning. This is the only thing I can do.'

He stared at her, unable to think of an appropriate answer. It didn't matter, for she hadn't finished speaking.

'When we were parted, and even when I was married to Iver, I learned how to take coins and earn more. I learned where to save, how to bargain.' Her face held an energy he hadn't seen before. 'I can do the same here.'

He didn't speak, but studied her, wondering why this meant so much to her. His gaze fell upon her ragged woollen gown and he asked quietly, 'You take care of others, I know. But when was the last time you bought something for yourself? A new gown or a ribbon?'

Confusion lined her face and she shook her head. 'Why would I need that? It's more important for our clan to have enough food to eat and supplies for the winter.'

'And clothes to wear?' he ventured, touching her gown. With a finger, he revealed one of the holes in the garment.

She stepped away from him. 'Don't, Bram. I'm fine the way I am.'

'Why would your needs be any less than anyone else's?' he demanded. 'You're my wife, not a beggar.'

She said nothing, as if she didn't quite believe she deserved more.

'You don't need to prove your worth, Nairna,' he continued. 'And you needn't sell your belongings, just to earn coins for our clan.'

She folded her hands, the guilty look returning. 'That wasn't what I wanted to sell. And it's not for me. It's for Laren.'

He stopped walking with her, resting one hand against a birch tree. 'Why would you want to sell something for Laren?'

She glanced around and admitted, 'Because she doesn't want Alex to know. It's something she's made, not anything that belongs to the chief,' she clarified. 'And I've promised to keep her secret.'

Bram didn't like the turn this conversation was taking. 'Nairna, no. You won't be involved in this.'

'She needs help,' his wife insisted. 'And I believe in her talent, even if Alex doesn't.' She sat down upon a fallen log, drawing her knees up.

The sadness in her voice tightened his chest. 'She should trust him,' Bram said. 'Alex wouldn't turn his back on her.'

'Look at them, Bram. He doesn't love her and he certainly doesn't care what she does. Why do you think she avoids the keep every day?'

He drew Nairna to her feet. 'What does it matter whether he loves her or not? He takes care of her and provides for their children.'

She lifted her eyes to his, and in them he saw a tiredness he hadn't noticed before. 'I don't want to be like them, Bram.'

'What is it you want, Nairna?' His voice held a hard edge to it and she flinched as if he'd struck her.

'I want to love you,' she whispered.

'Don't,' he warned. 'If you knew the things I've done—'

'You won't tell me.' She rested her forehead against his cheek. 'And I know it's tearing you apart inside.'

His hands moved to pull her away from him. A coldness settled into his skin, but she pressed again. 'What happened, Bram?'

He moved towards their house, staring at the hills surrounding them. For a long time, he said nothing, wondering if he should admit the truth.

But God above, she wanted to love him. He needed her to understand that he wasn't the man she believed he was.

'All summer I watched the guards, learning their habits,' he began, not meeting her eyes. 'What time they ate, what time they slept. I kept my head down and tried not to be noticed.'

She was listening intently, with far too much compassion on her face. Bram forced himself to tell her the rest, for he owed her the truth. He'd made an unforgivable choice. And it haunted him still.

'One night, after we'd been building a wall, I let myself fall to the ground. One of the guards came to see what had happened and I smashed a stone into his face. Then I ran to the opening we'd created.'

He rubbed at his eyes, but continued on. 'I shouted to Callum, ordering him to join me. But two of the other guards grabbed him. They held him and threatened to kill him.'

Nairna came up beside him and took his hand. She squeezed his fingers, as if trying to obliterate his guilt.

'I chose my life over Callum's,' he admitted. 'I ran when they could have slit his throat.'

'But they didn't.' Nairna leaned against him. 'Marguerite said he's still alive.'

'A thousand times I've wondered if I made the right decision. I left him there and swore I'd return for him. I risked his life on that. I didn't know if they would carry out their threat or not, but if I didn't leave, we were both dead.

'They let him go, because they had to chase after me.' He expelled a breath. 'I ran for the next two days, until I came to Ballaloch.'

When he'd finished, he expected her to pull away. He expected to see disappointment or revulsion in her eyes at his cowardice. Instead, she told him, 'It's not your fault. And I know you're going to free him.'

He stared at her. 'I can't forgive myself for abandoning

him.' With his hand, he traced the soft skin of her neck. 'I have to find him, Nairna.'

He let her go, not wanting her pity. Nor did he want to know what she thought of him now.

'Are you certain about this?' Laren asked. She held on to the leather-wrapped glass oval as though it were her firstborn child. 'I don't think they'll want it.'

'They're building a new kirk in Inveriston,' Nairna reassured her. 'Your glass windows will be the envy of every priest in the Highlands.'

'And what if it's not good enough?' Laren looked dismayed when Nairna gently took the glass from her.

'Your glass will inspire the monks,' Lady Marguerite insisted. 'It deserves to be part of the abbey.'

Although Laren still appeared unconvinced, Nairna hid the leather package within her cloak and went to where Dougal was waiting.

'Can you be back by nightfall?' she demanded.

'Easily.' The young man looked irritated that she'd even asked such a question. 'It's not that far to the parish.'

Nairna passed him the wrapped window, hoping that her plan would work. 'Demand seventy pennies, and when he offers twenty, take the glass and start to ride away. He'll come up in his offer after that.' She drilled into Dougal the right asking price, inwardly praying that he wouldn't come home with the wrong amount.

'I'll bring it back,' he promised.

'If I can rely on you, you can have the foal that my mare Anteria is carrying, after it's born.'

Dougal brightened and she suspected he would move the sky above them in order to sell the glass. 'By nightfall,' he repeated.

'Don't let it break,' Laren pleaded. And when he'd gone, she looked as if she wanted to chase after him and snatch it back. 'It will be all right, won't it?'

'The abbot will want more after he's seen this one,' Nairna predicted. 'Can you make them?'

'Of course.'

Laren's shoulders lowered and Nairna stopped to link arms. 'Don't be afraid. You have talent and I believe in you.'

The woman offered a faint smile, though she still appeared nervous. 'I hope he gets a good price for it.'

Marguerite took Laren's other arm in a show of support. 'He will.'

The house was now finished, and Bram stood back to look at it. Though it was well after dark, the men had lit torches, working together until the last segment of thatch covered the roof.

Tonight he would sleep beneath his own roof, with his wife. He'd even constructed a bed frame for Nairna and Alex had arranged for the mattress to be brought from the grain hut.

She might not want to be anywhere near him, after what he'd confessed about Callum. When he stared at the bed, he half-wondered if he'd be sleeping on the floor.

The slight noise of women approaching made him turn. Bram saw Laren and her daughters, along with Lady Marguerite and Nairna. When his wife drew closer, he stilled at the sight of her.

She wore a kirtle and matching surcoat of green silk embroidered with pearls. Her dark hair was braided back from her face, with a few long strands covering her shoulders. A small embroidered cap covered her hair with a trailing veil. The gown was one he'd never seen before—it clung to her body, outlining every curve. Her breasts filled up the fabric, and he could see the plump outline of them within the silk.

She was wearing one of Lady Marguerite's gowns; he was sure of it. And though it pleased him that she'd made an effort to cast aside one of the shapeless, grey gowns she usually wore, it bothered him that she didn't have a gown of her own of that quality.

'Nairna,' he greeted her.

She moved towards him slowly, with her dog trailing her. In her hands she held a drinking horn. Her lips parted and her green eyes were soft in the firelit torches. Bram tried to take the horn from her, but she refused to let go. Instead, she opened it for him, lifting it to his mouth as she offered him a drink.

The ale was cool, as if it had been kept underground. After the day's hard labour, nothing could have tasted sweeter. She let him drink his fill; when he'd had enough, she took the horn away.

'Do you like your house?' he asked.

She nodded, raising her eyes to look at the new structure. 'I'm glad they were able to finish it tonight.' Then she sent him a slight smile, before leaving him to stare at the sway of her hips as she returned to the others.

The way she spoke made him wonder if she had plans for this night. His thoughts filled up with ideas of everything he wanted to do to his wife beneath their own roof. The memory of the taste of her skin, the soft sighs she made when he touched her, was enough to send his desire raging.

The women opened up the bundles of food to share, but Nairna didn't join him. Instead, she stood at a distance, watching him from the shadows. He ate the venison stew that was passed around; although it tasted delicious, his attention was centred upon Nairna.

She moved among the others, thanking each of the men for their labour on the house. A few of them sent her smiles that were a little too friendly, and Bram stood up, joining her. He shadowed her, letting the other MacKinlochs know that Nairna was his. Possessive, aye, but they didn't need to be staring at his wife.

'What are you doing, Bram?' she asked, after she'd spoken to the last person.

'Protecting you.'

She raised an eyebrow at him, but he took her hand anyway. 'I hardly think that's necessary.'

'They're going to leave us,' he said darkly. 'As soon as they've finished eating.'

Nairna gave a faint shrug. 'Did you see Dougal among the others?' Though she kept her tone casual, he caught a note of worry in her voice.

'No.' Bram had been so busy with the building, he hadn't really thought about Dougal. But his brother should have been there. 'And why would you be so concerned about him?'

'No reason.' She shrugged, but her eyes were searching. They settled upon Laren, who also looked uneasy.

They were hiding something, and he didn't like secrets being kept from him. 'Nairna, what is this about? Where is my brother?'

Nairna sat down upon a tree stump, beckoning for her dog Caen to approach. The animal trotted forwards, settling at her feet like a faithful shadow. Bram recognised it as the distraction it was meant to be. He covered her hand with his own, upon the dog's head.

'Nairna, tell me.' It was a demand, not a request.

'He—he went to Inveriston.' She scratched Caen's

ears, and the dog rolled onto his back, licking at her hand. 'Several hours ago.'

'Alone?'

She nodded, clutching her hands together. 'He said he could be there within an hour. He knew where it was and promised to be back by nightfall.'

Bram released a stream of expletives. What in the name of God had she been thinking?

'He's four and ten, Nairna. Not a man. And he's certainly not old enough to go anywhere alone.' Bram stood up, his fury threatening to spill over. By God, he wasn't about to lose another brother to the English. Not because of any foolish attempt to earn money.

Nairna caught up and tugged at his sleeve, 'Bram, wait. He might have been delayed. There's no reason to think that he's not all right.'

'There are dozens of English soldiers patrolling the lands only a few miles from here,' Bram shot back. 'Any number of them would be glad to have a MacKinloch hostage.' He couldn't believe she'd done this. His brother wasn't a damned merchant.

When he reached Alex, he let out a terse order. 'Come with me. We're going to find Dougal.'

Alex's attention snapped to Nairna. 'What's happened?'

Bram tilted his head towards Laren. 'Ask your wife.'

Nairna and Laren exchanged glances and Laren was the one who paled, keeping her eyes averted from Alex.

'Where is Dougal?' Alex demanded.

Laren eyed Nairna with desperation, but finally answered, 'He went to Inveriston to sell some things that Nairna and I gave him.'

'What sort of things?' The chief stared at the pair of women and Bram recognised the concealed anger in his expression.

'Some…things we made,' Nairna answered. She looked at Bram, her eyes wild with pleading. She didn't want him to tell Alex anything. 'This is my fault. I apologise for putting Dougal in danger. I didn't think anything could happen near the parish kirk.'

Alex's chin snapped up. 'Do you think he's been taken?'

Bram shook his head. 'I don't know. But we need to search for him now, before anyone else finds him.' The two stood up, then Alex gave the order for a search party to form. The men gathered weapons and torches and Bram was just about to leave when he cast a look back at Nairna.

Her cheeks were pale, her eyes filled with regret. 'I'm sorry,' she said softly. 'I thought we could earn a ransom for Callum with the things we sold.'

He supposed she hadn't thought of all the consequences. But her naïvety might cost them his brother's life. Without another word, he turned his back on her and left.

Chapter Sixteen

The house was unbearably dark and cold, but Nairna didn't dare to light a fire. Her breath formed mist inside and she huddled beneath a woollen blanket left behind. Caen rested at her feet, his head lying on top of folded paws.

It had been hours since the men had left and she'd long ago dried her tears. She'd never meant for Dougal to be lost or hurt. Aye, it was her mistake, believing that the young man could go alone to Inveriston.

Fear tightened through every muscle in her body. If anything had happened to Dougal, Bram would hold her responsible. Her fragile marriage would crumble away until there was nothing left.

She'd hoped that tonight she could rebuild something between them. Marguerite had loaned her a gown while Laren had dressed her hair. It had been so long since she'd looked after her own appearance, but before they'd begun, Jenny had shown her a reflection in a polished mirror.

Nairna hadn't known she looked like this—like a wraith, dressed in grey as though she'd never left mourning. It was no wonder that Bram questioned what she wore. No man would want a woman who neglected herself in such a way.

Nairna drew her knees up under her gown. It had taken both Jenny and Marguerite to help her put it on, it fitted her so tightly. She couldn't take it off without Bram's help and she didn't even know when he was coming back. Or if he would return.

She had stared at the door for what seemed like hours, her eyes dry, while her heart grew more fearful. And when, at last, the door swung open, she nearly jerked with shock when Bram tossed a large sack at her feet. It was filled with coins, from the metallic jingle she'd heard. Yet her husband didn't look at all pleased.

'Is Dougal all right?' she asked.

'He's back at Glen Arrin, where Alex is meting out his punishment.'

'Punishment?' Appalled, she couldn't stop her mouth from dropping open. 'But we asked him to go. It wasn't his fault at all.'

'He was foolish enough to let himself be led astray by women. Aye, it's his fault.'

Nairna stood up, her temper flaring. 'Don't you dare lay a hand upon him. He did as we asked, and from the looks of it, he did well enough.' She kicked at the sack of coins, sending it a few feet away. 'It might pay the price of Callum's life.'

'The coins are false,' her husband gritted out. 'Hardly worth the stones at our feet.'

A rushing noise filled her ears, and Nairna forced herself to sit down. False? What did he mean?

Bram loosened the ties of the bag and withdrew a handful of silver pennies. He poured them into her palm, and she could feel, from the light weight, that they were indeed false. At the bottom of the sack she found useless bits of iron.

It made her sick to think of the priests trying to cheat Laren's artistry. Her beautiful glass was now gone and Dougal's efforts were for nothing at all. Nairna wanted to lash out at the unfairness, but what good would it do?

'I'm sorry,' she said. 'I thought it would help you.'

Her husband's grim expression made her feel even worse. She lowered her gaze, not knowing what else to say.

'We found Dougal a few miles east of the abbey,' Bram said. 'He was getting ready to set up camp for the night.'

'He wasn't hurt, was he?'

Bram shook his head. 'No. But you never should have sent him. I ordered you not to get involved.'

His arrogance and refusal to listen was starting to wear down her patience. 'I don't regret sending the goods to be sold. I only wish they hadn't cheated him.'

'There was no need for the ransom,' Bram continued. 'We'll fight for Callum.' He leaned against the wall beside the door, his hand reaching back to unstrap the claymore from his shoulders.

'Do you know where he is now?' Nairna asked, noticing the change in his face.

'Aye. The last messenger returned an hour ago, and told us where he was taken. We're going after him tomorrow.'

'Where?' she managed. 'Who took him?'

'Robert Fitzroy, the Baron of Harkirk.'

Nairna clamped her mouth shut, unable to believe it.

Harkirk's fortress was one of the strongest in the Highlands, thanks to her father's bribery.

'Then we have a common enemy.' She explained what her father had done to avoid bloodshed. 'They're bleeding the MacPhersons dry to fund their soldiers.'

Bram stared at her, with no mercy in his eyes. 'Not for long.'

He pushed the door open, stepping past the sleeping dog, and returned to the outdoor hearth the men had built earlier. The fire had died down to hot coals and Bram picked up a staff the width of his wrist. He used it to push several of the hearth stones inside their home, and when he closed the door behind him, Nairna could feel the radiant heat rising from the stones.

Even so, it did nothing to ward off the coldness surrounding Bram's demeanour. She doubted if an apology would change his anger, but she had to try. 'I never meant for anything to happen to Dougal.'

Bram seemed to be holding his temper back with the greatest effort. 'It's not as safe around Glen Arrin as you might believe, Nairna. We're lucky to have found him.'

She gave a nod; it seemed that he was trying to press down even more guilt upon her. Aye, she'd made a mistake, believing it was a simple matter of taking the glass to be sold. But now that they possessed a sack full of false coins, she realised that they had a different sort of opportunity. It was a chance to ransom Callum and lose little, from a monetary standpoint.

'Take the coins with you in the morning,' she advised. 'Lord Harkirk might not notice that they're false until it's too late.'

'Why do you insist upon offering a ransom, Nairna?'

he demanded. 'Don't you believe us capable of bringing him back?'

Nairna heard the stiff pride in his tone and suddenly, she was tired of arguing about whether or not he was strong enough to fight.

'It doesn't matter if you are or not,' she answered honestly. 'If there's another way to rescue Callum, why wouldn't you try it?' She moved towards him and his cheek twitched when she stood before him. 'Would it threaten your honour so much?'

He didn't answer and she realised that she'd struck a nerve. Though she didn't know whether or not he could fight, she'd just as soon avoid it when possible.

'If we ransom Callum with false coins, I'd consider that justice. Harkirk deserves to be cheated.' To her mind, it would help Bram get his brother back and keep the men out of harm's way.

'I don't play games with men's lives.' Bram's dark eyes narrowed. 'The risk is too great.'

Nairna wished he would stop being so stubborn and consider a way of freeing Callum without bloodshed. 'And you don't think about the risk of death? Someone will get hurt or killed if you try to fight them. Why wouldn't you want to try it?'

He moved past her, ignoring her suggestion. 'Because we're not like your father, paying for men's lives.'

Nairna had no answer for that. She'd once blamed her father for surrendering without a fight. She'd hated the thought of paying the English, arguing with him constantly about his loose way with coins. Had she changed her opinion so much, in these past few weeks?

Aye, she had. And it had everything to do with the man standing before her.

'I don't want you to be hurt,' she whispered. 'Or killed.'

Bram removed his shoes and she heard the rustle of his tunic falling to the ground. It had grown so dark, she couldn't guess whether he was wearing all of his clothes or not. She closed her eyes, warming her hands near the heated stones. A shiver broke through her at the thought of sharing a mattress with a man who despised her so much.

But he returned to her, his hand catching hold of hers. 'I've been training for weeks now, Nairna. I won't bother trying to convince you that I can fight.'

He pressed her palms to his chest and she could indeed feel the changes. No longer was he thin and wiry; she could feel the outline of new muscles in the rise and fall of his lungs.

When she reached his stomach, the ridges ended at the waist of his trews.

'I know you can fight,' she murmured. 'I simply don't want you to.' This wasn't about trust in his abilities. It was the unsettling fear that if Bram left her in the morning, he wouldn't come back alive. She knew Lord Harkirk and the large numbers of men who defended his motte. They would be slaughtered within minutes, if Harkirk learned why they were there.

Bram caught her hands and her heartbeat trembled within her chest. She could smell the scent of wood upon him and despite his anger, there was no denying the way she'd aroused him. His shaft nestled against her, when he drew her close.

'I'm not weak, Nairna.'

'I never said that. But what if the raid goes badly? It won't end, will it?' she whispered. 'Even if you do bring back Callum, there will be war.'

'Until we've driven the English out, aye.'

She broke free of him and the worry made her head ache. When she reached the opposite side of the room, she sat down on a wooden stump that served as a stool.

Bram returned to the bed and she heard the sinking sound of his body weight against the mattress. Her hands rested upon the silk of Lady Marguerite's gown and she felt like weeping.

The silence in their house closed over her and she stared at the bag of coins that lay at her feet. Though she didn't understand how Dougal had been cheated or why, there had to be a way to make use of them.

She glanced back at Bram and the mattress rustled as he rolled over. He wasn't going to use the coins, nor would he appreciate her interference.

But what if…she could use her father's help? What if Hamish could coerce Lord Harkirk into releasing Callum? Then, at least, they could avoid any bloodshed.

The hours were slipping away, and she listened to the sound of Bram's breathing, wondering if Alex would listen to her suggestion. If they travelled to Ballaloch and stayed with her father, they would know more about Harkirk's forces and what to do.

Silently, she reached for the sack of false coins, listening to her husband sleep—if, in fact, he was sleeping. He didn't move when she opened the door, nor did she hear him stir when she slipped outside.

Her dog Caen, however, stood up from where he'd been sleeping and trotted over to see her. Nairna reached down to touch his ears, thankful that he hadn't begun barking.

She planned to return to the keep for the remainder of the night and wait for Alex to awaken. If she spoke to the chief before they left, he might even allow her to accompany them.

The thought of returning home was a hope that filled Nairna with yearning. She hadn't seen her family or friends in so long. Surely her father would offer his men to help her, if she asked it of them.

The moon had slipped lower in the sky, and she hesitated, wondering if Bram was still asleep or not. Nairna held the bag of false coins and adjusted her cape to keep warm. She began walking downhill upon the path leading through the forest, with Caen at her side. Though it was still dark, she could see the torches lining the walls at Glen Arrin.

In the distance, the faint grey light of morning was on the horizon. She wouldn't have to wait too long for Alex to awaken.

As she walked further, she ignored the unsettled worry in her stomach. By the time Bram discovered her gone, she would be talking to his brother.

She could only hope that the chief would listen.

Bram wondered what on earth Nairna was doing. He'd watched her take the bag of coins before she made her way down the hillside. Damn her. Where was she planning to go in the middle of the night?

Though he wanted to throttle her for daring to leave, he took a few moments to prepare his horse. It would be easier to overtake her, since she'd gone on foot.

He hurried to get the gelding ready, and within minutes he was following Nairna. Once he reached the bottom of the hill, he urged his horse into a hard run to catch up to her.

He was torn between fury at her defiance and worry about why she'd left. *He* was the one meant to take risks, not his wife.

There. He saw her walking closer to the keep, with her dog at her side. Her hood had fallen back and she was several paces away from the gatehouse.

Bram gripped his horse with his knees, racing until he started to gain on her. Nairna glanced behind her; when she saw him, she stopped walking. It startled Alex, for he'd expected her to run from him, not wait.

When he reached her side at last, he leaned down and picked her up, bringing her across his lap on horseback. A flush of guilt covered her face, but she held on to his waist for balance.

Bram held her captive in his arms, demanding, 'Where did you think you were going?'

It occurred to Nairna that an explanation would only make Bram angrier than he already was. She was caught now; there was nothing else she could admit except the truth. He didn't bother to wait for her answer, but wheeled the horse around to take her back home again.

Weariness made her reluctant to provoke another argument, nor did she want to listen to more reasons of why she ought to stay home where it was safer.

A woman holds power of her own, Jenny had told her. *The power to bring a man pleasure.*

And though the idea of seducing Bram again was more than a little frightening, it was the only weapon she had.

He dismounted from the horse, never once letting go of her. He brought her inside the house, locking his arms around her waist. 'Did you think I wouldn't know that you'd left, Nairna?'

She wasn't going to bother trying to convince him of anything. It was clear he wouldn't listen to a single word. Instead, she reached up to his face, lifting her lips to his. She kissed him softly, as if to tame the beast.

Bram's mouth didn't move and the coldness made her wonder if she'd made a mistake. When she pulled back, his dark eyes glittered with fettered frustration. 'You're not going to soften me with a kiss, Nairna.'

She supposed it was naïve to think that were possible. So she ran her hands over his bristled face, down to his wide neck.

'Where did you intend to go?' he demanded, flinching slightly when she touched his shoulders.

'I wanted to talk to Alex,' she answered. She could feel the knotted tension in him, and when she slid one hand beneath his tunic the hot skin startled her.

He jerked back, drawing her hands behind her. But instead of feeling trapped, it brought his chest up against her body, making her breasts grow aroused.

'Why did you bring the coins?'

She lifted her eyes to meet his. 'You know why.'

His grim expression was barren of all emotion, as though she'd betrayed him. But lurking beneath the surface was something more. He was fighting against himself and though she didn't know what his thoughts were, she sensed that his control was slipping away.

'You're driving me to madness,' he said, releasing her suddenly. 'I don't understand you.'

'I don't suppose you understand what it's like for me, being left behind.'

He was standing near the bed, staring at the doorway. He looked as though he wanted to say something to her, but he hadn't decided what.

Nairna moved closer, her pulse thrumming like a

bird's wings. If she let him push her away, their marriage would be no different than it was before. 'You feel so helpless, afraid of what might happen.'

She came so close; she rested her cheek against his, tracing her fingers over the scars upon his lower back. 'I don't want there to be anger between us. Not now.'

He didn't answer, but she lifted her face, hoping he would kiss her. Bram held motionless, letting her touch him. For the longest time, she continued stroking his scarred flesh.

He lowered his forehead to hers, and she sensed him fighting the temptation. 'There isn't much time left, Nairna.'

'Then let us make the most of it.' She kissed him, no longer waiting for him to claim the right.

Chapter Seventeen

The light touch of her lips upon his was an invitation Bram didn't want to accept. He wanted to chastise her for leaving him, to make her understand that he was trying to protect her, not imprison her.

He took command of her mouth, letting her know that he wasn't at all in the mood to be cajoled. But when her arms wound around his neck, he started loosening the laces of her gown. The fabric was so tightly drawn against her breasts, he could see the outline of her budding nipples.

'This gown doesn't fit you,' he said against her mouth.

Nairna's hair had fallen wild against her shoulders, the cap forgotten upon the floor. Her green eyes were flooded with desire and need. 'Then you should take it off.' When he pulled against the laces, she stopped him. 'It belongs to Marguerite. Be careful.'

He wanted to rend the fabric from her body, tearing her free of the silken cage. Instead, he knelt down, lifting the surcoat away. Then he raised her kirtle from the hem. She wore nothing beneath the silken gown, not even a shift. His arousal deepened, seeing her bare skin.

Nairna lifted her arms to help him remove the dress and the sight of her large, firm breasts was nearly his undoing. He stripped the gown away until she stood naked before him.

He used his tongue against the smoothness of her throat, while he cupped her breasts with his hands.

'Bram,' she whispered, her breath hitching. Her eyes were hooded with desire, her skin prickled with goose flesh.

'I haven't finished with you yet.' In the darkness of early morning, her features remained shadowed. 'I can't see you the way I want to. So I'll have to find you by touch.'

He took her hand and brought her to the bed, lowering her onto it.

'You're going to wish you'd never left our house,' he said, stripping off his clothing. He needed to feel her naked skin against his, to know the response he'd provoked. She was shivering, but he used his body heat to warm her.

He wanted to be inside her when she came apart. He wanted to be encased in her satiny wetness, feeling her violent tremors squeezing his shaft.

'You're not leaving me behind this time,' she responded. 'I'll stay at Ballaloch while you go after Callum.'

'You're going nowhere, Nairna.' He kept her hands pinned, while he worked his mouth over her throat, using his tongue to encircle her nipples again. When her body spasmed at the dark pull of his mouth, he reached between her legs to feel the creamy wetness there.

'If you go without me, I'll only follow,' she whispered. Her hand slid to his thick erection, caressing his length. 'You wouldn't dare to tie me up like you did Dougal.'

'Don't tempt me.' He flicked his thumb over her hooded flesh, entering her with two fingers.

In response, she squeezed the length of his erection, sliding her palm up to the head. Her hand dragged over the length of him, caressing him in an erotic rhythm.

'I won't allow you to endanger yourself.' He gritted his teeth against the fierce sensation of desire that pulled at him. 'It isn't safe.'

'And what about you?' Nairna demanded. She rubbed the moist tip of him and her wet palm encircled him again. 'Do you think I want to watch you risk your life again?'

Bram pushed her hand away. 'I'm prepared for it, Nairna. You aren't.'

She gasped when he moved down on her, spreading her legs apart. He cupped her hips, tasting her intimate opening. With his tongue, he worked her swollen flesh, watching her responses to see where he should move.

She seemed the most sensitive at the hooded place above her entrance, and he teased it, watching her shiver. But despite his efforts to send her into a release, she wasn't responding in the way he'd hoped.

He moved to rest on his side while she laid upon her back. 'Touch yourself,' he commanded, bringing her fingers downwards. 'Show me where it brings you the most pleasure.'

She started to refuse, but Bram wouldn't let her deny him. He gripped her hand, bringing it down to her secret flesh. 'I want to know.'

Nairna's fingers spread out, but she didn't move them.

She didn't know what to do, he realised. She'd never explored herself; he would have to take the lead.

He brought her fingers to her wet centre, circling the opening. He showed her how to move, how to stroke.

She looked embarrassed, but he refused to let her shyness overcome her. At last, she closed her eyes, her hand moving. He watched as she raised her fingers above the opening to the swollen nub. She let out a gasp when she touched herself, increasing the pressure in a slow circle.

'Keep going,' he encouraged her, staring in fascination as she arched her hips. He was getting more aroused, watching her bring about her own pleasure.

Her swollen nipples tempted him and he reached out to take one into his mouth. Nairna cried out as he kept a wet pressure upon the tip, caressing the other with his hand.

Her breath came in shuddering gasps as she pressed harder in a rhythm that mimicked his own thrusting. 'Don't stop,' she pleaded when he released one of her breasts.

In response, Bram took the nipple between his fingertips, rolling it as he suckled the other. He felt the change in her body as she arched against him, releasing a moan as her body shivered with pleasure.

He nearly lost control, watching her shatter. When her hand fell away, he moved down, using his tongue to work the place she'd just touched.

Nairna came apart again, her body shaking violently. 'Bram, I can't. It's too much.'

'Again,' he demanded, sucking hard against her folds until she convulsed in his arms. She guided him up, taking his shaft in her palm and guiding him into her.

He slid inside with no barriers, only the tight, wet warmth that surrounded his erection.

Her breasts were pebbled in response, and when he withdrew and slid back inside, she let out a gasp, squeezing her walls against him.

It was like nothing he'd ever felt before. Even as he possessed her, plunging inside, it was as if she were pulling him deeper. She arched, wrapping her legs around his waist to take him even further.

'Go faster,' she urged, gripping his backside. 'Don't stop.'

He obeyed her urging, increasing the pace of his thrusts. She was taking him so deep, he didn't know how much more he could last. But then, when her head fell back, he grasped her hips hard, pumping with such speed that she came apart again, her body melting with wetness between them.

She met his rhythm with her own desire, bucking against him until he released his seed, burying himself deep. Nairna's legs held him around his waist, as if she wouldn't let him leave her.

He held her tightly, not speaking. There were no words, no attempts to touch her again. Simply silence.

Nairna held still, her body trembling with aftershocks. She'd always suspected that it would be this way between them and wished she could hold him like this for ever. Or at least a piece of his spirit, if her womb were to be blessed with a child.

A sound bumped against the doorway and she saw her dog Caen returning inside. He eyed Nairna as if to scold her for leaving him behind. Then he circled around twice before settling down in front of the door.

Bram propped up his head on one arm. 'He's not much of a protector, is he?'

'I don't know about that,' Nairna mused. 'If someone were to invade, they'd likely stumble over him.'

Bram caressed the skin of her hip for a moment before he withdrew from her body. The morning sun filtered through the crevices of their house and Bram stood up to get dressed. Already she saw the determination on his face.

'We're going together, Bram,' she reminded him. If he left her behind again, he would withdraw even more. Worse, if he didn't find his brother alive, he would never forgive himself.

Bram's face didn't falter. 'I'm not putting you in danger, Nairna.'

'I know that,' she amended. 'And I promise, I won't follow you to Harkirk's stronghold. As I said, I would stay with my father.'

'We're not going as far as Ballaloch,' was his answer.

Dismay pooled inside her, for she could sense the cold, vengeance-minded husband returning. She couldn't yet abandon her desire to intervene in another way. Her father had a tentative alliance with Harkirk—why couldn't he negotiate the safe return of Callum?

The sound of horses approaching made her reach for an older gown from among her belongings. She dressed quickly and opened the door, only to find the chief and a dozen men arriving, heavily armed.

Alex regarded Bram with a suspicious look. 'I thought you would be ready to leave at dawn.'

Bram glanced at her and Nairna flushed, not wanting to admit the reason her husband was late. Instead, she interjected, 'I'm going to travel with you. You'll stay at my father's house at Ballaloch and you can learn what you need to know about Lord Harkirk, before entering the fortress.'

Alex's expression was neutral as he thought about her offer.

'She's not leaving Glen Arrin,' Bram insisted. 'I won't allow it.'

'But she isn't asking to go with us to fight Harkirk,' Alex said. 'She's asking to visit her family and give us a place to make our plans.' He exchanged a look with Bram. 'It wouldn't be a bad thing to have the protection of Hamish MacPherson.'

'I am not bringing Nairna into this,' Bram argued.

'But my father may have a way of getting more information about Callum. It would give you an advantage.'

Alex studied her, as if trying to determine whether or not she spoke the truth.

Please believe me, she prayed silently.

Finally, the chief gave a nod. 'She comes with us, Bram. It makes more sense to stay with Hamish than to camp on our own. That would only draw Harkirk's men upon us sooner.'

Nairna sent him a grateful look, but the chief seemed uninterested in her personal feelings. Instead, he sent one of the men to bring back a horse for her while Bram prepared his mount.

Within another half-hour, Dougal returned, holding the reins of a mare Nairna hadn't seen before. When he came closer, he said, 'I didn't want your mare to be burdened while she's carrying her foal. This is Gavina, and she's got a calm temper.'

He didn't meet her eyes; Nairna understood that he was feeling guilty for having lost Laren's glass.

'Thank you, Dougal.' She accepted the reins of the horse. 'And I'm sorry for what happened last night.'

His mouth tightened into a line. 'So am I.'

She touched his shoulder. 'I know you're wanting to come with us to free Callum. But we need men to stay here, especially after what happened at Cairnross.' She forced him to meet her gaze. 'Please, will you protect Glen Arrin?' Amid the other men, she caught Alex's impatience. But this time, she didn't want Dougal attempting to follow.

The lad looked down at the ground and nodded. Nairna gave him a slight hug, causing his ears to brighten with embarrassment.

'Good. And there's something else I need from you.' She pointed to the doorway of their house, where Caen lifted a sleepy head. 'Will you watch over Caen?'

Dougal eyed the dog and Nairna added, 'He's quite a fierce animal, really. He'll tear out a man's throat if he threatens a MacKinloch.'

A slight grin perked the lad's mouth at her sarcasm, when the dog yawned and closed his eyes again. More than likely Caen would sleep through an invasion. But after Nairna finished packing her supplies, Caen woke up and got to his feet, trotting forwards. He sniffed at Nairna as she ordered him, 'Be good while I'm away.'

Dougal knelt to pet him, and Caen licked his hand. Satisfied that both would be safe after they left, Nairna mounted her horse and joined the others.

But as she followed the men, trying to keep in their midst, her husband's annoyance was palpable and he would no longer look at her.

Ballaloch Castle, two days later

'Harkirk's forces are growing stronger,' Hamish said. 'He's been demanding more funds from the clans and few are able to pay anymore. His greed knows no logic.'

'What of your family?' Bram asked gruffly. He knew it was a continual source of frustration for Nairna that her father had chosen to bribe Lord Harkirk instead of fighting the English forces.

'I'll admit, I have little left to give.' Hamish gave a shrug and gestured for them to join him at table. 'But the MacDonnell clan returned most of Nairna's dowry from her marriage to Iver. The replenished supplies will help us through the winter.'

Bram's knuckles whitened as he thought of Nairna's previous husband. Although he knew it wasn't rational, he viewed Iver as the man who had stolen her away from him. He couldn't stop the possessive feelings, but he was glad that part of Nairna's life was over.

His wife had disappeared above stairs, taking food with her and claiming that she was tired. Bram didn't trust her, and he wouldn't put it past her to eavesdrop.

Throughout the two-day journey, she'd said little to him. It was as if she were trying to become a soft-spoken, demure wife. Bram wanted to snort at the idea. Nairna was most definitely up to something, and though she'd convinced Alex she had no intention of interfering with Callum's rescue, he knew better.

The false coins had disappeared among her belongings, and he didn't doubt that she would put them to use. Though she claimed it was because she wanted to avoid fighting, he still wondered if it was because she lacked trust in his abilities. He'd done everything he could to rebuild his strength, but Nairna didn't seem to believe in him.

His mood grew darker over the next half-hour. He listened to Alex and Hamish discussing Callum's whereabouts; although his brother was going through each of the possibilities, Bram was growing more distracted. He was tired of waiting and the idea of negotiating a release sounded as if it would only drag out Callum's suffering. Were it up to him, he'd leave now and get his brother out.

At last, they agreed that they would speak to Lord Harkirk in the morning, asking for Callum's release while Bram and Ross infiltrated the English defences. Even if no decision was made, they would then have the knowledge they needed to launch an attack.

Satisfied, Bram returned to the room he and Nairna had been given. He found his wife curled up on her side, though he doubted she was asleep. He pulled back the coverlet and saw her bare skin. His body responded at the sight of her nakedness and he removed his clothing, slipping into the bed beside her. Nairna rolled over to face him, her expression pensive.

He waited for her to speak, to ask the questions he knew she was itching to voice. But she didn't say a word. At last he offered, 'We're leaving tomorrow for Harkirk's fortress.'

She gave a nod to show she'd heard him, then rolled onto her back to stare at the ceiling. 'I hope you get him back safely.'

'You don't want us to fight for him, do you?'

She remained silent for several minutes. Then she answered, 'I used to think my father was a coward for not facing them. I wanted him to fight for our freedom, rather than bargaining with the enemy.'

She reached for his hand and pulled it to her. 'I understand now why he made the choices he did. I'd rather surrender every last coin, if it meant keeping you safe.'

The haunted note in her voice gripped him hard, for she spoke as if she knew he would die. Her fear was real and he laced his fingers with hers in quiet reassurance.

'I'll return to you, Nairna.'

'You don't know that.' Her eyes gleamed with unshed tears. 'There are so many of them.'

He kissed the corners of her eyes, as if to take the tears away. 'It won't be a direct attack. Alex and your father will negotiate, while Ross and I try to find Callum.'

'Promise me you won't take any risks.' She traced her fingertips over his jaw, stroking his skin.

'I can't promise it won't be dangerous,' he admitted. 'But I have a good reason to return.'

She knew that nothing would keep him from this fight and her fears multiplied until she wondered if this was the last night they would spend together. She thought of the dried flower he'd given her and the gift of Caen. He'd built a house for her and done everything he could to give her happiness.

Her life with Bram was better than she'd dreamed it could be. And her heart was utterly lost at the thought of losing him.

'What is it, *a ghaoil?*'

She turned her head into the sheet, fighting back tears. 'I'm just afraid because I don't want you to be taken captive again.' She touched the scar that ran down his throat and he caught her fingers. 'I can't stop thinking about it.'

'I won't be a prisoner again,' he swore. 'I would surrender my life first.'

She knew it, but the idea of losing him was tearing

her apart. She embraced him hard, trying to hold on to him. She didn't want tonight to end with any distance between them. Her hand moved down, catching hold of his shaft. Slowly, she stroked him, coaxing his erection until he was hard. She moved upwards, easing his length inside her.

'Nairna,' Bram murmured.

'Just relax,' she said. She eased up, sinking back down until his length was impaled within her moist walls. The sensation of taking control, of bringing him pleasure, was a way of showing him how she felt.

His hands held her waist, guiding her up, before he sheathed himself within. 'You think I can relax while you're doing this?'

She rocked against him, forcing him to thrust deep inside. 'You needn't do anything. I'll take care of you.'

His answer was to withdraw, dragging her down until her stomach rested on the bed, her feet touching the floor. From behind, he spread her legs apart, his fingers probing her opening. 'No, Nairna. I'm going to take care of you.'

Abruptly, she felt him filling her and the thickness of him was shredding all the clear thoughts of her brain. She surrendered to the heady pleasure as he drew her hips to him, penetrating her in short thrusts.

She moaned when he quickened the pace, the rhythm bringing her swollen womanhood into full contact with his shaft.

'I love you,' she blurted out, shocked when a shaking spasm gripped her. Though she hadn't meant to confess the words, they had an effect upon her husband. He gentled his thrusts, going deeper, as if he were trying to caress her from within.

Though he didn't reveal any of his own feelings, she

sensed that he did care. He kissed her shoulder lazily while he penetrated her again. 'Do you want me to take you like this?' he murmured, filling her up with a smooth stroke. 'Or like this?' He took her hard, with a fast pace that stole her breath. Immediately, her body reacted and she fought to catch her breath.

'Faster,' she gritted out and he obeyed. He pumped inside, taking her with no mercy, his shaft slamming inside so hard, she bit back a scream. A spasm of ecstasy flooded over her, making her come apart with wicked release.

'Tell me again,' he demanded, reaching up to cup her breasts. His fingers pinched her nipples, but there was no pain, only a delicious pleasure that shot down her body into her womb.

'I love you,' she admitted. His hands stimulated her breasts while he finished his thrusts, driving so deeply inside that she felt like he'd stolen her mind, as well as her heart.

And when he at last found his own fulfilment, his breathing shuddered against her, his hips driving deep. Nairna's heartbeat thudded within her chest, while Bram rested atop her.

'I'm coming back to you, *a ghaoil*.'

She prayed he could keep that promise.

Chapter Eighteen

The circular defences of the English fortress were heavily guarded. Archers wearing chainmail stood at the gatehouse, while Bram spied more soldiers patrolling the motte-and-bailey structure. As Hamish led them inside, Bram felt the coldness rising up. His claymore was strapped across his back, hidden from view by his cloak. He kept his shoulders lowered, trying to hide himself from their view, but he counted soldiers, mentally reviewing their positions.

A second inner curtain wall enclosed a modest wooden structure that was starting to resemble a keep. From the layers of stone built up against the wood, Bram supposed that prisoners were being used for the labour. He kept his eyes fixed upon the ground, searching for the entrance to the prison. It would be a small opening, likely somewhere near the centre of the fortress.

Though he kept near the others for now, he was already planning to slip away to find the location. It might be that he could steal away while Hamish was speaking with Harkirk.

Hamish dismounted and led them inside the fortress. He'd worn his best tunic and a cloak lined with fur, making it clear that this meeting was indeed meant to be a negotiation.

Bram's gaze flickered to the Englishman and the ruthlessness in his eyes reminded him of Cairnross. He possessed an air of superiority, as if he owned the souls of the men around him.

'I have come with the chief of the MacKinloch clan,' Hamish began. 'He wishes to negotiate the return of his younger brother Callum, whom we believe to be a prisoner here.'

The English lord's face remained cold and impassive. 'I presume you are speaking of the one who was transferred to me from Cairnross.'

'Aye,' Alex interrupted. He stepped forwards, meeting Harkirk's expression with his own determination. 'I want Callum returned to us.'

'And what are you prepared to offer in return?' the lord enquired. 'Another hostage to take his place?'

An icy coldness rose up in Bram's throat, but he didn't flinch or turn his face away. Instead, he stared hard at the enemy, letting Harkirk see the unbridled hatred. Men had suffered and died in chains, innocent victims who had been taken to punish the clan members.

'You're going to release him,' Bram said quietly. 'The clans protect their own.'

'Do they? Then why is it that they've retreated to the north, hiding in the wilderness?'

'They're biding their time,' Bram answered. 'Joining forces together.' He lifted his eyes to the Englishman's.

'By keeping our clansmen as prisoners, you give us a reason to join together against a common enemy.'

Harkirk let out a rough laugh. 'Your barbaric fighting methods don't stand a chance against our cavalry. We'll defeat you, just as we did with Wallace's men at Falkirk.' A thin smile stretched his lips. 'And you know what they did to Wallace. He was drawn and quartered, like the traitor he was.'

He gave a flick of his hand and half-a-dozen guards came closer in a silent threat. 'MacPherson, we've nothing more to discuss.'

'One prisoner,' Hamish interrupted, lifting his palm. 'I am prepared to offer silver for his safe return.'

Bram's fists tightened when he saw the bag of coins Hamish withdrew from beneath his cloak. He recognised the sack of false coins and he held his breath.

'A contribution from our clan,' Alex intervened.

'You're prepared to pay a ransom?'

'For our brother, yes. But as for your other prisoners, you risk the wrath of the other clans by holding them captive.'

Harkirk signalled for one of his men to come forwards. Hamish reached into the bag and withdrew a few of the silver coins for inspection. The servant eyed them, then nodded to his overlord.

The English baron seemed to deliberate for several moments, before replying, 'Bring me Cairnross's prisoner.'

Nairna was waiting inside the courtyard when they returned. Her heart soared with thankfulness when she saw Bram and, most of all, the man they'd brought home with them. She didn't doubt it was Callum MacKinloch, for the man held the look of his brothers, despite his captivity. Yet he was different from Bram. Though he walked with a slight limp, it was the emptiness in his gaze that worried her.

Nairna rushed forwards to Bram, but he made no move to greet her. His expression was angry and all he would say was, 'Pack our belongings. We're leaving immediately.'

She couldn't understand what was the matter. He'd rescued Callum, hadn't he? 'What's wrong?'

Bram kept walking and she struggled to keep up with his pace. Nairna saw Callum enter the keep, leaning upon Alex for support.

'Wait for me,' she begged Bram and ordered one of the serving maids to bring food and fresh clothing to Bram's brother.

In the meantime, her husband had already disappeared into their chamber. When Nairna arrived, he was pacing across the floor.

'What is it?' She couldn't understand what had brought about his frustration.

'It was too simple, Nairna. I don't trust them.'

'Are you angry about the coins I sent with my father?' she asked, her face reddening. 'Did he have to use them?'

'He paid the ransom, aye. But when they learn that the money at the bottom is false, they'll—'

'The top layer wasn't false,' she admitted. 'Only the remainder. It's still worth a man's life.'

Bram took a breath, leaning his hand against the wall. 'I pray they don't find out until we're gone.'

She saw the immense guilt mingled with his confusion and frustration. Though she'd hoped that Callum's safe return would alleviate her husband's guilt, it didn't seem to have made a difference.

'It wouldn't surprise me if they attacked us on our way back to Glen Arrin,' he said. 'We'll leave at nightfall, when it's more difficult for them to track our path.'

He didn't feel safe, she understood. Not even here, among her father's men. 'All right,' she said softly. 'We'll go tonight.'

Nairna moved closer, sliding her arms around him. 'Something else is troubling you.' Whether he wanted her or not, she needed to offer him some form of comfort.

'Callum hasn't spoken once, not since we left Harkirk's fortress.' Bram drew her tightly against him, his hand clutching her hair. 'Not a word. It was as if he didn't know us.'

'That will change when he's home,' Nairna predicted. 'You'll see.'

'I left him there too long.'

While she held Bram, the burden of guilt pressed down on him so hard that she wished she could shoulder it for him. 'He'll heal. Give it time.'

But he let go of her, his face growing stoic. 'I hope so.' He walked to the door, and reminded her, 'Prepare our belongings. I'm going to see my brother now.'

He didn't wait for a reply, but closed the door behind him. A hard lump formed in her throat, but Nairna knew she could do nothing more. Bram had returned home to her unharmed, with his brother safe, and that was everything she'd prayed for. Yet, as she waited alone in her chamber, she feared that the demons of her husband's past were not at all gone.

They didn't stop to sleep on the journey home, nor did they take more than a few minutes to rest or eat. Nairna thought her legs would drop off from the gruelling pace, but the men were convinced that Harkirk would follow them. She'd nearly fallen asleep on horseback, once they'd reached the area surrounding Glen Arrin.

Tall green mountains rose up, while a light rain fell down upon them. Rivulets of water creased the mountains, while fir trees skirted the lower hills. Nairna's clothing was completely soaked, but she hardly cared anymore. It had done nothing but rain since they'd left.

And her husband hadn't spoken to her in that time, either, keeping at Callum's side. Now that it was daylight, she took a moment to study Bram's younger brother. With long dark hair and a bearded face that hid his features, he looked a great deal like his brothers. It was only the emptiness in his expression that made her understand that he had endured far more than Bram. Though she'd sent fresh clothing to Callum, he still wore the stained, ill-fitting clothing he'd worn for the years of his imprisonment.

When she'd tried to question why he'd refused the clothing, Bram wouldn't answer. He'd ignored her attempts at conversation, spending all of his time at Callum's side.

They stopped at a stream to let the horses drink and Nairna came closer to the men. She'd hoped to introduce herself to Callum, but they'd shielded him from her. It was only when they were moving back to the horses that she caught a glimpse of their brother's back.

His ragged tunic was the colour of rust and she covered her mouth when she understood why he hadn't removed his garments. They were coated in blood; it was likely that removing the clothing would cause him pain.

Nairna swallowed hard, remembering the scars upon Bram's back. He wouldn't talk about them, nor share anything about his captivity, but it was clear that Callum had suffered a great deal.

Once they started up again, she brought her mount beside Bram's. 'Your brother needs a healer.'

'I know it.'

'His clothing is stuck to his flesh, isn't it?' she murmured beneath her breath.

He nodded. 'We tried to take it off him yesterday, but he fought us. He's not in his right mind. He isn't aware of what's going on.'

'Is there something I can do?' she asked. 'Tell me and I'll arrange it.'

'There's nothing, Nairna.'

'I don't believe that.' She met his gaze with resolution of her own. 'He's alive. And we can help him recover.'

Her husband shook his head, a weariness in his eyes. 'There are some wounds that never heal, Nairna.'

That night, after they arrived home at Glen Arrin, Bram tried again to talk to his brother. Callum sat, staring into the distance while a bath of hot water grew cold.

'I'm sorry,' Bram murmured, though he knew the words meant nothing. 'We tried to go back for you sooner. For a time, we didn't know where you were.'

Silence. His brother made no response, gave no indication that he'd heard a single word. A knot swelled up in the back of his throat and Bram tried to think of something he could say that would get Callum to open up.

His brother's face was filthy, his hair matted with mud. Bruises and cuts marred the surface and his clothing smelled of blood and decay.

'Let me help you, Brother,' he pleaded. He took a step

forwards, hoping that Callum would let him closer. But as soon as he tried to reach for the tunic, his brother's mouth twisted into a snarl. Like a cornered animal, he refused to let anyone near.

When Bram reached out to touch him, Callum's knuckles smashed into his eye. Pain exploded from the blow and Bram released his frustration.

'Damn it, Callum, why won't you let me help you? I know you're hurt. I've seen the blood.'

But his brother refused to speak. Bram sat upon a bench, his head lowered, his hands shaking.

The door opened quietly and Nairna stepped inside. 'Has he eaten anything?'

'Very little.' Bram met his wife's worried gaze and she walked over to his side. 'I don't want to restrain him, but we need to treat his wounds before they get worse.'

'Will you let me try to help?' Nairna asked.

Bram lifted his shoulders in surrender. He'd done all he could; if Nairna could break through to him, so be it.

His wife bade him, 'Wait here. I'll return in a moment.'

Callum stared at the wall and Bram set a cup of mead near him. It remained untouched.

When the door opened again, Nairna entered with Lady Marguerite. Bram couldn't understand why, but the moment Callum laid eyes upon Marguerite, something stirred in his expression. Though he didn't speak, he stared at *her* instead of into the empty air.

'Let Marguerite try,' Nairna said. 'She met him weeks ago.'

From the way the maiden was already approaching Callum, it seemed that they did know one another.

Marguerite wore a sapphire silk gown trimmed with grey fur, her hair spilling over her shoulder, though it was covered with a veil. Callum watched her as though he were dreaming and Bram felt Nairna take his hand, guiding him out.

'We'll wait just beyond the door if you need us,' Nairna was saying. She led Bram into the hallway outside the chamber, closing the door all but a few inches.

'How do they know each other?' Bram whispered, peering through the crack in the door.

'He was beaten after you left,' Nairna said. 'Marguerite found him and tended his wounds. He was sent away the next morning.' She moved beside him, resting her head upon his chest while they both watched over the pair. 'He allowed her to help him then. He might again.'

Marguerite was speaking to Callum in soft tones, seated across from him. In the flickering light of the torch set within a sconce, Bram spied a tear running down the woman's face. She continued talking, though she spoke in the French tongue. And after several minutes, Callum turned his back to her. Lady Marguerite came near, still talking. And when she reached him, her hands came to rest upon his shoulders.

Nairna's fingers moved inside Bram's tunic, tracing the scars there. As if shadowing Marguerite's movements, his wife soothed his skin, her face pressed against his heartbeat.

He'd been like Callum once. It had been so hard to face the outside world, so hard to accept that he was finally safe. There would be no one to shut him up in the darkness. No one to strike out at him or cut him down.

'Are you all right?' Nairna murmured. 'Your eye is swollen.'

'I got too close,' was all he would tell her. But they

both watched as his brother finally allowed Marguerite to help him remove the bloodstained tunic. He exhaled a sharp hiss when she had to peel back the fabric from his skin.

When his bare back was revealed at last, Nairna's arms held him tight. Bram breathed in the scent of her hair, holding her close as the years of his brother's torment were revealed. By the Holy Rood, the sight of Callum's raw, unhealed flesh was enough to send his stomach turning.

Though her face turned white, Lady Marguerite said not a word. She merely soaked a clean rag in the cooled bath water and brought it to Callum, touching his face with it. Soothing him. Then she wet it again and lightly wrung it out before setting the cool cloth upon his brother's back.

'She's doing well with him,' Nairna whispered, moving out of his embrace. 'We should leave them be.'

'She's a maiden,' Bram argued. 'It isn't right to leave them alone.'

'He's not about to hurt her.' Nairna pulled at his hand. 'Look.'

Callum had raised his face to Marguerite's. Though his eyes held suffering, there was also relief there. There was no threat from Marguerite and his brother succumbed to her touch.

'Bram,' Nairna whispered. 'Come with me.'

He didn't want to follow, but his wife wouldn't let go of his hand. She led him down the winding stairs and outside.

The rain had stopped and the ground was soft beneath their feet, coated with a light moisture. He thought Nairna would bring them back to their house, but instead she led him to the grain hut, where they'd spent their first few nights. It was dark inside and the interior smelled of barley.

'He'll be all right,' she whispered. 'You kept your promise.'

'Why did you bring me here?' He wound his arms around her waist, not understanding her purpose.

'I know you'll want to stay close to him this night. So we might as well sleep here instead of in our house.'

He understood her intention, but he wasn't going to leave Callum alone that long. For all they knew, his brother had fallen into the madness that haunted the prisoners he'd known.

'You can sleep here, if you wish,' he murmured to Nairna. 'But I need to go back to the keep. Alex and I can take turns watching over him.'

She touched his lips with her fingertips, before pressing a kiss upon his mouth. 'I love you.'

In her eyes, he saw the yearning and something inside him warmed to it. But he couldn't voice an answer. He didn't deserve to be loved, not after all this. If he could have gone back and changed his fate, he'd have freed Callum instead of seizing the chance for himself. His moment of selfishness might have destroyed his brother.

'I'll see you in the morning,' he said to her, kissing her forehead before he left. As he left, his wife's face held a sadness, as if he'd hurt her physically. And though he felt her pain as his own, there was nothing he could do to change it.

Chapter Nineteen

The next morning, Nairna left the hut, feeling restless. It was early and the morning sky still held the darkened shade of purple. The air was heavy, with a chill that slipped beneath her wrap, making her shiver.

Bram hadn't returned last night, and she knew he'd spent the hours guarding his brother. Though she understood his desperate need to ensure Callum's well-being, it seemed more of a penance. Her husband couldn't let go of the guilt that plagued him like a disease, festering inside him, until he could see nothing else.

He'd been right; there were some wounds that didn't heal. The comforts Nairna had tried to give him over the past few weeks had done nothing to wipe out the memories of his imprisonment.

She worried that no amount of love would take away his sense of blame. Instead of accepting her feelings, he'd drawn away from them, as if he viewed her love as another set of chains.

She tried to tell herself that it didn't matter. In time, he would come to care for her again, as he once had. They wouldn't have a shadow marriage, like Laren and Alex. She couldn't live like that, with a husband who hardly saw her or cared what she did.

Alone, she walked outside, pulling her wrap tighter. She crossed past the rows of houses, letting her mind drift. More of the women had returned, and she saw one young woman speaking in a soft tone, shushing her crying infant, bouncing the child against her shoulder.

The sight of them twisted at her heart, for she wondered if she would ever hold an infant of her own. Her hands settled over her flat stomach, and she let herself dream for a moment. The thought sent a quiet ache of longing inside. Bram hadn't touched her in several days, and she didn't know when he would again. He was so caught up in tending his brother, he'd forgotten all else.

But she supposed that would change, in time.

When she reached the outer area of Glen Arrin, she started to turn back. The clan members were rising to perform their morning tasks and she scented the peat smoke rising into the air, as more bricks were added to the fires.

A flicker of light caught her eye and she turned back. Peering at the hillside, she couldn't quite tell what it was. Perhaps it was nothing, but it looked like the flare of torches. Her heart quickened with worry and she hastened back to the keep. If there were intruders near, Bram and Alex ought to know about it.

When she reached the interior of the keep, she saw an exhausted Marguerite resting upon a bench with her head upon the trestle table. An untouched plate of food lay nearby.

Laren came down the stairs, followed by her daughter

Mairin. Adaira slept in her arms, her head tucked beneath her mother's chin. Though she greeted Nairna with a smile, there was apprehension in her eyes. 'Callum still hasn't spoken. Alex and Bram had to subdue him. He flew into a rage when Marguerite left.'

'It will take time,' Nairna said. 'But at least they treated his wounds.' Glancing around, she asked, 'Where are Alex and Bram now?' She wanted to tell them about the possible intruders, as soon as possible.

Laren glanced upwards. 'They're both still with Callum, above stairs.' She led her daughter to sit down, and lowered her voice. 'I didn't tell Alex about the glass—I told him it was a tapestry.'

'Did you find out who cheated Dougal?'

Laren released a sigh and nodded. 'It was a travelling merchant. Dougal believed the man's praise and thought he'd brought back a great deal of silver.'

'At least the coins served a purpose,' Nairna offered. She told Laren about the unexpected ransom and about the lights she'd seen this morning in the distance. 'I worry that it could be Lord Harkirk's men, if they discovered what we did.'

The chief's wife paled, but she nodded. 'Tell Bram and Alex. I'll gather the women and children and arrange for them to be hidden.'

Nairna's skin grew cold at the thought of an impending attack. Her father usually avoided conflicts and she'd never been in the midst of a battle before. The idea of hiding from the invaders should have comforted her, but all she could think of was Bram fighting alone. The last time she'd seen him sparring with Ross, he'd been injured.

Though she wanted to believe that he was stronger,

she simply didn't know. And her fear overshadowed the hope that everything would be all right.

Laren was already waking Marguerite up and the young woman took Mairin's hand, following Laren outside. Nairna walked up the winding stone staircase to the chamber where Callum was staying. She knocked softly, and when Bram answered she saw the shadowed circles beneath his eyes. 'You didn't sleep, did you?'

He shook his head. 'Neither of us did. He kept waking up and fighting us off. I don't know if he's even aware of where he is.'

Nairna wanted to take his hand, to reassure him, but something in his expression made her hesitate. Alex stretched and gave her a nod in greeting.

'When I was out walking this morning, I saw torchlight in the hills,' she told them. 'Do you think any of Lord Harkirk's men might have followed us?'

Bram's face tensed, and he exchanged a glance with Alex. 'It's possible.'

'I'll inform the men,' the chief said. 'If it is an attack, send a runner to Locharr and alert the Baron that we may need his help.' He turned to Nairna. 'Tell Laren—'

'She's already gathering the women and children.'

'Good.' The chief glanced back at Callum, whose eyes were open. The man had clenched his hands together; from the expression on his face, he'd understood what they were saying.

'I'll need your help guarding the women and children,' Alex ordered his younger brother. 'Even Lady Marguerite.'

Callum gave a slight nod to show that he understood, and though his hands were shaking, he managed to take the sword his older brother offered. Nairna wasn't so certain whether or not the man was capable of guarding anyone, but she understood it was a way of protecting Callum, by keeping him with the others.

Nairna led the men down the stairs and outside to the place where she'd seen the torchlight. By now, the sun had risen, but the sky remained dark with clouds.

Bram and Alex climbed up to the top of the gatehouse, but Nairna saw the threat as soon as they did. Not a few raiders, as she'd suspected.

Instead, an army of men had spread out in the valley, their chainmail reflected in the light like hundreds of silver coins.

Lord Harkirk had brought his soldiers. And with him were Lord Cairnross's forces.

This was what he'd been waiting for.

Dougal clenched his dirk, hiding behind one of the huts as the MacKinloch archers began firing arrows against the English. The frightened cries of children were shushed by their mothers as Nairna and Laren helped them go into hiding.

The dark scent of soot brimmed within the air and a flaming torch shot through the sky, landing upon a nearby roof. The dry thatch blazed and Dougal moved further away, to find his own position of safety.

The last time the English had come, his brother Alex had shoved him down in the storage cellar with Lady Laren and the girls, as if he were naught but a bairn. They didn't believe he was capable of fighting.

Not this time. Dougal refused to stand back like a coward, hiding with the women. He could drive his blade into a soldier's ribs, the same as any of them. Now that he was four and ten, he was old enough to help his brothers. If he slaughtered a dozen Englishmen, they'd finally stop treating him like a child.

Men shouted as the flames began to spread, and the clang of swords rang within the courtyard. Dougal found a place behind a wooden cart, out of the range of the arrows, while he decided the best place to launch his own attack.

Best to wait for the right moment to strike out and remain hidden until then. His kinsmen had already begun to attack the English, their battle cries roaring amid the chaos.

A tightness constricted in his lungs and sweat coated his palms. But he wasn't afraid to fight. No, soon enough, he would run out and join the MacKinlochs. For now, better to stay here and wait for one of the English to come closer.

A flash of movement caught him by surprise, and an arrow shot past him, embedded in the cart only inches from his face. Dougal dived beneath the cart, his heart slamming within his chest. He'd never seen the English soldier approaching from the back side of the fortress. How had the man slipped inside?

Dougal gripped his dirk, a bead of sweat rolling down his face as the soldier drew closer. He had to make a decision. His pulse quickened, a thick terror rising in the back of his throat.

But then, abruptly, he heard the sound of a dog snarling. Seconds later, his enemy's knees buckled beneath him. Dougal rolled out from under the cart and saw Bram's wife Nairna holding a stone in her hand, her dog Caen at her side. She'd struck the English soldier across the head and the man lay motionless, blood streaming from his temple.

'Take his sword,' Nairna ordered. 'And all of his weapons. Quickly, before he wakes up!'

Her face was grey and she looked as if she were about

to be sick. Though he'd been trained to fight, Nairna knew nothing about it. She didn't belong here.

'Go back with the other women,' Dougal told her as he seized the unconscious soldier's sword. 'You shouldn't be near the fighting.'

'Neither should you,' she said. 'Come back with me.'

He was about to argue with her, when another motion caught his attention. In a blur, his mind and body seemed to separate. Another soldier ran forwards, his weapon aimed at Nairna. Though Dougal tried to cry out a warning, the words smothered in his throat.

Instinct took over and he rushed forwards, driving the sword into the man's stomach. The blade sank deep within and Dougal staggered backwards, suddenly aware of what he'd just done.

He didn't hear Nairna's words, nor did he know what was happening around him. Blood covered his hands and he couldn't seem to take a deep breath. His ears rang, his vision blurring.

Bile rose up and he ran to a corner of the palisade wall, heaving up the contents of his stomach. Humiliation was a bitter taste upon his tongue, for he'd just shown Nairna his cowardice.

Moments later, a gentle hand rested upon his shoulder. 'It's all right, Dougal.'

But it wasn't. He'd never killed a man before, never known what it was to see the look of shock and death within a man's eyes. The pieces of his boyhood fell away in that moment, and he understood what his brothers had meant when they'd wanted him to stay clear of the battle. It wasn't a glorified fight for honour, for death could come at any second, without warning.

He wiped his mouth, realising that his duty right now

was no longer to defend their clan and fight. He needed to bring Nairna to safety.

'I'll take you back to the others,' he said. 'You need to stay with the women and children.'

His brothers would want that. He would join with Callum and they would form their own defence for those who were too weak to defend themselves.

Bram fought off the faceless soldiers, knowing that they were outnumbered. Numbness settled over him and he fought to keep his movements controlled.

Letting the invaders seize control of their lands wasn't an option. And though his rage was rising with every man he struck down, he couldn't afford to release his emotions. He had to keep his family safe.

The armies had formed a perimeter, nearly surrounding their fortress. If they managed to encircle Glen Arrin, it was over. He didn't know whether the English intended to kill them all or show mercy upon the women and children. It was doubtful that their lives would be spared, unless he could get them away from Glen Arrin.

Bram swung his claymore hard, connecting with another enemy, bringing him down. He saw his chance to break free of the fight and raced towards the keep, hoping to find a way to get the women out, with Dougal and Callum's help.

He stopped short when he caught sight of Gilbert de Bouche, the Earl of Cairnross, entering the gates. Cairnross strode into their broken fortress with the arrogance of one who owned it. He surveyed the land, seemingly satisfied with the burning huts and the bodies littering the ground.

Bram didn't move. In his enemy's eyes, he saw the man who had tormented him. His claymore grew heavy, his weariness sinking into his bones. This man had ordered boys flogged because they were too weak from hunger to lift stones. Too many had died, unable to stand the suffering.

There had never been any remorse in Cairnross's face. He had treated the Scots as his slaves, as if they weren't fully human.

Doubts and fears rose up inside Bram, crippling his resolve. He saw Alex fighting hard, along with Ross. They would die before surrendering. As would he. But he couldn't let a man like Cairnross get to Nairna.

'I wondered if you were alive,' Cairnross said, lifting his sword. He was flanked by two soldiers, guards who would ensure his protection. 'You were a great deal of trouble as a slave.'

Bram kept his gaze fixed upon the three men. Though he longed to fight, he forced himself to wait. 'What is it you want from us?'

Cairnross glanced back at the rest of the fighting, a smug expression on his face. 'Harkirk intends to claim his rightful share of your holdings, after you tried to cheat him with false silver. And as for me—' He nodded to the guard upon his left, who departed for the keep. 'I lost many of my slaves on the night you attacked. I want compensation for the loss.'

'You weren't interested in keeping them alive,' Bram responded. 'You wanted them to work until they died, and that was enough for you.'

Cairnross shrugged. 'They served their purpose.' Near the gates, more soldiers streamed inside, only to be met by MacKinloch fighters.

Though Bram was glad to see his kinsmen striking down the enemy, inwardly, he grew colder, afraid that there was no way for them to win this fight.

'Being a traitor has its price,' Cairnross said. 'And our orders are to suppress any rebellion.'

That was it, then. They weren't planning to let any of them live. Though he'd suspected as much, hearing it was enough to make him grip his claymore and raise it towards Gilbert de Bouche. He might die this day, but he fully intended to take Cairnross with him, for what he'd done to so many men.

'Then I'll die fighting.' Bram started to swing his claymore when one of the guards came racing back.

'They're not here, my lord.' The guard's face was red and he was out of breath. 'We've searched everywhere. None of the women or children are inside the fortress.'

'They're in hiding, then,' Cairnross proclaimed. 'Burn them out.'

Bram's skin turned to ice. Most of the fortress was made of wood; if it burned down, it would collapse upon the storage entrance, burying the women and children alive.

The rage inside him was threatening to break out and he gritted his teeth to keep his control. He needed to fight for Nairna and the others, not letting his temper master him.

A cry he didn't even recognise came from his throat as he swung the claymore hard. The two soldiers guarded Cairnross, and his blade struck their wooden shields with no effect.

Cairnross moved away, giving orders to the other men to set the keep on fire. Bram fought hard against the two guards, not even feeling the exhaustion as his claymore became an extension of himself.

Ross came up from behind. The older man struck the soldier on the left, bringing him down. Bram finished the man on the right when the soldier's attention was distracted by the death of his companion.

But they were too late. Already, smoke was rising into the air, the keep blazing. He saw them adding oil to the flames, and as the conflagration spread faster, Bram knew there was no hope of saving it.

'Mary, Mother of God,' Ross breathed. He broke into a run, and Bram was close behind.

It was only a matter of time before the unstable structure collapsed.

Chapter Twenty

Nairna could smell the smoke filling up the castle keep. 'We can't stay here,' she insisted. 'We have to evacuate the others.'

Laren's hand covered her mouth, but she nodded. 'I know it. But they'll see us leaving and follow. We'll die if we try to go.'

Terror boiled inside her stomach, but Nairna saw no other choice. And when the scent of smoke grew stronger, she didn't waste any more time. 'I'd rather risk my chances with the soldiers than be burned to death.'

'Dougal, I need your help.' She touched his shoulder, wishing she didn't have to burden a boy with such a task. But their lives depended on it. 'We have to get the women and children out. They can go to our house on the ridge, but I need help keeping the soldiers back. Do you have a bow?'

He nodded, pointing to the back of the underground chamber. 'There are extra weapons hidden there.'

'Good.' Though she wasn't particularly good with a bow and arrows, she'd stand with Dougal and fight.

But only a moment later Callum emerged, holding two bows and quivers of arrows. Nairna tried to take one, but he refused to let go of the weapon.

His brown eyes held a darkness in them and a fierceness that frightened her. But she couldn't let Callum's madness interfere with their escape.

'Can you defend us?' she asked.

His eyes met hers and he gave a single nod. Nairna stepped back, unsure of whether or not trusting him was a good idea. But then Marguerite started to gather the women together and Callum caught the young woman's hand.

He held it for a fraction of a moment, meeting her gaze. Marguerite's cheeks flamed, but she nodded. 'I know,' she whispered.

The underground chamber had one exit that led outside to the back of the keep. Below it lay a large ditch that the men had dug to keep out invaders on that side, partially filled with rainwater. Nairna started to move forwards, but Marguerite stopped her.

'I know the way to your house, Nairna. I'll go first and lead them, if you'll help Laren gather the others. I don't know them as well as you do.' The young woman's face was tense with fear, but she seemed determined.

'All right,' Nairna agreed. She went back to the weapons, hoping to find a bow of her own. There was only a crossbow with a single bolt, and she took it. Dougal and Callum would need help, and though she wasn't experienced at fighting, she would do what she could to protect the women and children.

The smoke grew worse, a smothering odour that stung her eyes and burned her lungs. Some of the children started coughing, and Laren began leading them outside.

She held her own daughters, one over each hip, as the women followed.

Nairna joined her in gathering everyone together and Marguerite walked beside Callum. Though neither spoke, she saw the protective glint in Callum's eyes.

The two young men took their positions on opposite sides of the ditch, Callum near the keep and Dougal on the other side of the bank.

Nairna climbed down into the water with Marguerite. She gripped her skirts as she sloshed through the muddy ditch water, and they grew saturated, heavy from the soaked weight. Her dog Caen dived into the water, paddling across before he headed up the hill, shaking the water off.

Once Nairna managed to climb up the bank, it was clear that one of them would have to stay at the hillside to help the women get out of the water, particularly if they were holding young children.

'Go and take cover in the trees,' Nairna told Marguerite, setting down her crossbow on the ground. 'I'll stay with Dougal and help the women out of the ditch.'

Although the path leading to their house was towards the front of the fortress, a line of thick fir trees edged the lower part of the hills. If they stayed hidden, they could make their way to the ridge.

Marguerite obeyed and as more women emerged with their children, Nairna assisted them out of the water. Jenny joined them and she directed her maid to hide with the others. Meanwhile, she kept watching both sides for signs of any soldiers.

She worried about Bram, not knowing whether he was alive or dead. Though she understood that he would fight better without her, being apart from him was a physical ache that didn't diminish. The thought of losing him a second time made her heart go numb. She didn't think she could bear it.

No longer was he the boy she'd first fallen in love with. He was a man who'd experienced torture and darkness, almost losing himself to it. And though he might never love her in the way she loved him, it didn't matter. She wanted whatever part of him she could have. She held fast to the hope that one day he would see her with different eyes. One day, she would mean more to him.

If they survived this day.

Callum took his position on the bank beside the fortress, an arrow already poised in the bow, but his hands were shaking.

'Can he shoot?' she murmured to Dougal.

'I don't know.' The boy shook his head. And that wasn't at all reassuring.

Nairna knelt down in front of the ditch, holding infants while their mothers tried to climb out of the water. Her dog Caen rested at Dougal's feet.

The first group of soldiers came around the corner and Nairna's heart seized with fear.

Sweet heaven, she didn't know what to do. She handed a baby to his mother before reaching for the crossbow. She didn't know how to aim it, much less release the bolt. And she only had one shot.

Before she could even consider aiming the weapon, Callum released an arrow that struck the soldier's face. He followed up with a second shot that embedded within the soldier's heart.

Nairna stared at the man, struck speechless by what she'd seen. How he could have such skill after being locked away for so many years made little sense.

But the look he cast towards Marguerite was a quiet promise that he wouldn't let anything happen to her. And the soft smile Marguerite gave him made Nairna's heart ache, as the woman disappeared into the trees.

Dougal cried out a warning and more of the enemy emerged from the other side. He tried to fire an arrow, but it struck the ground. Shaking, Nairna lifted her crossbow. She'd never killed a man before and she prayed she wouldn't have to.

The soldiers charged closer with their spears, calling out for more men to join him. But just as before, Callum's arrows took the men down, some of the bodies crashing into the ditch water.

Laren led her own children through the ditch, bringing up the middle group of women. They disappeared into the woods, and Nairna sent up a silent prayer that they would make it to safety.

Only a dozen or so women remained, and the keep's tower began to crumble, the wood groaning under the weight. Nairna set down her crossbow at Dougal's feet, climbing back down into the ditch. She helped one of the mothers by picking up a three-year-old boy on her hip, ordering the others to get out.

Bram and Alex came up around the corner at a full run. Blood covered her husband's hands; Nairna didn't know if it was his or another soldier's.

She was so relieved to see him, she passed the child she was holding up to his mother, who had already climbed up the bank. The remaining women got out of the ditch and Bram crossed through the water, helping her up. As soon as he emerged from the ditch, he pulled her into his arms.

Nairna was shivering with cold, but feeling his arms around her made it easier to endure. She clung hard, and both of them saw at the same moment when the keep started to fall apart.

'Callum, dive!' Her husband roared out the warning, and his brother threw himself at the ditch. Callum hit the water, while behind him the wooden structure collapsed. Marguerite emerged from the forest, but Nairna let go of her husband and shoved the young woman back.

'He'll be all right. Take the women up to the ridge and I'll send him soon.'

Marguerite sent Callum a worried look, but she returned to the woods, hurrying with the rest of the MacKinlochs.

Bram helped his brother out of the water, while Nairna turned to Dougal. The young man kept an arrow poised in his bowstring, but he looked terrified at the idea of facing more soldiers. 'Go behind the women and take your bow,' Nairna ordered. 'We'll follow you in a moment.'

But just as Dougal disappeared, the soldiers came pouring around the corner from both sides. One archer fired several arrows towards the forest before Callum killed him.

Nairna cried out a warning to Bram and Alex, who split off to meet the men, their shields and weapons ready. She picked up her crossbow, her heart stopping when she saw a soldier swing his sword at Bram's head. A sound tore from her throat as she ran to her husband. Though she couldn't do anything to stop it, she released the bolt and it struck a different man.

Bram dived to the ground, skewering his attacker with his claymore. They were completely outnumbered and Nairna understood that she was not going to survive this attack. These men would show no mercy, not after all that had happened.

She reached Bram and helped him up. He kept his claymore steady, but the soldiers simply closed in on them, waiting for the command to kill. Nairna wrapped her arms around his waist, as if she could hold on to these last moments with him.

Callum held his bow steady, his eyes glazed as if he weren't really seeing the soldiers. He didn't move, nor did he speak.

Lord Harkirk entered on horseback from the right, while Lord Cairnross joined in from the left. Bram's arm tightened around her and he moved down to whisper in her ear.

'When I tell you to, I want you to run hard towards the others. I'll fend them off as long as I can, to give you an escape.'

In other words, he would sacrifice his life for hers. Nairna's eyes welled up with tears and she buried her face in his tunic. 'Bram, if I leave, it will lead the soldiers to the other women. Their only chance at living is if I stay here.'

He made no reply, holding her tight against him for a long moment. She let the tears fall and whispered, 'I'd rather die at your side than live without you again.'

Bram released her, his tone rigid. 'I'm not going to let you die, Nairna.'

He took a step away, raising his hands in surrender. Eyeing first Harkirk, then Cairnross, he said, 'If word gets out of what you've done here this day, the clans will unite. The war will continue and you'll have given them a reason for vengeance.'

He paused, choosing his words carefully as he stared at Lord Cairnross. 'I'll return willingly, as your prisoner, if you let them go.'

He'd once said that he would die before becoming a

prisoner again. But it wasn't at all true. He'd surrender his freedom, even his life, if it meant saving Nairna.

He drank in the sight of his wife, afraid it would be the last time he saw her. Her brown hair was tangled, her green eyes filled up with tears. Even now, she was a balm to his broken soul. She was everything to him and they'd had so little time.

The memories flashed before his mind, quiet pieces of the past that he tried to hold on to. And he realised then that leaving her was the hardest thing he'd ever have to do. He wasn't worthy of her love or being her husband. He'd made so many mistakes, born of his hotheaded ignorance and, now, his carelessness.

But he loved her. He hadn't believed himself capable of it, but the emotions swelled up inside, his need for her overriding everything else.

Cairnross gave a signal and two soldiers seized him. He went with them, hoping that they would agree to this. He didn't care what happened to him, so long as Nairna and those he loved were safe.

But once he'd given himself up, two other soldiers seized his wife. Cairnross rode forwards, his expression ruthless and coldhearted. 'You took my betrothed wife from me. It only seems fair that I take yours in return.'

'Don't touch her,' Bram ordered, the rage rising up inside. He could feel the anger clouding his judgement, transforming it into hatred.

'Perhaps I'll let you watch,' Cairnross mused. 'And when I'm finished with her, you can watch her die.'

The last hold he had upon his sanity snapped at the sight of Nairna's terror.

Bram unleashed the full force of his temper, smashing his head against the nose of the soldier holding him captive. Reality blurred, and somehow he had both a dirk and a sword in his hands. The first blade sank into flesh, and he fought with every last breath he had to give. He struck again and again, until he no longer knew what was happening.

He heard the sounds of battle, felt the slash of the enemy's sword, but still he fought.

For her, the woman he loved. The bloodlust roared through him, and he let go of all control, no longer caring what he did. He would die before letting any man touch her, especially Cairnross.

And when he felt the hands dragging him away, the last sight he saw was Nairna's stricken face.

Chapter Twenty-One

Her husband had fallen into such madness, Nairna feared she'd lost him. Sweat dripped down his face and his eyes were wild. Blood covered his hands and the body of Lord Cairnross lay fallen on the ground.

Nairna had never seen anything like it. The rage had broken free and Bram had moved so fast. He'd torn her free of the soldiers' grip, slaughtering them like a legendary berserker.

Alex shielded his brother, protecting Bram as they both fought. And then her husband had run to Cairnross, dragging the earl off his horse before killing him.

Now, Bram held his claymore with both hands, as if daring anyone to draw near. Lord Harkirk had disappeared and the soldiers were awaiting orders for what to do next.

Nairna didn't know. But when the archers pulled back their bowstrings, ready to take her husband's life, she ran to stand in front of Bram.

'Don't,' she pleaded with them. She couldn't stand

and watch him die. 'Please, don't.' Tears that streamed down her face, and she shielded him, even knowing she might lose her own life.

She didn't care. She needed to be with him, no matter that it might be their last moments. Bram's eyes were clouded and she saw no awareness within them. His breathing was ragged, his eyes glazed.

She closed her eyes, waiting for the arrows to slice through them.

Instead, she heard the roar of men approaching. From both sides, there were archers surrounding the enemy with bows drawn. Lord Locharr rode forwards in full armour with his MacKinnon clansmen. On the opposite side was another nobleman, dressed in regal finery. He was flanked by at least twenty men, and behind him were even more soldiers. They were heavily armed, with both archers and cavalry.

Within minutes, Lady Marguerite emerged from her hiding place in the forest and ran towards the nobleman. From the similarity in their features, Nairna suspected the man was her father.

The nobleman signalled for two of his men to guard Lady Marguerite, while they escorted her to his side. She spoke quietly to the man for a moment, before he gestured for the guards to take her to safety.

A moment later, the man glanced at Lord Harkirk cowering behind his soldiers. 'I am Guy de Montpierre, the Duc D'Avignois,' he said.

He rode forwards, staring down at Harkirk as if the Englishman were little more than an insect. 'I'd advise you to return to your own stronghold, unless you'd rather I discussed this attack with your king. I suppose he would be interested to hear of why you've stirred up more unrest in the Highlands.'

Lord Harkirk signalled for his men to fall back. He met the duke's stare, but was wise enough not to argue. Within minutes, his men retreated, followed by Cairnross's survivors. Nairna didn't breathe easily until they were gone.

Alex came forwards to greet the duke along with Lord Locharr, and between the three, Nairna overheard talk of alliances.

But there were still matters she wanted to address with the duke. She let go of Bram and moved forwards.

'Your Grace,' she said, dropping into a curtsy. The nobleman turned a curious look upon her and waited for her to speak. 'What about the death of Lord Cairnross?' She worried about Bram and whether or not the English nobles would accuse him of murder.

The duke eyed the fallen body of Cairnross. 'Should anyone ask, I will bear witness that the earl was killed in battle.'

Nairna closed her eyes with thankfulness and Alex sent her a reassuring look.

'And there's something else,' she blurted out, despite his impatient look. 'Lord Harkirk has been demanding payments from the surrounding clans, in order to secure peace. I believe you would gain the support of many men were you to use your influence to stop the bribes.'

'I will see what can be done,' the duke answered.

She sent him a grateful smile, as he turned to talk again with Lord Locharr. Satisfied that she'd done the best that she could to help her clan, Nairna turned back to Bram. His fist still gripped the claymore and his expression remained stoic.

'Bram,' she whispered. 'It's over.'

Her relief was so great, she went into his arms. But

he never responded. Never moved. His palms gripped the claymore as though everything depended on it.

She couldn't pry the hilt out of his grasp and Alex came over to help her. When at last he took the claymore from his brother, Nairna tried to guide Bram home. She needed to do whatever she could to bring him out of his darkness.

He let her lead him up the hill, but his hands were cold. Alex followed, and after a short distance, they found Callum crouching atop a flat stone, his bow and arrows held in one hand. He was fixated upon Lady Marguerite, watching her with her father.

The longing on his face made Nairna ache for him, for there was no hope of a match between a duke's daughter and a third son. He seemed to know it, and after a time, he turned away and joined them.

When they reached the ridge, Nairna told the others what had happened. Most of the women wept with relief, taking their children in their arms as they started on the walk home.

Alex looked at his wife as though he wanted to pull her into his arms, but Laren remained frozen in place. She watched her husband, her expression filled with an unnamed emotion. Then he helped to bring Bram inside, while Laren stood alone with their daughters.

Nairna was the only one who saw the pain on Alex's face.

'Will you be all right with him?' he asked, eyeing Bram, who was seated on the bed.

'Aye.' Nairna poured water into a basin and retrieved a cloth to tend her husband's minor wounds. 'Go to Laren. She needs you.'

There was a slight shift in Alex's face, but he nodded and left. Nairna hoped that he would indeed go to his wife and reconcile with her. Though Laren had put on a brave face for the sake of her girls, the woman had been terrified.

When, at last, Nairna was alone with Bram, she picked up the cloth and soaked it in the water. Her hands trembled, so afraid she wouldn't be able to break through to him. She brought the cool cloth to her husband's face, smoothing away the dirt and blood. Then she pulled his tunic free, lifting it off to bare his chest. There was an angry cut on his arm and she washed the dried blood away, thankful that it wouldn't need stitching.

'Nairna,' he murmured, when she brought the cloth over his scarred back. Awareness had filled his eyes, and he reached up to take her hand. 'Are you unharmed?'

'Aye.' She cupped his face, pressing a kiss onto his mouth. 'We're safe now. And your brothers. Everything will be all right.'

Bram bowed his head, resting his bloodstained hands on his knees. 'I would have died for you, Nairna. Willingly.'

'I didn't want you to die.' She stepped between his legs, lifting his arms around her waist. Right now, she sensed that he needed her, needed a physical comfort. She kept her arms around him, sitting on his lap.

'I don't regret killing the English. Especially Cairnross.' He tightened his arms around her. 'They might hang me for that.'

'The Duc D'Avignois will speak on your behalf,' Nairna reassured him. 'I believe he will protect our clan from the English.'

He sobered. 'Then we owe him a debt.'

She touched his back. 'We'll ally with Marguerite's family and offer protection to one another. She was grateful to you for rescuing her from Cairnross.'

He gave a slight shrug of acknowledgement, but it didn't appear that he truly believed the danger was over.

'Bram, what is it?' she prompted.

He closed his eyes, as if he didn't know what to say. Nairna sat beside him, waiting for him to speak. At last, he said, 'Tonight, I wasn't afraid of my own death. I was afraid of yours.'

He took her hand and brought it to his face as if drawing strength from her very touch. 'When I thought he would harm you—' He broke off, holding her hand so tightly.

'He didn't. You kept me safe,' she murmured. She held him tightly, knowing that there was more he hadn't said.

'You asked me what it was like,' he said quietly. 'As a captive.'

She took a breath, not wanting to reopen such raw wounds. 'You can tell me about it later, Bram.' She stroked his hair away from his face, leaning down to kiss his mouth.

'No.' He took her hand and touched it to his throat. 'You should know everything. And then you can decide if you want to be with me.'

How he could even think she could bear to be parted from him, she didn't understand. But right now, he needed her to listen, and though she didn't truly wish to hear it, the confession might ease him. Nairna touched the scar upon his throat, then brought her lips to it.

But he turned his back to her, showing her the scarred surface. 'Six years ago, my brother was beaten until he couldn't stand. I lost my temper that night and used my chains to strangle the guard.

'It didn't work. As a punishment, they cut me with their knives. One cut for every day of the year.'

Nairna was sickened by the thought of such torture. 'You survived it.'

'I prayed to die, at first. After I healed, I vowed that I would master my temper and bide my time.'

He rested his forearms on his knees, lowering his head. 'But when I had the chance to escape, I risked his life. Callum might have died that night.'

'He didn't. And I don't think he blames you for leaving him.'

'Did you?' he asked softly. 'When I left our wedding, did you blame me for leaving you behind?'

She wanted to say no, that it hadn't mattered. But it wasn't the truth. She'd been devastated when he hadn't returned. Many times, she'd grieved for him, wishing that he hadn't gone home with his father.

'At the time, I understood why you left,' she admitted. 'You needed to go with your family to defend Glen Arrin. But I never expected to be a widow so soon after our wedding.'

'When I escaped from Cairnross, I almost didn't return to you,' he admitted. 'I thought you were better off, believing I was dead.'

'Why did you?'

'Because I needed to see you. The image of you, of your smile, had given me a reason to hold on.'

She embraced him, closing her eyes as his strong arms came around her. Though she wished she hadn't remarried another, she let go of the past years, for she now had the man she loved.

'I don't deserve you, Nairna. Today, when I almost lost you, I realised how much I need you.' He brought her hand to his heart and she could feel the pulse beneath her palm. 'I love you. And though I'm not the man I once was, I want to be a good husband to you.'

'You already are,' she whispered. She pushed away his tunic, caressing his warm male skin. Lowering her mouth to his pectoral muscles, she kissed him gently. 'You're all that I need.'

He pressed her down onto the bed, fully aroused. She welcomed the thick feel of his erection against her softer flesh.

He removed her clothing, then his own, before lying down beside her. She took him into her arms, shivering when his mouth covered hers.

'I have years to make up for, Nairna. If you'll allow it.'

She opened her arms to him, and with his hands and mouth he caressed her skin. Her nipples puckered and he kissed each of them, cupping her breasts as his mouth moved lower.

'When you touched yourself the other night,' he murmured, dropping a kiss upon her stomach, 'I was watching you. I wonder if I've learned how.'

With his fingers, he entered her womanhood, caressing the secret flesh that was already moist for him. Nairna gasped, lifting her hips as he withdrew his fingers.

'I'm not going to use my hands, though.' He sent her a wicked smile, raising his hips to hers. With a shallow penetration, he entered her, coating his shaft with her arousal. Then he took his length and used it to rub against her hooded flesh. The thick pressure made her grow swollen, sensitive to every stroke. He teased her, moving in a slow rotation that made her arch against him.

He ground himself against her, with both hands upon

her bottom, until she hooked her leg around his waist and took him deep inside.

'I haven't finished with you,' he said, moving slowly.

'Haven't you?' She kissed him, taking his tongue into her mouth while he penetrated her fully in slow strokes.

In answer, Bram stopped moving. He withdrew, leaving only an inch of his manhood inside her, while his thumb moved up to touch her hooded flesh. He used a soft rhythm to caress her, and she grew wetter as he quickened the pace in a circular motion.

'I love you, Nairna,' he said, his eyes locked upon her. She cried out as he intensified the pressure, guiding her towards the shimmering pleasure she needed so desperately.

'And I love you,' she whispered, arching her back and shuddering as the first swollen wave broke through her. As she started to tremble, he drove inside, and she gripped his length, letting him feel her release as she climaxed.

She saw his own pleasure tightening, and he took her body in swift strokes. 'I'll never leave you again, Nairna. You're mine, for always.'

The intensity of his lovemaking and the way he held her made her lose control of her own body. She stopped thinking about what was happening and simply let herself go.

When another storm of release overtook her, she took his mouth in a kiss. Bram ravaged her mouth until he let out a groan, losing himself in his own fulfilment.

'I love you,' she breathed. 'Now even more than I did then.'

Her husband rested against her, their breathing growing steady. 'It will take time before I can be the man you want.'

'You're already the man I want,' she said. 'And what you endured has only made you stronger.'

Bram's answer was to take her in his arms and love her again.

Chapter Twenty-Two

Winter came and went, and although there was still unrest in Scotland, the clans were united by a common enemy in King Edward Longshanks. Bram and Alex had supported Robert the Bruce, and that spring they saw him crowned king of Scotland. The fight for Scotland's freedom had not ended, but it had taken a turn for the better.

When Bram returned from Scone, he noticed a transformation in his wife. Laren had given Nairna free rein to handle the household and she'd spent the past few months sorting through the accounts, selling unneeded items and trading with the merchants.

His wife indeed had a talent for making money, just as she'd once told him. Because of her efforts, they were starting to rebuild Glen Arrin. With nothing remaining of the original keep, his brother Alex had redesigned the structure into a true castle.

Bram shielded his eyes from the morning sunlight, watching his kinsmen and brother Callum as they lifted stones, laying mortar to hold them steady. His mother Grizel was ordering her grandchildren around, using a wet thumb to wipe a smudge from Mairin's face.

And though she had never once apologised to any of them, Grizel had made herself useful in the household, assigning tasks to everyone until it ran smoothly. Nairna had found a way to manage his mother, by letting her believe that she had control.

Despite the way things were improving at Glen Arrin, Bram hadn't seen any improvement in his younger brother. Ever since Lady Marguerite had left, Callum had grown more morose, the silence continuing. He spent his time either rebuilding the walls of the keep or practising with his bow and arrows. Sometimes he disappeared for days on end.

Although Bram held out hope that one day his brother would fully heal, he wasn't certain it would happen. Time would tell.

In the meantime, he had brought a gift for Nairna back from Scone, one that had been given by the new Scottish king. Robert the Bruce had given many tokens to the chiefs who had offered their support.

Although Bram had returned last night, he hadn't had time to give it to Nairna. They'd spent every hour in each other's arms, until neither had slept well.

'I've been looking for you,' Nairna said, greeting him with a warm smile. Her hair was veiled, and at her side Caen wagged his tail in greeting. 'I was hoping to ask you about the sheep.'

Bram kissed her, adjusting the bundle beneath his arms. 'The sheep?'

'Yes. I'd like to purchase more, to increase our flock. I think, with the additional wool, our women could weave cloth to sell. The sheep are mating well, but not quick enough and—'

'Not quick enough?' A mischievous thought occurred to him, and he teased, 'Were you wanting me to coach them on how to satisfy their females? Is quicker really better?'

Shocked, she turned bright red. 'No, that's not I meant and you know it.'

He bit back his amusement. 'Or perhaps they should be mated more often?'

Nairna's blush deepened, and she shook her head in exasperation. 'Now, stop. You are quite good at satisfying a woman, I'll be the first to admit. But I don't think it's necessary to share that knowledge with the sheep.'

He laughed and picked her up, moving her around in a circle. 'I'll share everything I know with you, Nairna.'

When he set her down, he handed her the package. 'I brought you something. It's a gift from the king.'

She tore open the package and saw a length of crimson samite and a necklace formed from perfectly shaped pearls. 'Bram, do you have any idea what these are worth?' She clasped the package to her as if it were their clan's salvation. He could read her thoughts, and immediately he stopped them.

'You cannot sell a gift from the king. They are meant for you to wear. Sew a gown from the samite, and when we go to meet with him, you'll wear the pearls.'

She held still, not speaking. Bram took the pearls from her and fastened them around her throat. 'I know you are trying to take care of our clan. But you have nothing of your own.' He rested his hands upon the matched pearls. 'Years ago, I gave you pebbles and pretty stones. But these are what I wanted to give to you.'

She turned to look at him. 'Bram, I don't need pearls.'

'I want you to wear them for me. I want to see you in the gowns and jewels you deserve.'

'I can't accept gifts like these. Not when our clan needs so much.'

'You would offend our king if you don't take them.' He pulled her into his arms. 'It's a mark of your status, as my wife. Give our people a reason to be proud of their lady.'

'I'm not their lady.'

'You are. In every way that Laren cannot be.' Though she started to argue with him, he cut her off with a kiss. 'It's not a criticism of her, only a fact. You enjoy being in charge of the household more than she ever did.'

'I suppose.'

'Now, a good wife would offer thanks to her husband for bringing her gifts like these.' He settled his arm around her waist. 'Unless you'd rather I spent my time talking to the sheep.'

She shook her head, sending him a shy smile. 'Thank you, Bram.'

He held her in his arms, stroking her hair. 'Would that I could give you everything of your heart's desire. One day, perhaps.'

She lifted her face to his. 'I already have my heart's desire, Bram. You're standing here before me, alive and well.'

Bram leaned in to rest his cheek against hers. 'But you want a child, too.'

A faint smile crossed over her face. 'There's hope. It's too soon to tell, but it's possible…in winter.' Her hand went to rest upon her midsection and Bram covered her fingers with his own.

The light on her face made him kiss her, for he wanted nothing more than to see Nairna happy. He loved her so much, there weren't words enough to say it. He could only show her, every day, for the rest of their lives.

And he intended to do just that.

* * * * *

REQUEST YOUR
FREE BOOKS!

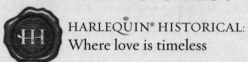 HARLEQUIN® HISTORICAL:
Where love is timeless

2 FREE NOVELS PLUS 2 FREE GIFTS!

YES! Please send me 2 FREE Harlequin® Historical novels and my 2 FREE gifts (gifts are worth about $10). After receiving them, if I don't wish to receive any more books, I can return the shipping statement marked "cancel." If I don't cancel, I will receive 6 brand-new novels every month and be billed just $4.94 per book in the U.S. or $5.49 per book in Canada. That's a savings of at least 18% off the cover price! It's quite a bargain! Shipping and handling is just 50¢ per book in the U.S. and 75¢ per book in Canada.* I understand that accepting the 2 free books and gifts places me under no obligation to buy anything. I can always return a shipment and cancel at any time. Even if I never buy another book from the Reader Service, the two free books and gifts are mine to keep forever.

246/349 HDN FC45

Name _____ (PLEASE PRINT)

Address _____ Apt. #

City _____ State/Prov. _____ Zip/Postal Code

Signature (if under 18, a parent or guardian must sign)

Mail to the **Reader Service:**
IN U.S.A.: P.O. Box 1867, Buffalo, NY 14240-1867
IN CANADA: P.O. Box 609, Fort Erie, Ontario L2A 5X3

Not valid for current subscribers to Harlequin Historical books.

Want to try two free books from another line?
Call 1-800-873-8635 or visit www.ReaderService.com.

* Terms and prices subject to change without notice. Prices do not include applicable taxes. N.Y. residents add applicable sales tax. Canadian residents will be charged applicable taxes. Offer not valid in Quebec. This offer is limited to one order per household. All orders subject to credit approval. Credit or debit balances in a customer's account(s) may be offset by any other outstanding balance owed by or to the customer. Please allow 4 to 6 weeks for delivery. Offer available while quantities last.

Your Privacy—The Reader Service is committed to protecting your privacy. Our Privacy Policy is available online at www.ReaderService.com or upon request from the Reader Service.

We make a portion of our mailing list available to reputable third parties that offer products we believe may interest you. If you prefer that we not exchange your name with third parties, or if you wish to clarify or modify your communication preferences, please visit us at www.ReaderService.com/consumerschoice or write to us at Reader Service Preference Service, P.O. Box 9062, Buffalo, NY 14269. Include your complete name and address.

Harlequin® Blaze™ brings you
New York Times *and* USA TODAY *bestselling author*
Vicki Lewis Thompson with three new steamy titles
from the bestselling miniseries SONS OF CHANCE

Chance isn't just the last name of these rugged
Wyoming cowboys—it's their motto, too!

Read on for a sneak peek at the first title,
SHOULD'VE BEEN A COWBOY

Available June 2011 only from Harlequin® Blaze™.

"THANKS FOR NOT TURNING ON THE LIGHTS," Tyler said. "I'm a mess."

"Not in my book." Even in low light, Alex had a good view of her yellow shirt plastered to her body. It was all he could do not to reach for her, mud and all. But the next move needed to be hers, not his.

She slicked her wet hair back and squeezed some water out of the ends as she glanced upward. "I like the sound of the rain on a tin roof."

"Me, too."

She met his gaze briefly and looked away. "Where's the sink?"

"At the far end, beyond the last stall."

Tyler's running shoes squished as she walked down the aisle between the rows of stalls. She glanced sideways at Alex. "So how much of a cowboy are you these days? Do you ride the range and stuff?"

"I ride." He liked being able to say that. "Why?"

"Just wondered. Last summer, you were still a city boy. You even told me you weren't the cowboy type, but you're…different now."

He wasn't sure if that was a good thing or a bad thing. Maybe she preferred city boys to cowboys. "How am I different?"

"Well, you dress differently, and your hair's a little longer. Your face seems a little more chiseled, but maybe that's because of your hair. Also, there's something else, something harder to define, an attitude…"

"Are you saying I have an attitude?"

"Not in a bad way. It's more like a quiet confidence."

He was flattered, but still he had to laugh. "I just admitted a while ago that I have all kinds of doubts about this event tomorrow. That doesn't seem like quiet confidence to me."

"This isn't about your job, it's about…your…" She took a deep breath. "It's about your sex appeal, okay? I have no business talking about it, because it will only make me want to do things I shouldn't do." She started toward the end of the barn. "Now, where's that sink? We need to get cleaned up and go back to the house. Dinner is probably ready, and I—"

He spun her around and pulled her into his arms, mud and all. "Let's do those things." Then he kissed her, knowing that she would kiss him back, knowing that this time he would take that kiss where he wanted it to go. And she would let him.

Follow Tyler and Alex's wild adventures in
SHOULD'VE BEEN A COWBOY
Available June 2011 only from Harlequin® Blaze™
wherever books are sold.

brings you

USA TODAY *bestselling author*

Lucy Monroe

*with her new installment
in the much-loved miniseries*

Proud, passionate rulers—
marriage is by royal decree!

Meet Zahir and Asad—two powerful, brooding sheikhs
and masters of all they survey. They need brides,
and marriage in their kingdoms is by royal decree!

Capture a slice of royal life in this enthralling sheikh saga!

Coming in June 2011:
FOR DUTY'S SAKE

Available wherever
Harlequin Presents® books are sold.